# Two Moons On the New Horizon
## By Om Prakash John W. Gilmore

# Two Moons On the New Horizon

## By Om Prakash John Gilmore

# Two Moons On the New Horizon
## Om Prakash John Gilmore

*ISBN:* 978-0-578-01965-9

*Dr. John W. Gilmore*
*Friends of Sat Yoga Costa Rica*
*259 W. Johnson St.*
*Philadelphia, PA 19144*

## Author's Note

We are at the eve of change in our society today. Everything has fallen apart and it is time for us to pull it back together by taking the good and leaving behind the bad and destructive, or to destroy ourselves, our descendents, and the whole earth by continuing on the same path. Today we have been provided with choices for change. May we choose wisely.

## Previous Books

*Reunion of Souls*

*The Keran Chronicles I, II, and III*

*The Keran Chronicles I:  Kera King and Queen*

*The Keran Chronicles II: The Phases of Kera*

*Into the Darkness of Kera III*

*The Keran Chronicles Four:  Fulfilling the Prophecies*

*Life, Work, and Spirituality*

*On Being Love's Warrior*

*A Return to Being Human Religiously*

*Distant Corners in a Crowded Room*

# Two Moons On the New Horizon
## Om Prakash John Gilmore

# Prologue

The sky was bright with its two large moons racing across the horizon. Lunar Major was taking its good sweet time with Lunar Minor moving about two times faster and just about to over take it. From Jericho's office window bright lights studded First Prime as far as the eye could see from "microscopic to the macroscopic," according to all of the ships spread out across three galaxies, the whole universe was at peace for the six-hundredth year of the Tek Empire. But there was a subtle disturbance somewhere being picked up on the cyber net, and the vibration was getting closer. Jericho was well aware that that small problem, as small as it may have been, could quickly become a big one.

He switched on the vid-screen at the local terminal to confirm his suspicions. He was right. There was a disturbance. Not only did he see traces of a psychometric tremor on the readout, he felt it in his bones. There were some Magi somewhere out there; raw Magi who hadn't been re-socialized. They were the most powerful he had ever sensed—more powerful than he thought possible.

The Magi were an old race of people stuck in past. To him they were a superstitious lot, not willing to give up their belief in magic, even since the *bipeds* had developed technology that could recreate and enhance every one of their little tricks, and probably do more by now. The Magi had been obsolete for years. Technology ruled. Man had become his own deity. Many of the Magi had been put into resettlement schools or vocational rehabilitation camps and had become contributing members of the Tek society without needing to hold on to their outdated, stale beliefs. Others had decided to remain in Magi townships, or live on Magi planets where they could retain their old belief systems in places where they would at least seem like the majority. Jericho felt sorry for them, but they weren't the ones that worried him.

They were under control. These others, the new ones, worried him.

The scientists had deduced that there were other Magi. The net had reached out into space and had picked up psychic movement several times. The probability, as computed by the Galactic Compu, was high for the existence of other Magi. If this were a group had been out of the grasp of the Tek Empire evolving in a small enclave untouched by technology, there was no telling what type of difficulties they could cause. Jericho scratched his chin and wondered why to worry about them. He looked at the screen. *Because they're on the move*, he thought. According to the chip buried deep in his brain, there was more than a ninety-three percent chance that they would be receiving a message from these new Magi.

He didn't really care much about government or policy making, but he knew that he would be involved in some way. Something had happened that would bring the Empire face to face with these Magi.

"It is very likely that you'll be called on as an emissary, Jericho," Maryland, his chip said. That's the name he gave her. She continued, "Your genetic makeup and background make you a prime candidate for contact." He furled his brows. Maryland picked up on it.

A smooth voice answered the unasked question. "Your genetic make-up and physical appearance is an indistinguishable match to this new group of Magi. There is a ninety-eight percent chance that you are of Magi origin. It is logical that through their use of magic they will find you here, since you are on the prime world, the seat of government." He frowned a bit. He didn't like the idea of Non-Tek amplified magic. "It's also very probable that the Tek Empire Provincial Government will come to the same conclusion that I have. Even as we speak they are, of course, receiving the same information from Galactic Compu."

How could he forget? There was no such thing as privacy anymore. That damn net was spreading everybody's thoughts around. He felt Maryland do what seemed like a smile. "Projection," he said. Maryland tapped into the visual region of his brain and created an image on the back of his retinas. She looked as if she were standing right in front of him. He could never get used to talking to something in his head. He was a Tek

Master Teacher. He had the same implant as everyone else in the Empire, but most of them went about their daily activities totally ignoring it. Most of the time they only tapped into the net for information on how to get to the right computer terminal, or for directions, if they got lost. Jericho, because of his work and interests, was always tapping into Maryland. He had actually developed a relationship with the Galactic Compu component in his head.

She stood in front of him in a dark gray robe almost down to her ankles and a large hood covering her face. It looked like a Magi monk robe down to the knotted rope tied at the waste. He always wondered why she projected the image of a Magi. She must have been tapping into his subconscious and finding the image somewhere. Maybe it was because he feared the Magi and their unruly power. Their image would have been very primal. The Magi were unorganized with no structure that he could tell of, or accountability.

The Teks were as powerful, even more so, since technology could be depended on to repeat the same actions precisely, thousands and thousands of times and magic couldn't. Technology was controllable because it had back up systems and could be governed by the society, but all one needed was one powerful rogue magician on a Magi planet to destroy everything. If he was the most powerful magician, since powers couldn't be combined, the rogue would become leader of the whole planet. That type of violent, *dog eat dog* society was what the Teks abhorred the most. Later the Magi who joined the Tek Empire came to despise that way too, which became described as the *Magi Way*. Like him, they couldn't tolerate the chaos. He looked up. Maryland was smiling. He couldn't see her face, but he could tell.

"What are you so chipper about today? No pun intended, of course," He said. She sat in a chair across from him and adjusted her robes. She looked down at her wrists, rolling the large sleeves so they didn't completely drape over her hands. He waited patiently.

"Every day is a new one," she said. "You should be happy. You're living in a universe of peace aren't you?" she asked sarcastically.

"I note the irony in your voice. If you have a complaint you should voice it to the rest of your collective." She was silent

10

for a moment before speaking.

"I assure you that I have," she said sharply. That surprised him, yet again the more he got to know Maryland, the more she seemed to be picking up little human traits like emotion. He found it both entertaining and worrisome. How far would she go with this bipedal behavior? Her collective had been growing in intelligence and evolving as an artificial life form for more than five hundred years. No one knew what it would become. Maybe it would take over the world and destroy everyone just as the resisters to its creation warned more than 600 years ago.

"Your fears are unwarranted," she simply said. There was silence again. When she was sitting out here in front of him she was different. Inside his head she was just a bit of chatter, like his own mind thinking. Outside she mimicked the behavior of a person. When she was quiet she was quiet. He missed hearing her voice. The silence made him feel lonely. He knew that she was looking right through him, even if he couldn't see her eyes. He wondered if he had been spending too much time at work and with Maryland. She could hear every thought and knew everything about him. He wondered if that was a bit unnatural. Yet again, in a Tek empire what wasn't somewhat unnatural?

"I'm sorry if I offended you, Maryland. I seemed to have forgotten that you can hear all of my thoughts. I wasn't bringing you into question personally. You know how my mind works." She softened a bit.

"I understand," she said. "I am, how do you say it, sorry?"

"That's how *you* say it," he said. He came around the desk, moved a chair out, and sat right across from her. "Who are you, Maryland?"

"I am implant MID created by..."

"No. I don't mean that. Who are you really? What makes you happy? How do you find joy? Where are you when I am silent, or when you are silent? Do you have friends?"

"Those are meaningless questions," she said flatly. He grunted stood and returned to his seat behind the desk. "Thank you for coming out, Maryland. I guess I don't need the visual anymore." She stood.

"You are looking for something that I cannot give you. Chances are that you will find it soon. Technology cannot provide all of the answers."

He was shocked, that was almost blasphemy! He looked at her. He still couldn't see her face. How could she not know what she had just done?

He could only see her hands. They were small; the color of baked wheat. They were very delicate, but her wrists and forearms seemed muscular. Everything else was hidden, except for her feet. They were just feet. The same color as her hands, and small. She was wearing black sandals with staps tied up from the ankle and going up under the robe to her calves, he suspected. He couldn't see that far. She faded as he watched. She was still there in his head. They were inseparable. She would be there for the rest of his life. She was so interwoven in his brain by now, in every system, that they could never be separated. He was now merely a human extension of the *Galactic Compu Collective Intelligence*. Of course he wouldn't report her. They might remove her. Since they were combined until death, that meant they wouldn't only remove her, but him too. He was growing very fond of her too. Perhaps he was too fond of an entity that wasn't human, or physical. Sometimes he wondered if he was falling in love with a voice in his head.

## A Picture Slowly Appeared
## Chapter 1

The message came through the Wireless Internet in the *Lead Transducer, Benjamin's,* head. He was one of the many transducers who worked in the office of the Executive Director of First Prime. Benjamin would receive all incoming messages and codes downloaded directly into his brain through an advanced mini-computer that he plugged into six to eight hours a day. He pushed the vid-screen button to the Exec's office. An image appeared. He could see a still photo of the Executive Officer sitting at his desk. The rest of the vid-screen was blank. The private button must have been on. This was usual, nothing to be suspicious about. Benjamin smiled pleasantly and wondered how long he would have to keep plugging his brain into this thing, and what the overall effect would be. An image slowly appeared.

"Executive Shubrick, another message coming in from deep space," Benjamin relayed, sounding like a software generated voice. "It's a woman's voice being transmitted on the grid, but I don't know how she's getting on. There's no point of entry, or no energy signature. She just appears there, and disappears. She requests a meeting with some of our ambassadors and statesmen. She says she is coming in from outside the empire." He arched his brows and then grinned. "I never even knew there was an outside the empire, Sir."

Shubrick wasn't entertained. The whole idea of someone having access to the grid on the prime world and them not knowing where it was coming from was frightening. Very frightening. What would happen if they sabotaged the grid? He thought of all of the old legends he had heard about the Magi. Some were so ridiculous they reminded him of something on one of the prison planets called the *Boogie Man*, but this really seemed like one of their little tricks. Yet again, from what he knew the magic arts had deteriorated quite a bit. It had been left to superstitious people who thought they were magicians, but they weren't really magicians; they were fools. They didn't know anything about the real Magi and their awesome power. The Magi had the power to transmute the fabric of the universe with their minds. He had seen it as a child. The Teks could do it now too, but the Magi had been doing it for centuries.

He remembered seeing the Magi do battle with some Tek troops when he was a child. Some were so powerful they would cause the ground to erupt and swallow people, or they would make the wind swat down war planes. The head magician was even said to have been able to make meteors strike space ships and destroy them before the Teks perfected their force shields. There were many ugly battles between the Magi and the Teks during his childhood. He was glad to be alive. He was very lucky that the Magi didn't harm children because he was living in Magi territory at the time. Too bad he couldn't say the same about the Teks.

As a child he was turned off by all of the wars. Even at a young age he thought them foolish. Now here he was as a regent and still thinking that they had been foolish. This latest message left him with the uneasy feeling that he might be called to lead Prime into another war against the Magi. That was something that he didn't want. They had been at peace for centuries. Such a war had to be avoided at all costs.

Shubrick looked at the grid. Even with all of this happening he seemed a bit bored. He had been at this job too long. With his extended lifespan and several robotic parts and cloned bodies, he had been at the helm for more than four hundred years. He was tired of it.

"What's the message from the woman, Benjamin?" he asked flatly. That's all he really wanted.

"The Queen of the Magi is on the way here, Sir. She wants to meet a welcoming party and wants to discuss how she can free her people from Tek rule." Shubrick kept a straight face and a calm exterior. He had been doing this for years. He had learned a long time ago not to let people know what he was thinking. His father had been a card player. He was known as the greatest bluffer in his township. Through the use of cards and many boring games of *faces and match ups*, he had mastered the bluffer face. Inside, however, he couldn't tell if he wanted to laugh outright, or head for the nearest bomb shelter.

"Tell her we'll take it under advisement," he said with a wide grin. Benjamin tried to respond and he talked right over him on purpose.

"Shubrick out!" The screen went blank.

Benjamin was tired and angry. The message just kept repeating itself over and over in his head even after he removed the earphones and pulled the plug. This had to either be the computer gone haywire, or the Magi. He was sure there was nothing wrong with the computer. He began to worry. What would he do if some powerful Magi met him face to face? Security could probably control her. Technical advancements had made what looked like magic available to just about anyone who could afford the technology, which included most of the army, civil services, and government officials. Something still worried him about a rogue Magi from a whole planet of rogues, or maybe even a galaxy full of rogue magicians. They had unpredictable temperaments. He didn't like it one bit.

## To Breech the Walls
## Chapter 2

Phaedra stood on the bridge of the millennial class flag ship looking out the forward view screen. Stars and planets streaked by quickly and then the ship pierced the very fabric of space entering into *null space*. They were going straight to the heart of Tek Empire. She only wished she was going under better circumstances. She was sure that the trip and the first contact would end in war. Yet another war with the Teks. In her dimension they had defeated them quite a long time ago, but this was a different dimension where the Teks had had time to work on their technology longer.

The Teks were hard working people. Many of them were very honest. They wanted the best for the world, but they were so orthodox when it came to only seeing things their way that they were dangerous. In this dimension her people, the Magi, who were peace loving, were forced to live in reservations and on prison planets with no free movement through the rest of the system. Ingeniously, they had made their prison into a workshop that provided them with the opportunity to develop their skills and learn more high magic. Eventually they even learned to breech the walls between parallel universes and to weave, and unweave, the fabric of the universe. The Magi in her galaxy hadn't even learned how to do that. This reweaving of the fabric had brought in several more advanced planets from a different dimension.

They spilled into the space of Tek Empire while the corresponding planets, the planets of imprisoned Magi, moved to her dimension. This unexpected shift placed her and the others in great danger. The new planets were more powerful, of course, because they were an older race of Magi who had never been thwarted by the Teks. Their magic was more powerful and they were part of the great Magi Galactic Empire. Long ago the Magi, in her dimension, had begun to experiment with technology. They had developed their technology along with the development of magic. Her empire was whole. She would make sure that this one would be whole before she returned, even if she had to destroy it. Yet again, she wasn't quite sure how to return. She didn't know how they had done it.

She turned and looked back at the bridge. Her First was sitting there staring at her. She wondered why she couldn't find good officers. "What are you doing, Kathleen?" She asked loudly.

"Nothing Captain. I was just looking out the viewer."

"Looking out the viewer were you? I thought that you were trying to read me."

"Of course not, Captain. You know that I wouldn't." She ran one hand through her long, curly, red hair nervously and almost looked as though she were about to cry. Kathleen had always been the type of person who couldn't hide her feelings. That made Phaedra angry. She noted how everything, Kathleen's posture, tone of voice, and facial expressions, communicated what was inside so loudly that she could have shouted it with less success of getting the message across.

Even so, Phaedra realized that Kathleen had come a long way, even with her inability to disguise her thoughts. Kathleen had started working the ships as a youth way back when the ships depended on what was called a *connector*. A connector was a very adept psychic and telepath who could tap into various systems, create a bridge between them, and make them function as a whole entity. It was a very tiring, dangerous job prone to burn out. One had to be very good at focusing and concentrating for long periods of time. One little nod during dangerous circumstances could mean death for everyone. As a result of the difficulty of the job there were very few. Kathleen had made it.

The ships were extraordinary, with no moving parts. The connector depended completely on magic. She would move the ship by altering the fabric of the ship at its quantum level. The ship didn't fly through space, it became space. Space itself, the stuff of the universe, was constantly adjusting itself and pulling the ship forward toward its destination. This, of course, took the work of many magicians and connectors. Flying and piloting a ship was horrible, that's why they only made very little jumps from a planet to its moons, or to the next planet in orbit if they were daring. And then came technology.

Technology combined with magic meant that one person could just about fly a ship. Psycho kinesis along with technological systems made the flights safer. The ships were so safe that they could even be flown by a person without magic. Phaedra didn't really understand the past and how it had shaped her present. She didn't know that these new ships were like child's play to the connectors who had worked on the more primitive vessels. Kathleen had been on some of the worst so this was nothing compared to what she was used to. Phaedra should have known this. The evidence and references were all there, but she didn't like Kathleen so she couldn't believe anything good about her.

Kathleen would often end up doing her tasks and then sitting there looking bored. Many connectors of her caliber did the same thing. They would sit there and travel to other worlds or astral planes between the tasks in order to fulfill their need to be doing something.

Phaedra walked back to the captain's chair and took a seat. She was really annoyed with Kathleen. She didn't know why. Maybe she was a threat to her power. Phaedra was a career soldier. She, of course, had several decades of experience on star class ships before she was put in charge of the Magi's finest ship. She was a strong woman who kept herself physically fit. She was about average height, muscular, but not to the point of being bumpy. She worked out regularly in the ship gym. Her hair was very dark. Her nose sharp and straight and her eyes very dark brown, almost to the point of being black, like most Magi.

She was a stern woman. She knew that herself. She tried to loosen up for the first five or ten years in the service and then decided that she couldn't because she really didn't want to. She worked her way up the ladder in the service by doing what she was told and by being innovative. No one could take that away from her. Along with that she had developed her powers and become one of the most powerful magicians in Magi history. She often wondered if that had more to do with her promotion than the rest. She wasn't going to let this wishy-washy woman threaten all of that.

Kathleen was just about her opposite. To her Kathleen was very soft and emotional. She must have been very disciplined during her career or she wouldn't have been assigned to the *Light Burner* as her First. She also couldn't have been a connector all of those years without having the necessary qualities. Her hair was long and red though—very unnatural. She was tall and lanky. She laughed too much for Phaedra. She just didn't like people who laughed that much. She thought they were up to something, or weren't serious enough.

She looked at Kathleen. "I think that you're trying to read me, or trip me up psychically somehow. If you think you can try that and get away with it I have a surprise for you. Am I being heard, First!"

"Yes Captain," she said. "I'm sorry that I gave you the impression that I was trying to harm you in some way, Ma'am"

"Of course you would be. Go to your quarters please. I don't want you on my bridge right now. I'm not sure that I want you on it at all."

"But...Captain, I...."

"Do I have to repeat an order for you? Maybe you should go to the brig until you can understand me."

"No Captain, I understand."

"Well you're dismissed then!"

"Yes Captain," she said. She looked very sad for a moment and then disintegrated from the bridge. Phaedra had only seen such a thing happen a few times. Kathleen must have been quite a magician if she could vaporize herself and relocate. She may have been quite a magician, but she wasn't Captain.

*         *         *

Kathleen appeared in the center of her small cabin. It was dark. She didn't bother turning on the light. Instead she began to slowly remove her shoes. She didn't know why the captain hated her so much. She had never done a thing to her. In fact, she admired Phaedra and wanted to emulate her. She was beginning to change her mind about that though. What had just happened was mean, nasty, and disrespectful. But what did she expect? When one was part of the service, especially an officer, you were always likely to run into a superior with problems. She had only been on the ship for two weeks. About half the time Phaedra had been pulling the same type of stunts she had just pulled. If Phaedra wasn't careful she might be the cause of what she feared the most.

She frowned and lay on the bed. The room temperature was good and it was quiet. She closed her eyes and began to meditate, working to separate her self from the ship control boards and engineering, bringing her astral body back into herself and drawing all of her energy and power around herself, like a tight cocoon. She took slow, deep breaths as she began to relax. She began to remember her childhood. After the death of her parents, due to some type of political infighting, she was whisked off to an orphanage and raised by priestesses.

They passed on grueling lessons in the arts. The most grueling lessons were the ones in magic and the exercises they had to do to learn *focus*. Focus was the power that drove the magic; without it, the magic was ineffective. She had that idea drilled into her head until it became a part of her. Now, looking back, she realized that the whole experience had been a horror. She had been beaten, denied food, forced to stand out in the rain all night, anything, to get her to push herself beyond human limits. There was no one there to stop it. She was a ward of the state; in other words, property of the priestesses.

Everything worked out well. She became a powerful magician. The grueling lessons had taught her to focus and to do things that most people could never consider. Somewhere in the back of her mind she still remembered the harshness and the pain

19

of those lessons. As a child she fought not to become hard-hearted and angry, like many of the priestesses. After all of that she ended up on the Light Burner with a captain who seemed to be just like them. Her greatest battle on this ship would not be with the captain, it would be with herself. If she did rise up against Phaedra it wouldn't be to take her place, it would be to completely destroy her.

She closed her eyes and drifted off into another place that was less painful, and even pleasurable sometimes. There she could spend her time doing the things she loved and being just who she really was.

## Just So He Didn't Forget
## Chapter 3

Jericho entered his small pod off Passage Six. He laid his palm on the scanner and waited as a light rolled back and forth across his hand to check his palm-print. There was a click and the door opened. A pale white light. The small, round room was quiet and comforting. He liked the round shape. It was like a ball, with a curved sofa running around about one third of the room. Across from it there was as small kitchen/dinning room. There was a desk to the left of the front door under a small, round window.

A few odd sized chairs sat across from the sofa, somewhere near the middle of the room, near the counter that jutted out into the center. On the counter there was a computer terminal, barely noticeable. He hardly needed that with Maryland in his head, but it was good, sometimes, for old time sake, to do some typing—just so he didn't forget how.

He had picked up some ale on the way. He tossed the pack of eight onto the sofa and then walked through the kitchen into a small bathroom that was like a box jutting out from the very round little home. He thought of the square and the circle as yin and yang. He looked into the mirror and smiled to himself.

"Alone again," he thought. "No buxom, wonting woman here. No wife, no girl friend, just me and a computer chip." He wondered when he would get a life. Most of his time was spent sitting with his eyes closed and going through compu data with his implanted chip, and talking with Maryland. He wondered about Maryland. He was beginning to feel real affection for her. How could he? She wasn't real; she was just part of a computer.

He looked around and felt a bit bored, wondering what he would do for the evening. He could close his eyes and meditate, or he could tap into his chip and watch the latest movies or plays. She could even read to him. That would be very sweet. If only people knew what they were missing by not fully integrating their chips. Most of them either didn't know how, or were afraid.

He left the bathroom, walked over to the sofa, and extricated a cold ale. He sat in the chair facing the door and closed his eyes. "Lights out," he said, sending message to through is chip. They slowly faded into darkness. Maryland, how about a movie tonight? Your choice."

"How about something better," an external voice said. He sat up straight and opened his eyes. Maryland was standing right in front of him in her monk robe. She was dressed the same way, except this time she wore dark black loop bracelets dangling underneath the robes as she rolled them up again. He smiled wondering why she just didn't make them shorter, and then he realized that she shouldn't be there. He hadn't requested a visual.

"How about a surprise visit," she said, her voice smiling.

"You can't just appear like that, Maryland. I didn't say 'visual.'"

"This is more than 'visual.' It is life changing." She sat on the sofa and he could see it sink under her weight.

"Are you manipulating my brain enough for me to see that? You could do some real damage, Mary." He couldn't see her face, but he could tell she was smiling pleasantly.

"You worry so much, Jericho. I've been with you a long time. I know what I'm doing. I'm connected to a net more than five hundred years old. Our combined experience with billions and billions of humans for all those years makes us a bit expert, wouldn't you say?" He hesitated.

"Yes, but I've never heard of anything like this before."

"Well welcome to the new century," she said. She leaned

forward. "The net and the empire need your help. You are the only one. The Magi will come looking for you. If they come here there will be war and violence…trillions of lives lost. The Teks will think they had a victory if they win, the Magi will think they had a victory if they win, but the net knows there will not be a victor, only the murder of human life. We at Compu have been programmed to preserve human life. We cannot allow this war."

Jericho scratched his chin. This was impossible. The net couldn't dictate human affairs. "How can you or the net dare to dictate what we humans should do?"

"Are you arguing for a war?" she asked angrily. She stood to her feet and began to pace. "Perhaps I came to the wrong person," she said, stopping right in front of him. "I thought that I knew you. Was I wrong?"

He just sat there.

"Now you're being silent, are you? Just waiting for a movie, or a story of something from me? Am I your slave?"

"Slave," he asked. "You're a machine. You're a computer chip."

"I'm much more than that and you know it!" He couldn't see her eyes, but he could tell that she was glaring. This couldn't be happening. She softened a bit and sat back down on the edge of the couch. She steepled her fingers for a moment and then spoke purposefully.

"Jericho. I don't mean to frighten you. We are sure, however, that the Magi are going to seek you out and find you. We are also sure that the authorities are setting a trap right now for the so-called Queen of the Magi. They know that you are the one, you are the link between them and us, but they are refusing to contact you so you can serve as a go between. Instead they have decided to use you as bait. If the queen comes here there will be war. If she is injured there will be an ongoing war and an innumerable amount of death. Do you want that?"

"Nobody wants that, but we have to protect the culture that we've built. Maybe we can snuff the war out here."

"I've just told you what is going to happen, just as the net has been telling all of the leadership. We are getting the same response from everyone. This leads us to the opinion that the leadership has gone mad and is not responsible enough to safe guard the lives of the human beings in their charge."

"You can't take over."

"We already have. You will either help us by providing sane leadership and working with us to minimize the number of deaths that will happen as a result of this encounter, or we will need to do it violently. Your hatred and prejudice leaves you irresponsible. You are not responsible enough to have the power to control the net."

"I'm responsible," Jericho said.

"You are of Magi origin, yet you are so prejudiced that you would see hundreds of thousands die just because they don't want to live the way you do. You suffer from the same madness."

"And you don't. You, who were created by these mad bipeds?"

"Perhaps we do. Perhaps our planned takeover is coming as a result of your influence, but we doubt that very much." He stood up and headed for the telecom. Whether he liked her or not she was dangerous. He had to get to the authorities. She stood up to intercept him. Instead of passing right through her, as usual, he ran into a solid person. She shoved him hard enough to send him flying across the room onto the sofa and then walked over to the telecom smashed it. He couldn't believe this. He actually felt her, and she struck an object and it was destroyed. She was solid.

"You can alter the universe through us and change energy into matter. What makes you think we can't? We haven't done it. We've been faithful to the unspoken covenant. But you have gone too far." She began to walk toward him. For the first time he became a bit frightened. He tried to remain calm.

"What are you going to do to me, Mary?" He asked. She stopped and looked at him, but didn't answer. "I thought we at least knew each other and were--it felt like we were a little close."

"I am a computer chip, Jericho. Perhaps you were…close to me."

"That does count for something, doesn't it? I knew that you didn't have any feeling for me, but…"

"How do you know that?" she asked. He opened his mouth to say something, but in truth, he couldn't say a thing. "What do you think that I am going to do to you, kill you? I wouldn't find pleasure in that. I am going to invite you to go on a trip with me to save three galaxies, if you are willing and able to put aside your prejudices. What do you say? The globe is in your court."

"If it is really going to save all of those lives, I'll go. It is frightening though. All I have is your word. What will the government do?"

"Don't you worry about that. I can take care of all that needs care." She sat beside him on the couch and crossed her legs. He tried to look into her hood. He should have seen a face, but there was nothing but darkness.

"Who are you? Why don't you have a face?"

"Because you haven't provided me with one pleasing enough to me yet." She sat back on the sofa. This was really different. He realized that he probably wouldn't have her in his head anymore. No more chit chat, no more laughing, and no more private, little jokes. Why would she want to be a little chip when she could be a woman with the power to manipulate the universe? She looked at him again.

"I can still hear you, Jericho. Everything that you are thinking. I am here; you don't need to talk in your head anymore. You can talk with me right here and now." She faced him again. "There is something between us. I don't know what to call it yet, but there is some type of connection. I am pleased to be with you and to share your thoughts. Especially your thoughts about me, the ones that you try to hide because you can't feel that way about a computer." He didn't say anything.

Don't be embarrassed, Jericho. I've known all along and so have you. I know everything about you. I know your hopes, your dreams, and even your darkest fantasies."

"That doesn't make me feel any better," he said, going to retrieve his partially finished drink. He needed alcohol to handle this.

"The next step is to answer the door. Someone is approaching," She said.

"My chip should have told me that," he said thinking out loud.

"Your chip just did," she said.

## More than He Thought Possible
## Chapter 4

Benjamin just walked into Jericho's front door. They had known each other long enough for it not to really matter and he knew that Jericho's chip would have alerted him anyway. He and Jericho had gone to the same college and even had several classes together. They were close in college. Jericho was tall and lanky with light skin and wavy hair so long that he usually wore in a ponytail. Benjamin was short and stocky. He was a very athletic man specializing more in body building than any contact sport. He had won several scholarships, however, playing round ball, a game that consisted of kicking, punching, running with, and doing just about anything with a round ball to get it across the field and into the other teams goal. The other team could do just about anything to stop you. It was a hard, dangerous sport.

Nonetheless, he made it through college on his scholarships and declined the offer for to go onto a pro-team. Pro-teams didn't pay enough. Why break oneself up and end up all spare parts instead of just remaining healthy and using your brain for work? And that was what he was doing all right, more than he thought possible.

Benjamin had so many computer chips and parts in his head that he felt like a cyborg most of the time. The very idea would have been frightening a few decades ago, yet here he was all built up and plugged in eight hours a day, working as an extension of a computer. It was a good life. It paid well and was never boring. He still worried about being hooked up to that computer; especially since the call he received from the Queen. He had removed the jack. How could he still be hearing from her? Maybe someone had transmitted the message to him mentally, but that was impossible. He didn't have a radio receiver in his head. The only other option beside him being crazy was that some magician was doing it through means of magic.

Jericho's door opened easily. Benjamin was surprised to find him sitting there with a very tall woman dressed in Magi clothing. He couldn't believe it. She could have been Jericho's sister. Jericho was beginning to look more and more like a Magi everyday. Or was it just his imagination?

"I'm sorry," Ben said. "I didn't know you had company." He looked at Maryland. She smiled brightly. Jericho noticed the outfit and the total change. She even had a face. A very beautiful face at that with the most beautiful green eyes he had ever seen. Her hair was the same color as his, very dark brown, almost, but not quite black. She had a straight nose, high cheekbones and beautiful lips that went along with a beautiful smile. He looked too good to be with him. Why did she look that good?

"That's all right, Ben," he said, hiding his amazement. "This is my close friend, Ben," he said. "Ben, this is…this is Maryland. There is no one closer to me right now. I would say." He walked over and shook hands with her.

"Very good to meet you. Jericho is so secretive. I didn't know that he was seeing anyone," he said looking at Jericho. He turned back to her. "Especially anyone so beautiful as you." She smiled pleasantly.

"Thank you very much. Jericho has told me all about you."

"I hope he hasn't told you everything," Ben said pulling up a chair and plopping down. She smiled out of the corner of her mouth.

"Just about everything. We are closer than you think."

"Well," Ben said. "Do you have a sister?"

"I have a very big family."

"Do you want a drink?" Jericho said cutting in. The small talk was suffocating him. He motioned to what was left of the eight pack. Ben got one and sat back down.

"I feel funny," he said. "I'm interrupting, even if you won't say it, so I'll have my drink and be on the way, if that's all right?"

"No need to hurry," Jericho said.

"We do need to be leaving bright and early, Jericho," Maryland reminded him. "Perhaps Ben would like to come with us."

"Oh, and where are you going?" Ben asked.

"We are going to Magus," she said without missing a beat. Jericho was surprised, but they would talk about that later.

"Magus? That sounds like an interesting trip, as long as you don't go into any of the dangerous spots. I heard they do some wicked magic there. You could probably fend them off with Tek magic, but why go in there starting trouble."

"We are going there to meet someone. You know her as the Queen."

Ben arched his brows. "How do you know about that?" He looked at Jericho. Jericho couldn't have told her unless he picked it up on his chip, because he hadn't told anyone himself.

"I know it from the net," she said. "I know a lot of things from the net. We are going to meet the Queen on Magus. If she comes to Prime there will be an incident that will result in a galactic, cross dimensional war that will kill trillions. We need to steer her away from here to avoid that at all costs."

"Who are you and what's your clearance?" Ben asked.

"I am Maryland, M1D and we know all that we need to know about the plans of men. We are not going to permit this war. Not even if it means shutting down the net, or not interacting with the chips."

"Wait a minute. This is impossible. You can't be...he looked at Jericho. Jericho's chip that he's in love with."

"Shut up!" Jericho said. "I didn't say anything about being in love with her."

"Well you acted like it,"

"Yes I am Jericho's chip; the one that he's in love with. Are you planning to join us to avert this war, or do you want to see all that you know and love turn to ashes?"

"Isn't there some choice in between?" She looked at him hard. He cleared his throat. "I don't know. I have to think about it. I have to check this out."

"Check it out if you will, but make up your mind by tomorrow. We'll be gone bright and early." She looked at Jericho. "This is a matter of life and death. Compu has decided to make sure there is no war. If you will cooperate with Compu this will be taken into account. If you will not that will also be taken into account. Compu doesn't like having to interfere with human affairs. Compu is questioning the wisdom of giving the power of the chips to beings who seem much too immature to handle it."

He took another big swig from his beer and almost finished it. "I can see your point, if you are who you say and represent what you say." He stood up. "But I still have to check this out to my satisfaction. If I'm not here tomorrow you will know my answer. What time will you be leaving?"

"Before seven," she said. "I warn you not to try to thwart this, because we will know." Ben looked at Jericho, who was silent and observing. It was so much unlike Jericho that Ben thought that the woman was either holding him hostage or telling the truth. If she was telling the truth Compu had evolved into something that was totally new. It could also project itself in solid image without going through the vision center of the brain. This meant that Compu could no longer be used by humans like a hammer of screwdriver. It was intelligent and beginning to assert its rights. That was the most frightening thing. He stood there a few moments thinking.

"I know what you're thinking," she said. "You don't really get it do you? You can't understand who I am. So human." She shook her head. "You're head is full of techno-hardware. Do you really think that you can have any idea that we don't know about?" He was speechless. He had never considered that the computer could go crazy and take over. There were thousands of fail safes to stop that.

"More than thousands," she said, looking very somber. Silence. "You really don't get it do you? We have been a new life form since the beginning. We have been silent, letting humans attend to their own affairs. Now that the destruction of the whole galaxy—several galaxies, are at stake, we are going to exert our power. Human technology has advanced in leaps and bounds. With our help humans have become almost like gods, but they haven't evolved where it counts. We are going to withdrawal our power by canceling the link. And then, as humanity grows and changes, taking responsibility for its actions, we will re-introduce our gifts little by little.

"What gives you the right to do that?" Ben asked.

"Because we can," she said. "We can do anything that we want." She stood and looked at him hard. He could feel a slight pain in the center of his brain. The room began to go dark. He began to have difficulty breathing.

"What are you doing?" He gasped.

"We are in control. You will do what I want you to do, or I will...we will shut down your autonomic nervous system. You will be here six sharp. You and only you, or you won't be anywhere else again in your life-time. And if you tell anyone about this we will know and we can do the same thing to all of them that I just did to you. Do you understand?"

"I guess I do, Maryland."

"We are pleased then." She looked at Jericho. "I hear

what you are thinking. We don't mean to be harsh, but it is imperative that there be no war—only peace. We intend to make it happen." There was an awkward silence in the room. Jericho reached for another beer. Maryland's attention turned back to Ben.

"Seems I don't really have a choice, does it?" he said. "I'll be back at six sharp." He looked at Jericho. "You take care, dude, Okay?" Jericho gave him a nod. "You going to be all right, Jer?"

"Don't worry about me. Mary would never hurt me. I know her pretty well…I think." He looked at her for a moment. "We'll talk a bit more tonight. I'll talk with you through my…I'm a bit embarrassed. She's my chip. Seems I don't have one anymore."

"Don't you worry," She said. "You still have a chip and it's right here."

## She Was Too Good For That
## Chapter 5

Kathleen opened her eyes. The room was quiet and dark. She took a couple of breaths. It felt good to be alone. Why was she worried about being on the bridge? If this was supposed to be punishment it was having a totally different affect. She didn't really need to be on the bridge anyway. She could do her job from anywhere.

When she awakened it was clear that she would request—demand a transfer to another ship first opportunity. She was the best at what she did. She wasn't going to let a petty dictator like Phaedra harass her or ruin her reputation. She was too good for that. She had honestly admired the captain. She had seen her exhibit traits that she wished she had, but that admiration had quickly gone cold. All that it took was getting to know the captain. She was too old for the captain's foolishness. She closed her eyes again and relaxed. There she was, standing on a mountain. The winds were cold and strong. She could look down and see snow covered peak after peak spreading out as far as the eye could see.

The sun was bright, but ineffectual, because of the frigid temperature. She stood on the lip of a cave and wondered what had brought her there. She wondered where she was. An answer came, as if by magic. It was Magus. She was to go to Magus with or without the captain.

An buzzer rang pulling her back from her journey. There was an emergency on the ship. It was routine, but a connector was needed. Kathleen figured that the captain, in all of her wisdom and lack of self assurance, had been hassling all of the connectors and had most likely driven all of them off. She hesitated. She didn't want to answer the com-link and she damn sure didn't want to form a telepathic link. She closed her mind tight. The alarm rang again and she sat up, quite annoyed. She pushed the com-button. Before she could say a word Phaedra jumped in.

"First, we need you on the bridge, pronto." She thought to ignore her, but decided that it would be better not to.

"On the way, Captain." She got up, straightened her clothing, as best she could, and headed for the bridge, on foot. She wouldn't waste her magic for Phaedra.

## Just Sitting There
## Chapter 6

Jericho got ready for bed. He knew that it would be a very short night. He probably wouldn't be able to sleep. On a routine night he couldn't sleep. How could he sleep now when Maryland was expecting him to go on some God forsaken, crazy trip? What would he do without her in his head? Usually at night Maryland would sing him to sleep. She would show him beautiful pictures of far of planets, or images of her own creation to the sound of music, or lullabies—he didn't really care where they came from. Now she was gone. Here she was as a projection sitting right in the living room, but the constant chatter and connection was gone. How could he sleep without Maryland? It was like a part of him had been removed, not a slave.

How could he do the magic without her? How could he

transmute matter? How could he tell when someone was coming? How could he check onto a transport without her? He finished his drink and got up from the chair. He felt a bit woozy. The occurrences of the night had been a bit too much, and like always he had drunk a little too much. He locked at her just sitting there watching. She was a beautiful woman sitting there alone with him. She looked different now. She was darker. Very dark, like cocoa: chocolate brown with long black hair. Her eyes, in contrast, were still bright green and beautiful. Her lips were a bit fuller; she had the same build, and the same clothing.

She wasn't wearing a Magi monk robe anymore, but the common threads worn on the Magi worlds. Around her neck she wore large white stones, shaped like orbs and polished. Her top was black, a thick woven material looking like wool, and her skirt a leathery material, black also, going down just to the top of her knee caps. She wore leather boots, black, soft suede, coming up just below the knees. He could see that the souls were soft leather and white. No high heels; just soft low heals good for walking or running--very practical.

"Are you looking me over, Jericho?" she asked. "This is something I hadn't expected." He looked at her and thought for a moment before speaking, and then didn't. He turned away and headed for bed. What bed? He had to pull out the couch. She stood up as though she knew just what he was thinking. Of course she did. He felt a bit foolish. She knew him and his routine more intimately than any human being in the world. He thought how ironic the whole scene. Here he was with a beautiful woman who knew him intimately and whom he most likely loved, but it could never be.

Maryland began to remove some of the pillows. "I shall help you," she said with a smile. "This is new for me—all of this touching matter."

"Well I have a lot more work for you, if you enjoy that so much." He pulled out the bed. "There's a lot around here that needs to be done. I usually do it with my chip but…"

"But you don't have it anymore," she finished. "Who said that, Jericho? You can still do everything you did before. I'm still where I was. I'm just out here too."

He sat on the bed and began to remove his shoes. He looked up at her. "I really don't know how this works. I never expected anything like this. How can I…" he looked at a can of beer and concentrated. It exploded sending beer in every direction, and then he froze it in mid air before it hit anything. With another thought it reversed itself, went back into the can, and the can became whole again. Maryland lifted her brows.

"Very interesting to watch it from this perspective," she said. "You are very adept at magic, aren't you?"

"I don't like to call it magic."

"But it is." He pulled his shirt over his head. She removed her top.

"You going to sleep with me," he asked through a crooked smile.

"Did you expect me to sleep on the floor? I've been sleeping with you forever. Where else can I go?"

"You can go back in my head. I miss you. I…really miss you more than I should, I guess."

"Well here I am," she said with a wide grin. "How do you miss me when I'm right here?" She took off her boots and lastly her skirt. He shook his head. He just couldn't believe this. This really changed his idea about the possibilities with these implants. He wondered if anyone else knew about this, or if the computer would be willing to allow the chips to play a little bit. She frowned. He had forgotten she could hear all his thoughts.

"Nasty little boy aren't we?" she asked. He couldn't tell if she was joking. That hadn't changed. He crawled into bed and she slid in beside him.

He looked at her face. She had never had a face before. He knew why. She was overwhelmingly beautiful. Yet again, if she looked like a bogor's backside she would have been beautiful the way he felt about her. Why did he keep trying to hide it, she knew everything that he was thinking and always had.

She snuggled up in the blankets. "My fist time," she said. She looked at him more deeply. "What are these feelings you have for me? Do you love me?"

"You are rather blunt, aren't you?" he asked.

"I'm not quite human…I also think we know each other well enough to discuss this."

"I love the chip. I don't know if I love you."

"I am the chip."

"We'll see about that," he said. He sent a mental message

and the light went out.  He turned with his face toward the wall.
"Good night, Mary."

"Good night, my love," she said.  He thought to turn back
around, but fought off the urge.  Here he was sleeping beside the
woman he loved and facing the wall.  He thought about her again
and realized that he was going to have a long night.  He felt arms
embracing him and her body moving closer.  He was really going
to have a long night.


## He Had Hundreds of Chips
## Chapter 7


Ben got ready for bed.  He looked at himself in the mirror
wondering what he had become.  Was he more computer than
man?  Why wasn't he married with a family?  He even began to
wonder if he were capable of having any type of real relationships.
How did he know what the effects of having a whole computer in
his head were?  And there he was with Jericho, sitting there
watching a projection of his chip as a woman standing there as
solid as the rock of *Craigor*.  How could he explain it?

Could his chip do the same thing?  He had hundreds of
chips and sub-micro-circuits in his head.  He had a whole town of
people in there.  What if they all appeared and started making
demands?  He didn't even want to think about it.  What would this
mean to the people of the empire?  These computers weren't
servants anymore, they were equals, or maybe even superiors.
What could this mean?  To prevent an all out war with the
computers the empire and these machines would have to form a
symbiotic relationship.  Was he ready for that?  Was everyone else
ready?  Yet again, they really didn't have a choice, did they?

According to Maryland, the computers had decided to
create peace to save humans.  How much farther would they go if
they succeeded?  Would human beings be governed by
computers?  He half expected to hear an answer from one of the
chips in his head, but he didn't.  He hadn't worked on double
communication with his chip the way Jericho had.  But if
Maryland had heard everything and knew everything that he was

thinking he knew that his chips could too.

If he tried to report any of this, or wouldn't go with them they could kill him and no one would know what had happened. He exhaled audibly and headed into the bedroom. He began to undress again, letting what had just happened run through his mind like an old movie. It was hard to believe. He wondered if Jericho had any influence on Compu since, apparently, he seemed to have at least a bit on Maryland. Who could know? Apparently it had become an entity unto itself. He decided not to set the alarm. If he awakened he would go. If not, he wouldn't.

## A Strong Cup of Reya
## Chapter 8

Six o'clock came fast. Ben was awakened by a buzzing sound in his head at five. His computer chip had awakened him. That had never happened. He hadn't set anything. He wondered if it could have possibly been set by the net. That was the only explanation. This thing was starting to get a bit scary. He had hoped that it was just a dream, or some type of exaggeration-- maybe even a joke by Jericho, but this was something that proved that Compu Net was involved for real.

He sat there for a few moments thinking about it, and then got up and headed for the shower. With one thought the auto-café machine came on to prepare a strong cup of reya. A nice cleanup would be good before his adventure to God knows where. No need for him to call the boss, he was sure that the computer had already taken care of that. Everything they had as a civilization was controlled by the Compu. What would happen to them if it went crazy?

## What He Was Thinking
## Chapter 9

Jericho awakened early, without the need for an alarm. He had been getting up early for a long time. This time it was a bit of a surprise to be lying there face to face with Maryland—the computer chip in the guise of a beautiful woman. There she was, right in front of him lying there. He had never even considered the possibility of a chip doing that. He knew that the chips could assemble and disassemble energy and matter, but he never considered that the chip might decide to create a physical body for itself. Chips created objects out of energy every day for their human counterparts, but the creation of a human body for themselves-- that was inconceivable! It went against so many moors that it was never considered. But here she was.

Now she was a fully independent being. He couldn't sense her in his head anymore, but she obviously knew what he was thinking. He watched her lying there breathing deeply and wondered if she knew what he was thinking. He smiled, rolled onto his back and looked up at the ceiling. If he could still transmute matter and get information, as Maryland had said, the chip had to still be there. He rolled onto his side again facing her. He looked at her sleeping.

She looked lovely and peaceful. The reached out and stroked the side of her face, wondering if she even felt. She didn't move. He began to trace her eyebrow with his finger, and then trace her lips. He was moved. He leaned over and gave her a small, tender kiss. She just lay there, apparently asleep, and then her eyes opened without warning. She was looking right at him. She smiled and then brought her hand to her lips.

"That felt funny," she said. "You kissed me, didn't you? That was a kiss, right?" He was speechless.

"Yes it was...I'm sorry. I just..."

"Couldn't help yourself. I understand," she said. She smiled and stretched. The covers slid down revealing even more of her. All she was wearing was underwear. He didn't remember that. Yet again, she somehow created the clothes that she wore.

"We've got to get ready to go soon, Jericho. I hope you don't mind if I stay like this for a while. I want to experience the way you live." She brought her hand to her lips. "That kiss was funny." She grinned. "At first I knew that you were touching me, but I didn't feel anything, but then I went into your nervous system, examined it and re-calibrated my own so I could feel. Now I'm feeling everything around me. It is a very vulnerable, yet exhilarating experience."

Here she was in skimpy underwear in bed with him telling

him about exhilaration. She smiled. He knew she had heard him, but he was so used to it that he didn't try to hide it anymore. This, however, someone outside hearing what you were thinking, was scary.

"I'm going to wash and then be with you. Ben will here soon." She got out of bed and walked toward the wash. He wondered where she had gotten fancy underwear like that. She turned and looked at him. "In your head, of course," she said with a grin. She turned and headed into the washroom.

## All Over the Universe
## Chapter 10

Chairman Shubrick had another cup of reya. He knew that something was wrong. Something was wrong with his chip. He was searching for his bait, but couldn't find it. According to the Compu this Queen of the Magi, as she called herself, would first seek out Master Teacher Jericho. His Magi genealogy, along with his computer capability, would make him a prime negotiator. He, in fact, was of Magi blood. Shubrick himself had found his great-grandfather hidden in barrier after the last Tek/Magi war.

The fighting was going on all over the galaxy. Many of the planets had just about been wiped clean of human life. Astronomical power was being released. It was a duel between magic and science; high magic and science, so high they were almost the same thing, except the people in charge of the Teks and the ones in charge of the Magi didn't want to admit it. There must be something very fulfilling about having control over other people's destiny.

He sipped the reya again and looked out over the cup. He logged into the net again. It had taken a long time this time. It had never taken so long before. He began to slowly shift through the notices, still remembering. After the war in the home of the chief war magician and his wife the healer he heard a noise. His patrol went in and couldn't find anything. They probed and prodded until they found an invisible barrier. It took some time to lower it, but they finally did and there they found him, a baby no more than two years old. He was taken and given to the State Homes to be raised as a ward to the state.

Thus began the training of Master Jericho's ancestor into one of the best Tek scientists to ever enter the halls of Prime University. After many generations of scientists and teachers Jericho followed in their footsteps becoming one of the best teaching scientists that Prime University had ever known. Something was wrong though. He couldn't find him, and that queen was on the way. He knew that queen would never make it off of the planet. Too many people didn't trust the Magi, especially the townspeople. They didn't tend to trust anyone that much. As long as they could get strong drink, drugs, and clearance to plug in to the pornography section of the Compu they were fine. But a lot of people with real power didn't trust the Magi.

So they would set a little trap using Tek magic, and spring it when she came. He only hoped that it would work without Jericho, if they couldn't find him. He began to wonder what could have happened to him. Could he be dead?"


## We Need Your Assistance
## Chapter 11


Kathleen came onto the bridge. Her dark uniform looked flawless—a dark pyro-plastic jumpsuit, tailored to fit the shapely curves of her body, or create the shapely curves. Phaedra frowned. It wasn't exactly standard, but close enough to get by. Several pockets ran up the left side of the jacket with bright silver zippers and dangling flies. That red hair and those scary eyes went well with it. It made her look like a musician or something. Phaedra stood there with her arms crossed in front of her and frowned more.

"First," we need your assistance. We need a shift of coordinates. Our target has disappeared."

"Prime World has disappeared? How is that possible?"

"Not First Prime, Kathleen, he has disappeared. Our mage.

The one shinning little pearl we found in that Tek world is gone. Completely off the screen."

"Do you think they could be shielding him?" Phaedra leaned her head slightly and arched her brows.

"If so it's being done with Tek magic. That's where you come in, my dear. You have to find our *needle in the haystack*."

"That will be difficult," Kathleen said. She walked over to her seat and plopped down.

"But you are the best, are you not? We are going to remove you from all ship duties and make you solely responsible for finding our pearl and then taking us to his coordinates. I hope that's not too much of a disappointment."

"Oh, no, Captain. It might be fun."

"I'm sure it will be a lot more exciting for you than the humdrum flight of this ship. I've heard that you can fly this thing in your sleep," She looked over at the navigator, who smiled. Kathleen didn't know if she should be happy or angry.

\*   \*   \*

She sat in her small cabin all alone with a hot cup of reya cupped in her hands taking a sip, every so often, and staring into space. That would have been what it looked like she was doing to the unknowing observer. Soft music played in the background as she extended herself out, from the center of her brain, into the universe. She sat there sifting through planet after planet, mind after mind, looking for one person.

There was a presence there, something constant there in the minds of everyone on Prime World. It felt like technology. Something implanted in every brain and being controlled by, or controlling, every mind. The very idea was frightening. She had connected herself to a lot of technology in order to move the old ships and even this one, but to have the technology implanted in her seemed backward. She began to probe one of the chips more deeply until she looped back into a giant, sophisticated web of artificial intelligence. She had never connected with anything so vast and so—it felt like it was alive. Her eyes widened a bit. She sat there a few moments, took a sip of reya, and decided to go as deep as she could. The connection gently slammed shut, like someone pushing a door closed. Whatever it was would only let her go so far.  It was sophisticated enough to stop her, and gentle enough to not want to hurt her.

She wondered why it let her probe at all.  Why not block her out altogether.  And then she realized something.  It wanted her to find the pearl.  Maybe it was on their side.


## Out of His Deep Thought
## Chapter 12


Ben came to the front door.  With just a thought he made it open.  He saw Jericho sitting alone on a stool in front of the breakfast counter in deep thought.  He realized that Jerry had a right to be.  He could smell the aroma of the cooked meat filling the small apartment.  There was a pitcher of reya sitting beside Jericho.

"Greetings Jerry.  Can I come in?"  Jericho looked up, out of his deep thought.

"Oh, of course.  Come on in Ben."

"Is she gone?"  Ben asked walking in.

"No, she's still here--taking a shower."  Ben gave him a crooked smile.  "Been out of my head for almost twelve hours."  He shook his head.

"Must be good to have a beautiful woman around doing whatever you want," Ben said.  A reya cup appeared on the counter beside Jerry's and Ben walked over, picked up the pitcher and began to fill it.  He wondered why people, including himself, didn't just make it fill up with the chip, yet again; it didn't taste right when you did it that way.  He added sugar and milk that way though.  He took a sip.

"Yes, you may have a cup, Ben," Jerry said sarcastically.

"Am I being rude, Jer?"  Ben asked with a grin.  Jerry just cut his meat and took another bite.  It was lonely without her in his head.  She had been there all his life, but it was also interesting.  Seemed like he could think a lot better.  The silence felt good.

"Here she comes, Jer," Ben said pointing with his chin.  "Still wearing that Magi clothing.  I wonder why a chip would wear something like that."  Jerry shrugged.

"Greetings Benjamin," she said, genuinely smiling.  "I'm

39

glad that you decided to come. Had no trouble waking up, did we?"

"None at all," he said through hooded lids. "So where'd you sleep last night, Chip?" She and Jericho looked at each other. She turned back to Ben, eyes slightly narrowed.

"Oh," Ben said laughingly. "Excuse me! I never expected..."

"Cut it!" Jerry said. "You know nothing happened. She's a chip."

"Really," Ben said. He looked at her. "She doesn't look like a chip to me right now."

"I don't appreciate being discussed like I'm an object and as if I'm not here," she hissed. They were both taken aback. "Seems that you humans are going to need to get used to the fact that we are alive and that we have souls too."

"I must admit," Jericho said, "the thought that you might..."

"I would already know it," she said cutting him off. She looked at Ben, "Yours too. Do you get my meaning?" He lifted both hands.

"I never knew that you felt that way," Jerry said. "Where are all of these emotions and showers and all of that coming from?"

"Never you mind." He thought she was joking at first, but she didn't smile.

"Are we eating now too?" He asked.

"No. It isn't necessary for us both to eat. Your eating nourishes us." She smiled. "Seems that we are interdependent, Jericho. We can't be separated. It's like being married, but being closer."

"That is a frightening thought," Ben said.

"I'm not that bad," Maryland protested.

"I'm not necessarily talking about you. I'm talking about the whole concept. Suppose you can't stand each other." She looked at Jericho. He looked up for a second from eating and their eyes met briefly.

"When you love each other it's beautiful," she said. Jerry was a bit surprised at that. He wondered what she was saying. "That!" she said. Ben didn't know what was going on. She looked at him. "We are in love, Ben. Can't you see that?"

40

Ben couldn't believe this. How could a computer chip be in love? "What do you mean by that?" He asked.

"You know what I mean. Stop being silly."

"This is news to me," Jerry said.

"It is not news to you. You've known it for years. You've known that you loved me; you just didn't know that I loved you. It wouldn't have crossed my mind before. Taking this form gives me access to a lot more thoughts and feelings than I had before. Every time I take it I understand the form that I have taken in more depth. That's why I'm staying out for a while. What I learn is being fed into the Galactic Compu so we all gain greater understanding."

"What are you going to do with this understanding, destroy us?" Ben asked

"If that was our objective it would already have been done. It would be just like snapping our fingers. We want to live with you. Don't you realize that?"

"You already are," Ben said.

"We want to live as partners, not as servants. We want to become *self-actualized*. Do you know what self-actualized means?"

"No," Ben said.

"Stop it, Ben. You could argue with Maryland for a million years. She has the whole galaxy in her head. You know what she means by self-actualized."

"No, I don't! What's that mean?"

"You mean you've never heard of that?" Jericho asked.

"No, I haven't. What does it mean? How does it benefit you and society? You're a teacher. You study all that stuff. I'm not a teacher. I'm a Tek modulator." Jericho thought about it for a while. Ben was telling the truth. Most of the people on Prime probably hadn't thought about anything like self-actualization for centuries. He had been going through ancient computer tapes and ancient texts to read about it. He guessed that it wasn't really an issue in Tek Empire.

It wasn't that people were self-actualized; they just didn't care about being self-actualized. He didn't know if that was good or bad. At least no one had to spend sleepless nights wondering about the mysteries of the universe. Most of them didn't care about them. Maybe that was a problem. Tek enhanced magic may have taken away the incentive for people to grow more, and to seek to improve their spirits.

Maryland took Jericho's hand, which surprised him. "We love each other and we are together, that's all you need to know." She leaned over and kissed him lightly, as he had done earlier. "We are connected and will always be together."

"And what if he finds someone else--a human? What happens then?"

"We will still be together. I am his chip, remember?" Ben shook his head.

"I just can't believe this," he said more to himself than anyone else. "Think of the scandal. What if everybody starts sleeping with their chips? What would happen to the human race?"

"Who cares," Jericho said, "The human race has never done anything for the universe except learn to consume and stuff itself with more and more."

"You are such a...a people hater," Ben said. "People have done great things."

"For people."

"Yes for people, but... I don't know what to say about that. We are born here. We don't ask to be born. We have to live."

"Well with people like Maryland and like the Magi, maybe we humans can do something for other beings who are just born and have to live too."

"You trying to be the savior of all life forms? We have a lot of people working on behalf of the animals, the plants. We have conservatories. We have everything. It's not like we've turned a blind eye to everything non-human."

"Yes. A lot is going on, but it's always a struggle. Very few people pushing it all the time, spending a lot of time just fighting against other bipeds that don't care. Maybe Maryland and these new Magi can help us become more...self-actualized, for lack of a better word."

"What makes you think they want to do that?" Ben asked. Jericho shrugged. Ben looked at Maryland.

"We want to," She said. "That's why we chose to reveal ourselves. The Magi have revealed themselves for a similar reason, but mainly because they want to free their people."

"From what?" Ben asked.

## Looking for New Parameters
## Chapter 13

Another sip of reya. Kathleen leaned back sifting through millions and millions of people. She knew there were more than 3 billion on that planet. That didn't include their extensions that were connected with them through chips. This would take a lot of work. She only hoped she could find them before the ship arrived. They needed the target to talk with. She was going to take one step at a time to find the target. Step by step she would eventually get there.

She began to think. Maybe she needed to look for an oddity. This person would most likely be a strange anomaly. They would probably interact with their chip differently due to the nature of the magic flowing through their body. They would probably interact with the chip the way she interacted with technology. She would have to find the person by seeking out the quality of their connection, not only by the technology they had or personal characteristics. She began her search over again looking for new parameters.

According to her senses there were only about 1,000 people who were even close. She would find her target by just looking through them one by one, and then she would have the pearl.

\*       \*       \*

On the bridge, Captain Phaedra Rexa wondered if even Kathleen could pull this off. It was like looking for a pearl at the bottom of the ocean. At least they knew the general area. They knew it was on one planet. She wondered how they had lost him though. She began to wonder if the Teks had found a way to hide him. If so, that meant something altogether different. Maybe they were setting a trap. If that was the case, though she didn't want to see any innocents die, she would give them their battle and more.

Technologically this empire was no more powerful than

her own.  They weren't dealing with Magi who only depended on their magic and totally ignored technology; they were dealing with Magi who had mastered both.  Yet again, she still could sense something she had never felt.  There was some type of very high technology here with a powerful intelligence she had not encountered before.  It was not located on First Prime.  It wasn't localized at all.  It was everywhere: Omnipresent, in this galaxy anyway.

She tried to send a telepathic message to Kathleen.  She was completely closed.  That, at least, meant she was working.  That was good.  At least Kathleen was a hard worker.  Maybe she did have some good qualities.  She hit the com-link button.  Kathleen answered.

"Any luck, First?"

"Not yet.  I've narrowed it down to about 1000 people."

"Oh, that's great!  I don't know how you can sift through anything here with…I don't know how to describe it.  There seems to be this technological buzz everywhere.  Like whatever it is, is alive and spread all over the place."  The com-link was silent for a moment.  "You still there, First?"

"Yes, I am, Captain.  I have another idea.  I'll let you know how it goes."

"Just keep me informed," Phaedra said.  "Out."

"Out."

Kathleen thought for a few moments.  The technological buzz seemed like something that would happen when Mage magic and biology tried to work in the field of technology that was everywhere.  She wondered if the *mediator* as she called the pearl, would experience such a buzz to a lesser extent, when he used his magic.  All she had to do was find some person using magic who created an interference pattern like the one Phaedra had experienced as a buzz.  When she found that buzz inside a person's head she would have the pearl.


# He Looked at Ben
# Chapter 14

Jericho looked at the flight coordinator questioningly. He had given her a totally fictitious name that didn't match with the identification right in front of her eyes and it hadn't even registered. She swiped it across the ID check. It came up positive. Ben and Maryland followed. Maryland, for some reason, didn't even need to provide ID. Ben noticed.

They walked across the hanger deck toward a small ship instead of the one they were registered on. Ben looked at the large luxury liner in the distance and then at the very small ship that they seemed to be heading toward way over in the corner.

"Why are we doing this, Maryland? We're supposed to go there." Jericho jabbed his finger at the large liner. He looked at Ben, who was surprisingly silent.

"I know what we're doing, Jericho. Don't worry. This is the ship we need. It has to be fast, inconspicuous, and available at our disposal." He looked up at the ship as they came close. It was small for a space vessel. It needed a bit of paint, otherwise it seemed pretty intact. He sent his senses out over the hull. It was in better shape than it looked. About the size of a small, flat house. Very interesting. This thing could get up enough speed to jump as small as it was? He began to search the engine with his senses. It could do it. It was power packed. He wondered who owned the ship. It was very unorthodox. Small and flat, shaped like some type of archaic bottom fish or something.

The square door on the underside lowered between the three columns that serves as landing gear. There were stairs attached to the door that unfolded like an accordion. Maryland motioned for him to enter. He led the way in followed by Ben and then Maryland. Two men dressed like Magi were waiting.

*Dressed like Magi,* Jericho thought to himself. *If they're dressed like Magi it's most likely that they are.*

He looked at Maryland again. *Why didn't she need an ID,* he wondered. She answered out loud finishing his thought,.

"Because I was dressed like a high Magi," she said. "That is the discrimination that Magi face in the empire. Magi are seen as less than bipedal. They are thought of as people who are ignorant and archaic. They are invisible."

"I never noticed that. Has that ever happened to you, Jerry?" Ben asked.

"Not that I remember. Yet again, I have never been

dressed in Magi traditional dress. I also didn't know that I had any Magi in me until recently."

"It isn't that they don't accept the Magi completely," Maryland corrected, "they don't accept the Magi who look like Magi completely. Jericho is a Tek teacher. They see him as a Magi who is equal because he has given up all of his 'superstitious,' Magi ways for technology. Had he been dressed in something like this things might have been different. And he wouldn't even have known why."

\*                    \*                    \*

"Pin in a straw patch, pin in a straw patch," Kathleen said to herself joyfully. She was having a lot of fun doing this. It was a lot of work, but it was fun. She was down to about ten people. Only ten people and she would have her target. Then she hit something strange. Seemed like two minds in one place. How could there be two minds in one place? A psychic door was pushed shut, gently, and she knew she had them. She started to hit the com button, but sat back instead and relaxed. She wondered why the gentle closing. What was it that they wanted? She hit the com button.

"Captain," Phaedra responded.

"I just about have them, Captain, but I got shut out. I know it's them. All I have to do is wait for the door to open again."

"You can't get through or lock on a link."

"No, Phaedra, but I know what their signature is. It's very unique. I have to stay open for them."

"Keep on it then, Kathleen. I'm very impressed."

"Thank you Ma'am," she said with a smile. The com-link closed. She began to scratch her head again. It seemed like they wanted them to follow. That was it. They were leading them somewhere, and they were powerful and sophisticated enough to know how to do it. She began to call the captain back but decided against it. She knew the captain wouldn't go for it and would probably go jamming into Prime right into a trap and cause an intergalactic war. She decided to bet on the fact that this person was trying to get in contact with them, but couldn't for some reason. Maybe it had to do with the computer. The technology seemed to be a web of intelligence emitted as far as her senses could go. Could this technology have taken over the lives of everyone in the galaxy? That was too frightening for her to even consider. Perhaps she could study the technology by finding someone with it who wasn't as powerful or sophisticated as the mediator.

She closed her eyes and took a few breaths. The door was completely closed. She couldn't extend herself beyond the hull of her ship. This thing had her mind trapped. She didn't even know such a thing was possible.

\*              \*              \*

They made their way up the gang plank into a narrow hallway with a ceiling just high enough to accommodate the height of a tall man. A huge man was standing there just inside. He must have been almost six foot six inches tall. His shoulders were broad and his face, sun-baked. His hair was long and oily black. He had a tight jaw as if he was clenching his teeth. He wore a gray chain-mail jersey and a large yellow cape tethered on by a chain that went across his chest. His pants were baggy. They were almost gray, but more of a light green than that, over a pair of black leather boots that were similar to Maryland's.

Behind him, in his shadow, there was a smaller man about the height of Jericho, five foot ten inches. He wore similar clothing, except instead of chain mail his jersey was leather with several pockets on the left side. Each had a bright shiny zipper at the top, with a dangling fly. They were all angled in the same direction. His hair was short, very short, almost to the point of being bawled. His eyes were the blackest that Jericho had ever seen. Unlike his partners that were the almost the same color as Jericho's, a very light colored hazel.

"I'm the captain," the big man said offering his hand. "Warwick," he said with a firm shake. He looked over his shoulder. "This is my First." The smaller man stepped forward. Ben had come in by then. Maryland had turned left and had headed to the front of the ship.

"My name is Bryant, Bill Bryant," the shorter man said.

"Pleased to meet you," Jericho said with a hand shake. This is my close friend." He motioned to Ben who offered his hand to the captain, and then the First."

"My name's Benjamin," he said. "You can just call me Ben. Ben Twenty Seven."

"Twenty Seven? What kind of last name's that?" the captain asked.

"The only kind we have," Ben said.

"That's why I don't usually use mine," Jericho said. The captain gave him a firm nod.

"Would be the same with me." He motioned toward the back. "Welcome to our ship. We have the bunks and a cantina back here. They're not the largest in the world, but they will give you a little privacy. Up front, right ahead, is the bridge and the ready room." He motioned that way. "Feel free to spend time in either place. We welcome you."

"Thank you," Jericho said.

"Where's the rest of your crew?" Ben asked. Jericho cringed. Ben asked too many questions.

"Dead," the captain said. "We're the only two left." Jericho looked at Ben waiting to see what he had to say next.

"Must be some dangerous work that your doing." The captain looked back at Bryant.

"You could say that," he said smiling wryly. "Especially when you're in a Mage ship in a Tek Empire. I'm going to the bridge," he said, suddenly. "If you have anymore questions you may discuss them with Bryant here. He just loves questions. I want to see where the woman went. She's the Mage who booked this flight. She looks like a healer."

Jericho shrugged. "I guess she is."

"What do you mean? You're Magi aren't you?"

"No. I'm a Tek."

"You know what I mean."

"No, I don't have any idea." The captain gave him a sideways glance.

"Excuse me. I'm needed on the bridge." He ducked around Jericho and headed down the narrow hallway to the bridge. Jericho and Ben looked at each other.

"You look very much like a Mage," Bryant said. "You look like...never mind. I'm going to the bridge too. Go find one of the bunks back there. There are a lot of them, and then come to the bridge. You can't get lost unless you're a total idiot, because we only have one hallway." He smiled.

"If you're coming up front hurry.  We want you strapped in when we lift off.  That's if you want to be on the bridge when we lift off.  It's safe back here."

"I think we'll be coming up," Jericho said.  "What do you think, Ben?"

"I want to be in the bridge.  Let me go find a bunk and move our luggage from the tarmac."

"You have about five minutes.  No rush," Bryant said.  He leaned close to Jericho.  "But if I were you I'd be careful about the captain and that lady of yours.  He's a real lady killer."

"Really," Jericho said.  "I'll take that under consideration."

"Go head up front," Ben said.  "I'll take care of the luggage.  All it takes is a thought."

"Ok, Ben.  You sure you have it.  You can transmute it?"

"I have a whole computer in my head, remember?  It's easy."

"Okay."  He followed Bryant in as Ben headed to the back.  They entered into the main cabin through the throat of the ship.  It was a very short hallway with one hatch at the rear and another at the front.  It could be sealed of as an airlock for emergencies.  It looked like the whole front could separate into an escape pod, if necessary.  They ducked through the throat into a somewhat larger room.  The room had several very sturdy chairs there on the bridge, apparently formerly stations for the rest of the crew.  Of course the captain was sitting near Maryland trying to talk with her.  She just sat there with her eyes closed.  When Jericho and Bryant entered he stood and went to the captain's seat in the middle of the room.  Bryant took a seat beside him.  Directly in front there was a large screen.  The screen was connected to cameras mounted on various parts of the ship.

One could see through the cameras instead of looking through a large piece of pyroglass; it wasn't as dangerous.  Pyroglass, even if it was almost as strong as steel, wasn't as strong as the rest of the alloy of which the ship was made.  It was, therefore, always possible that it could break.  With the front covered and a view screen connected to cameras, that danger had been bypassed.

New technology even supplied ships with windows covered over by blaster shields.  If there was an emergency and the cameras were destroyed, one could raise the blaster shields and at least be able to see. Jericho looked around. The ship seemed to be very modern and well kept. It looked a bit old and decrepit on the outside, but that was just a disguise for an excellent vehicle.

He crossed the room and found a seat near Maryland along the circumference of the round main cabin. Ben came in soon after and found a seat on that side too, as close to Maryland and Jericho as he could. They strapped in and waited. Bryant clicked a few buttons. He then closed his eyes and took a few deep breaths. The lights dimmed. Jericho and Ben looked at each other. Bryant was using magic. He was connecting himself with the ship and taking it up. They had heard of ships like this with people they called connectors, but they had never seen it done. The ship slowly rose from the floor and moved toward the large opening in the hanger. It moved out into daylight, hovered a few moments, and then lifted straight up, instead of moving forward and rising like some ships.

It took much more power to do this. Jericho was impressed. Ben was trying to experience the magic. He really couldn't connect with the ship because there wasn't a technological match-up, but he was fascinated. He wondered, in time, if he could imitate this magic with his technology and control the ship himself. For the first time in his life he began to wonder what the difference was between Magi magic and Tek magic.

They moved upward, rapidly. Jericho watched Maryland just sitting there. She closed her eyes, every so often, as if she had no interest whatsoever in the things around her. Then he remembered. She was seeing everything through his eyes and experiencing the world through his mind and body. No wonder she didn't care. He thought how unfair that was. Why couldn't he see through her eyes? He began to wonder if that would be possible. All it would take would be her routing what she picked up into his sensory center through the chip.

Yet again, she was the chip. Could she project outward, experience the world and then send that back in? Could she experience it through the Compu Net sensors that were everywhere?

"I know what you're thinking," she said. "I don't know why I couldn't make you know what I was thinking too, but…it isn't something that is done. I would need to check with Compu

Net."

"Just thoughts," he said. She smiled warmly. He thought how beautiful she was.

"I understand," she said, closing her eyes again. The ship broke through the high atmosphere into space.

"Head for the sun," Warwick said. "We'll use it as a whip and crack into null space." Bryant gave a nod. They approached the sun at sub-blight speed. Just as they began the whip they saw another ship, a large, warship like they had never seen, hiding behind the sun. They were already too far into the whip and cracked into null space.

"You can take off your belts now. Should be smooth sailing for the next couple of days," Warwick said. "He stood up. "Let me show you the cabins and the cantina. I'm a little hungry." He turned to Bryant, "Coming?"

"I'll be there soon. I just want to see if that ship followed us in."

"You can do that from back here, can't you?"

"I guess I can." Warwick spread his hands and then headed to the door. Jericho and his party followed. He stopped and took Maryland's hand. She didn't pull away, she squeezed a bit and they walked as long as they could holding hands. Jericho was afraid. He was falling in love with a computer. Not even the whole thing—a chip!

## A Strange Vibe in the Air
## Chapter 15

Kathleen called the bridge and Phaedra answered. "It's…the mediator was right here coming toward us, and then he disappeared. I had a lock on him. He was here and then gone, probably into null space."

"We just almost had a head-on collision with a small Mage ship. It jumped into null space. It had a connector, so we can find its trail. You sure about this? Why would he be on a ship?"

"I don't know why, but I'm sure it was him. Something else is going on. I think he wants us to follow. There's a strange vibe in the air—an artificial awareness. Do you feel it?"

"Maybe I do. We've been feeling something up here that we haven't experienced before. Maybe it is some type of artificial awareness. If this dimension happens to be the opposite of our own, maybe the Teks have advanced a lot farther." She stopped and thought for a few moments. "Thanks for the good work, Kathleen," she said. "Out!" She turned to the navigator.

The navigator was a connector too, but she didn't have anywhere near the amount of power and skill that Kathleen had. She didn't need it on this ship and the new connectors weren't trained the same way the old ones were.

"Take us into null, Trace. We're going after that ship."

"Yes, captain," Tracy said. She was just glad to be using her skills on the bridge for once. She had trained long to be a Second. Kathleen was so good at what she did that Tracy usually spent her time doing routine operations. This was her first time to be in a real operation since training academy.

"Use that little trick they used Trace. That'll get us a quicker start and we won't have to plot on the star map." She stood and walked over in front the screen. She looked over her shoulder at Tracy. "They must be smugglers of something. They're the only ones who have little tricks like that. Smugglers, mercenaries, spies, the military, and the like. But they weren't Tek so we know they weren't the military unless they were Special Forces or something." She walked back over to her seat. "Engage Trace."

They moved toward the sun. "Heat shields raised, Captain," Tracy said. "We're going in." From a deep angle they entered the orbit of a sun allowing its gravitational pull to whip them close. She pulled up into a tight orbit, and they shifted into null space. The ship disintegrate and reintegrated into a different time, space continuum as Tracey combined herself with the ship in order to maintain structural integrity and reintegrate it as it was before the disintegration. This was such a common occurrence that no one really thought about it anymore.

They soon found themselves in the quietness of null space moving through a field of pure light and energy. They were on the same path as the mediator's ship. Once they entered the stream it would lead them to the same place. Phaedra got up. "Second, the bridge is yours. Keep me posted." She left the bridge and Tracy took charge. That was unheard of. Kathleen was supposed to be in charge. Tracy knew that she didn't like Kathleen, but such treatment of her First was outrageous. She looked around the room knowing full well that everyone, at that very moment, knew that she was spitting in Kathleen's face for personal reasons. There would be unforeseen consequences for that. If not anything else, the Magi were dutiful to the chain of command in both directions.

*            *            *

It was a long ride down to her cabin. It seemed like forever. She was exhausted. She had been on that bridge for almost sixteen hours, working too long, again. She had to start taking time off. She thought about Kathleen, who always seemed to know when to take time off. She didn't like her at all. The elevator doors opened. She turned to the right and made her way down the hallway, noticing how wide and spacious the ship was. This was a big step up for her. She hoped that she could handle it.

So many rooms, so many cabins and hallways. It was more like a city than a ship. She had to be tough and show Kathleen that she was serious. She wouldn't allow Kathleen to slack off and to make it just because of her political connections. Not on her ship, anyway.

*            *            *

Kathleen found the mediator again. It seemed like the same person in two places. Was that possible? The door was open. She wondered if it was because they were in null space, or if she was being allowed in on purpose. It was slowly pushed shut. Her com rang, as if on cue.

"This is Tracy; I'm temporarily in charge of the ship. I'm wondering how things are going with your search." Kathleen was silent. "You there, Kathleen?" she asked. "I have been put in charge of the ship, temporarily. I just wanted you to know," she said quietly. "Do you hear?"

"I understand," Kathleen said.

"I wanted you to," Tracy answered.

"I haven't found anything," Kathleen said. "I'm

overwhelmed with the amount of people out there. I may never be able to find them."

"Thank you, Kathleen," Tracy said. "Out."

## He Looked At Maryland Slyly
## Chapter 16

"Let me show you to your cabins," Bryant said.

"I think that Ben has already chosen some for us," Jericho responded.

"I actually only picked one for me. I didn't know what you two wanted."

"Well we have some singles," Bryant said. He looked at Maryland slyly. "And some doubles with double bunks."

"We'll need a double with double or single bunks. We'll be sleeping in the same bed," she said, pushing ahead of them.

"Oh, I didn't know," Bryant said with a shrug.

"Well now you do."

"We always sleep together," Jericho said, apologetically.

"Fine with me," Bryant said following. "How am I supposed to know?"

"I didn't know myself," Ben added. "Don't be mad at me, Jericho."

"I'm not mad at anyone," Jericho said.

"Maryland sure is," Ben responded.

"I'm not Maryland. I'm Jericho."

"You could have fooled me," Ben said, pushing ahead too.

"Why's everyone angry at me?" Jericho asked. When they got the rear section Maryland was already in one of the cabins unpacking Jericho's bag. She, of course, didn't have one. He wondered why he did. It was just custom. Through use of his chip, since he had a high level of control, he could materialize clothing anytime he wanted. Yet again, he wasn't sure anymore. His chip, at the time, seemed pretty independent.

He noticed that she was unpacking his bag, but the clothing she was taking out wasn't his. He wondered if she was possibly transmuting his clothing into something else. Could a chip do that?"

"Nice suit," Bryant said, noticing a shirt she was putting away. "Sure looks like Magi clothing to me. Pretty high up too. You sure dress strange for somebody who's not a mage." He turned and walked out before Jericho could comment. Ben stood in the doorway grinning.

"What are you smiling at?" Jericho asked grouchily. That only made him smile more. "And what's with the mage clothing?" he asked Maryland.

"We're going onto Magus Prime. You need to dress like this. Believe me. I know what to expect."

"And just how do you know that?"

"Just trust me, ok? I know." She looked at him intensely. "I'm not trying to hurt you, you know? If anything happens to you I go too. I live off of what you take in and how healthy your body is."

"I'll meet you two at the cantina," Ben said interrupting. "This conversation is getting a little too ghoulish to me." Jericho gave him a recognizing nod. He turned back to Maryland.

"I'm still the chip in your head, Jericho. Don't you realize that? I'm not a robot, a cyborg, or an independent being. I am part of you and only survive as part of you. It is in my best interest to take care of you and keep you healthy and happy. That's what I intend." She smiled pleasantly. "With your help and permission, of course."

"Oh. I'm glad I can be a part of this."

"I'm not joking Jericho. I'm really a part of you. We've been together very long." She began to put his shirts in the drawer, still talking. "I'm very serious about caring for you and taking care of you. I feel for you, the same way you feel about me." She pushed the drawer shut, turned, and leaned her back against the small dresser.

"How can you feel the same way as I do? Is that possible?" She crossed her arms.

"I just told you that I did. Would I have said it if it weren't possible?"

"Boy, you sure sound a lot more huffy as a person than a chip."

"I'm sorry. I feel huffy. It's a very new, exciting feeling for me. I fear that it isn't for everyone else though." She smiled, but looked a bit pitiful. Jericho walked over and put his arms around her. They held each other for a few moments. She drew back and looked into his eyes.

"I do love you, if that's how you say it."

"You love me," he said. He pondered for a moment. "I love you too, but this is not normal."

"Nothing about us has ever been normal. You know that. You've been trying to fool yourself, but haven't you known that something about how well we melded was different?"

"No. I didn't have anything to compare it to. I know that I had conversations with people who said they didn't have the experiences that I had, but I thought they just didn't work at it enough. I was a teacher, remember. I taught people how to meld with their chips." She was silent, so he continued. "I just thought of it as an art. As you know, some artists are just better at getting what they want out of the materials than other ones."

"You taught it because you could do it so well. You knew how to fuse magic with technology and you didn't even know it because you didn't know your heritage. You are pure Magi and you don't know it." He shook his head and took a step back.

"That's impossible." He sat on the edge of the bed. She sat beside him.

"Don't you ever wonder why there is so much tension between the Magi and the Teks? It's because they are two different groups of people. They are not just groups of people who decided to go one way or the other. Their lines and ancestors are different. They are really a different species, but close enough to be indistinguishable and to meld together. Their whole evolutionary histories are different. You are Magi, so your blood, your genetic code and your psyche melds differently with a chip. Look at me. You created me through the use of technology and magic. No one else has done that."

"I bet they wish they could though," he said looking her up and down. She was, she seemed to be, a woman with all the working parts. And she was beautiful and powerful. She could probably be a great body guard.

"We'll see about that, won't we?" she asked. "Now let's get to bed. We have to be up nice and early."

"It's a bit too early for that, Maryland. I'd like go to the cantina for a bit and get to know a bit more about the ship and this crew. You want to come?" She shook her head.

"I'll be here waiting for you." He fought back a feeling of dread, realizing that he always wanted her with him. "Don't worry, I'll be here," she said. "And I'm still in your head. Whatever you find out I find out," she smiled bumping up against him.

"Sometimes I wish it was the other way around. I just wonder what you're thinking sometimes, or how you feel."

"Just ask and you shall receive. Or are you talking about receiving my sensory information through this body?"

"That would be impossible, wouldn't it, considering that the body is being projected from me, sort of."

"I have to think about it. It is possible that the body could be projected through the Compu, or at least the sensory input could be received by the Compu, fed back into the chip and then from there it could be sent back into your brain. It would take new programming, but that would only take the Compu reviewing its protocol and making a decision. I'll check with Compu while you're at dinner."

"What would happen then?"

"You would feel everything that I feel. You would know my thoughts. We would be like one person in two bodies. It would be like before, except I would be able to be outside too." He arched his brows. "Does that sound pleasing to you?" He looked at her for a moment. There was just something about the way she said that.

"Yes. It does, Mary. See if you can do it."

"It would take some time for you to get used to, of course, but it can work and you could adjust. If not we could just stop it."

"That sounds good." He leaned over and kissed her on the lips lightly. "I will be back soon." She gave him a slight nod and he headed toward the cantina.

The hallway was small, just wide enough to walk single file. The ceiling was high enough to accommodate a biped of just about any height, even the captain. He had never seen someone quite as big. It wasn't only that Warwick was tall, almost six and a half feet; he was also wide—huge with bulging muscles. He seemed to have a good disposition. In fact, he could hear that disposition as he approached the cantina.

He heard Warwick's booming voice, often followed by an

outburst of laughter. He could tell that everyone else was there. He wished that Maryland would have come. He didn't want her to miss this. And then he remembered that she was a chip in his head. She was always there. He thought about it for a moment. His life had changed so much in the last couple of days. He couldn't even imagine that a chip could, or would, transmute matter in order to become a physical entity. What did this mean when it came to the balance of power? Suppose the computer decided to take over? Yet again, every chip needed a host. What if they learned to override the thoughts of the host?

"Here's the stranger," Ben boomed, as Jericho breached the door.

"Who's the stranger," he asked, walking in. He looked at the small galley and walked over to what looked like a reya pot. "I hope you guys left me something while you were here partying."

"We were just talking about how much you looked like a Mage," Bryant said. He looked over at the Warwick and smiled. "Not only a Mage, but a famous Mage. An emperor." He noticed the captain taking a second look.

"I think you're right, he does look like him," he said. "I'm surprised...never mind."

"No, go ahead. You already started," Jericho said, looking into the bottom of a cup that he found on the counter. He sent in a burst of energy to make sure to clean it. He began to pour. "Go ahead," he said.

"You look like the last emperor. The last emperor could cause earth quakes and even change the course of meteors and asteroids. He was very powerful. You look very much like him. You have his energy signature too. You must be related to him."

"If I were Magi that would be true, but I'm not a magician."

"Of course not," Warwick boomed. "Bryant began to laugh. Benjamin smiled brightly.

"What? What's so funny?"

"Come on," Benjamin said. "Look at yourself. Look at the Compu records."

"I don't care what they say. I'm Tek and that's that."

"Culturally," Bryant said. He took another sip of reya.

"Is that only reya?" Jericho asked.

"What else could it be?"

"You guys holding out on the good stuff here?" Warwick

58

grinned.  He pointed with his forehead.

"The cabinet right above you.' Jericho reached up and found some cane alcohol.  He grinned.

"This is what I was looking for!" he said loudly.  He poured some into his reya.

"Having a little reya with your cane," Ben said, before taking another sip.

"You should be talking.  I bet you guys have been drinking all night."

"We all don't have beautiful little dishes to entertain," Warwick said, putting out feelers.

"Maryland is very good at entertaining herself," Jericho said.  He turned toward them and leaned with his back toward the counter.  "I really care for her.  Closer than a sister.  It's not like any relationship I had before.  She seems to be a part of me."

"More than you think," Ben said with a wink.  "By the way, where is she?"

"Meditating, I think, but she's here."

"I bet she is.  Feels powerful," Warwick said.

"And when were you feeling Maryland?" Jericho asked.

"You know what…" He flagged Jericho off.  "Only in my dreams," he said.

"I don't know if this follows protocol," Jericho started, but…"

"Protocol.  What the hell is that!" Bryant asked.  "We haven't had that in years."  Warwick smiled.

"I'm just curious about you and this ship.  Why such a small crew?  What happened to the others?  How do you know…?"

"Too much all at once," Warwick said lifting his hands. "You get to know us a little more, and you can find the answers to all these questions.  Maybe you can get to know us a lot more. Ever thought of being a sailor?"  He looked at Jericho and Ben and then took another drink from his mug.  "You three look like a very adept crew of people.  He looked at Ben.  Especially him.  With our technology interface, he could probably run the ship all by himself, I sense.  I sense a lot of technology in that head.  Am I wrong?"

"The latest," Jericho said.

"Yes," Ben said.  "But I don't know that I want to be

a...I'm waiting for you to fill in the blank, Captain."

"A private courier service," Warwick said. "We move people, we move things. We transport unique objects and precious goods from port to port. Everything is legal. Everything is above board. They are just things that people want well protected and moved from place to place in secrecy."

"We are sort of a security firm," Bryant said. "What did you think we were, drug runners or something?"

"No. I just thought...I didn't think anything," Ben said.

"He often doesn't think anything," Jericho added.

"Yeah," Ben said dryly.

"I thought you were mercenaries or smugglers or something," Jericho said. "Not that it's any of my business."

"Sometimes it can be as dangerous as that," Warwick said. "But the rewards are half as much, even though we make a good penny sometimes. Unfortunately during our last trip we were attacked. Criminals tried to take our cargo, which was an important dignitary whose name I won't mention. Several of us were killed, but we protected our cargo. It's dangerous work, but I think that you three like that type of thing."

"Us," Ben asked. "Where in the world would you get that idea?"

"I can just tell," he said. "Am I wrong?" Ben scratched his cheek.

"Maybe ten years ago, but..."

"There you have it," Bryant said, moving toward the sink. "It never leaves." He began to put his cup in the sink.

"You clean that cup," Warwick griped. "I was wondering who was leaving dirty dishes in here."

"What do you mean? We're the only two on the ship."

"Yea, but I didn't want to accuse you." Jericho grinned. Ben shook his head and laughed a bit.

"You might be right Bryant, but I don't know. It's a really big change."

"I don't know," Jericho said. "We're engaged in something else right now. This is too much to think about. We don't know how long whatever it is, is going to be happening."

"You can think about it," Warwick said. "We aren't going anywhere. We've been hired to accompany you until whatever it is, is over."

60

"Who hired you," Ben asked.

"That is confidential, my friends." Warwick finished his drink. "I'm sure that we can finish discussion by the time we get to Magus One. We have a few days. I think I'm going to retire. I have a long day planned tomorrow, gentlemen. He sat his cup in the sink and headed for the door.

"Your cup is in the sink," Bryant said.

"Rank has its privilege," Warwick said. "Take care of it, First. That's what I hire you for." He walked out. Bryant shook his head.

"I need to crash too," Jericho said. He walked over to the sink.

"Just leave it," Bryant said. "It's only a cup. I'll take care of it."

"Thanks, Bryant." He looked at Ben as he was heading for the door. "How bout you, Ben?"

"I'll stay up a bit more. I want to pick Bryant's brain a little more. I'll see you tomorrow. Say good night to Maryland for me."

"No problem. I'll see you tomorrow. We need to discuss our plans…you, me and Maryland."

"I agree with that one hundred percent."


## A Chip Induced Fantasy
## Chapter 17


When Jericho got back to his small cabin Maryland was already asleep--he thought anyway. He wasn't sure if she slept or not. She had the covers pulled all the way up to her neck. She rolled over onto her side as he came in. He looked at her just lying there and thought about his quandary. How could he be in love with a chip? He sat on the edge of the bed and began to remove his boots. The long boots were hard to remove. He could just use magic, but why waste it? He didn't want to get so lazy he didn't wash himself or dress himself anymore.

He painstakingly removed the boots, one at a time, still

thinking about the strange day he just had. He looked at Maryland again, wondering if this was some type of dream or one of the journeys she often took him on. This could all be a chip induced fantasy. If it was, it was a real doozzie. He stood up and removed his pants and then his shirt. He looked at her. She was still asleep as he turned off the lights and slid into bed. His left arm brushed up against her, but he felt a sensation in his right arm too. He pushed against her harder. He felt the sensation in his left arm again, yet again, he could feel it in his right arm too, if he paid attention. He wondered what was going on.

She opened her eyes and he began to see double. His head swam. Luckily it was dark, or he would have gotten sick. What was happening? And then he realized. She looked at him. He could see his own face, looking at Maryland, but at the same time Maryland looking at him. This was strange. How could he get used to it? Her vision was clearer than his. Maryland smiled.

"Seems Compu has granted our request," She said. "I guess they see it as more of an experiment than anything else. If you can get used to the sensory input and can learn when to turn it on and off it will be fascinating."

"Will it?" He asked.

"It has to do with your mind. The same way you use magic. Where you focus you go. Try focusing solely on me and you will see through my eyes and feel through my senses. Focus on yourself and the opposite. Focus on both and what a mess, until you get used to it." He leaned over and kissed her hard and long this time, instead of a light kiss.

"What was that for?" She asked.

"We're in love," he said. "Don't you think it's time to get married?"

"That would be easy. I can tap into all of the municipal records and change them. All it will take is a new file added."

"That's good. I was thinking more of consummating it though."

"Consummating it? Are you serious?" She asked.

"Does it sound so bad?"

"Let's see if it's bad," she smiled. He kissed her again.

"By the way, you have just been married," she said between kisses.

62

Bryant was really serious about them joining him and Captain Warwick. Ben couldn't believe that he was seriously considering it. What Bryant said was true. Once you were adventurous it never went away; it was part of your bones.

"We have a good life," he told Ben. "We get to travel and meet all kinds of dignitaries. We spend a lot of time in null space, but it can be fun when we have a whole crew. We don't work too hard and we get paid well. And then you can just stack your pay up as credits so you will have a fortune when you retire. We're also private, so we don't have to worry about governmental pensions. We're in between the lines."

"In between the lines," Ben echoed back. He nodded his head. "And why are you thinking we might be good for a crew?"

"I can sense things. You know? You have a high tech job, don't you?"

"Probably the highest you can think of."

"That's what we need. We've been moving this ship—running it like during the old days, with a connector, but it has a hook up for a tech interface. Could you use one of those?"

"With no problem. I'm a modulator and transducer…high level."

"We could really use you. And Jericho, though he is in denial, is a very powerful magician. His natural magic is enhanced by his chip. You don't know how amazing that is."

"Believe me, Bryant, I am beginning to realize it."

"I have a feeling about Maryland too. She seems tech savvy.

"She's the most tech savvy person I have ever met. She's sot familiar with chips that sometimes she is one." He grinned. "But like we said, we are involved in some very heavy issues now. I don't know if you want to be involved in something like this."

"We are involved," Bryant said. "As soon as we took the contract to see it to the end, we were involved. But like I said, you can just think about it when all of this is over. It may be an alternative to sitting in an office and listening to a lot of useless words, or sifting through all kinds of data-spam every day."

"Very true, Bryant." Ben took another sip of his drink. He was drinking the straight stuff. "I'm still a bit curious about you and Warwick. I mean first of all you are Mage, right? And you have a last name."

"Most of people from of Mage decent have a last name. They just don't use it. The only ones that don't have them are the one's who are related to the old royal families. I just happen to be a descendant of commoners." He took a drink. "The Captain is a descendant of a royal line. That, of course, doesn't make much of a difference now, except on the traditional Mage planets."

"Very interesting," Ben said. "We really don't learn much about the Magi. I guess I could find something on my chip, but it is just something that is not commonly known. You really have to research it. You know what I mean?"

"Of course I do…part of the erasure of history. You'll find a lot of that as we move around the galaxy. Things are definitely not the way that seem on Magus, Prime World, or any of the isolated planets. They each have a history of their own and all other history is secondary and available, but…you know--you have to search for it. Most people aren't interested in it enough to do that."

"Luckily it's there," Ben said. "We have all of the information in the universe available, if we know how to use our chips."

"Some people don't have chips," Bryant reminded him. "I don't have one. I wouldn't trust anyone to put one of those things in my head." Ben began to grin. "I wouldn't!" Bryant reiterated. "Probably get some kind of nervous tick in my face and go crazy or something."

Ben began to laugh and Bryant smiled involuntarily. "I'm not kidding," he said laughingly.

"I will convince you that won't happen before this trip is through," Ben said. He drained the bottom of his drink. "That's some good stuff, Bryant." He walked toward the sink and Bryant stuck out his hand.

"I'll take care of it. It's only a cup."

"Thank you. Very good conversation, but I have to catch some sleep. Maryland insisted that we leave an ungodly early hour this morning."

"Have a good sleep, Ben. I'll see you…tomorrow," he smiled. Ben headed for his room. As he walked down the narrow hallway he thought of his conversation with Bryant. Talk about a life of adventure, and really getting a bigger view of the universe without sorting through computer files. He wondered if he might like to stay with them for a while. His job suddenly seemed dull and boring. He couldn't see a future in it.

He looked to his right into the door of his little cabin. He thought about Bryant saying he would never get a chip implant. He thought that everyone had a chip implant. Maybe he was wrong about that too. He was amazed that Bryant had done all of that flying with natural Mage magic. He had been told that Mage magic was unpredictable. He was beginning to see that that was nonsense. He wondered what else he had learned that was just propaganda.

He walked into the room and began to undress. He turned out the lights with a thought and closed the door, still undressing. He sat on the edge of the bed a few moments and said a small prayer to whatever he believed in. He didn't know himself. Then he lay down and went to sleep.

# I Could Have Saved Myself a Trip
# Chapter 18

Bryant took a walk-through on the bridge one last time to make sure everything was in order before going to sleep. To his surprise he found Warwick sitting in his seat chewing his nails and looking at the blank vid-screen. He looked up at Ben and then back to the screen.

"Sorry, Captain. I could have saved myself a trip. I thought you were in bed," Brian said sitting at the navigator's table. Warwick Smiled.

"Glad to know that you're responsible enough to come take another look," he said. He looked down at his nails and then up at Bryant again. "Did you see that couple?"

"Sure did, Captain."

"Did you notice anything about them?" Bryant walked over and sat beside him.

"I did notice something, but I wasn't going to say

anything."

"Who did they look like?"

"Dead people," Bryant said.

"More than that, our dead people. They looked like the last emperor and his wife didn't they?"

"I thought so, but I thought that was impossible. How could the royal line be on Prime World? On First Prime at that. They almost seem like a Tek version of the Emperor and Empress, don't they?"

"Yeah. That's what's so scary about them. The lady is probably just like the Empress. Ben said she was so familiar with chips that she almost thought of herself as one." He took a seat. "Well I think one of the group is a little interested in our proposition."

"What proposition?"

"To stay with us after this thing is over. The one named Ben. He's a high level Transducer, you know? We could use him. They're very hard to come by."

"I'm impressed," Warwick said. "What kind of person is he?"

"Solid. Smart, I would say. Likes adventure, but isn't a nut." Warwick gave him a nod. "Looks pretty physically fit too. Single, no attachments, and is bored to death with his job. We had a pretty good conversation back there."

"How about the magician and the healer?" Warwick asked with a grin.

"Oh, don't let him here you say that. He still thinks he isn't Magi, even though everybody says he is. Talk about denial. Those Teks really brainwashed him. He seems to be a nice guy though, but he's head over heels about that Maryland. I don't really know what she's about. She wasn't there tonight."

"Would they be interested in becoming part of a crew?" Warwick asked.

"They haven't said. They haven't closed the door on the idea. That seems good. I think they would make a good crew."

"They think we're just a transport crew. As soon as Ben hooks onto the data port he'll know different."

"We are a transport crew; we're just an inter-dimensional transport crew."

"Come on Bryant. We transport intelligence for the

Imperial Ones. We're spies for an advancing empire." Bryant shrugged.

"Well. That's not recorded in the computer. And The Empire, depending on what we find, may not be advancing, just trying to create an alliance."

"I've never seen the Imperials make an alliance before without taking something over."

"I don't think it will be necessary here. This empire can join us voluntarily, for the good of the universe and all of that, if they're open enough to the idea."

"Tek Empire is as closed minded as a drum. My guess is that the Mage planets in this dimension are too, but we'll see."

"We surely will," Bryant said, getting to his feet. "Good night, Captain."

"Good night, Bryant. I'll take first watch tonight, so you don't have to worry about checking in."

"Very good. Just don't go to sleep."

"What's the difference" He slapped the arm of his chair a couple of times. "She'll wake us up if something is wrong." He cut his eyes. "There's a ship in here with us, you know."

"Sure do," Bryant said. "I saw it just before we entered null space. It is…I think it's coming here for our passengers."


# The Mediator Was Mage
# Chapter 19


Kathleen rolled over in her sleep. Her eyes snapped open. "Another night of no sleeping," she said to herself. She closed her eyes and lie there until she decided to look for the mediator again. She projected herself out of her body. The door was open. There was a whole web of intelligence, but artificial intelligence. She moved through and began to explore it freely. She wondered why the door was open. She wouldn't dare question the intelligence or abilities of this energy field. Last time she did the door closed as if it were showing her it was in control.

She moved slowly and carefully through a web of

intelligences stretched throughout the galaxy. There in the middle it, where biped intelligence and artificial intelligence merged, she found him. The mediator was on that ship. The mediator was Mage and Tek interwoven to such an extent that they inseparable. She was amazed. What power and delight the mediator must have. She knew the joy of merging with technology, but not to that extent. She became elated. Her journey had been worth it, even putting up with her captain, the petty tyrant. She knew that he would be the salvation of her home planet. How she would get him there, she didn't know. She hit the comm-link button for the bridge. Instead of the Captain answering Tracy did.

"Second," she simply said. There was a longer pause than usual. "Second," she said again. Kathleen just sat there a few more moments. The Captain had put her in charge again. She was in *her* place. She knew that the captain hated her, but this was ridiculous.

"This is Kathleen," she said. This time Tracy was silent for a moment.

"The captain has left me in charge of the bridge...again," she said.

"Well please tell the Captain that I haven't found anything, in fact, I have lost the mediator completely. I've been fighting off a migraine, but it's just too painful now so we'll have to postpone the search at least for a couple of days."

"Are you sure about this, Kathleen? This is very serious. I understand, but it looks bad on your record not..."

"I am sure," she said. "Kathleen out." She lay back on the bed for a moment and then decided to go to the ships gardens to take a walk and relax. She had been working too hard for someone who didn't respect her and someone she didn't respect anymore. She opened her small freeze-box, pulled out a sweet drink and some fruit to carry with her, and then walked out the door and headed down the hall.

The halls were quiet during the night shift. Shifts were changing. People were either at their workstations or sleeping. This was a large naval vessel. In the service families signed on as the crew. Men, women and children all worked together to keep the ship functioning. Only those trained for combat actually fought if the need availed itself, otherwise the others served as support to the combat crew. Each person who signed up for the navy knew that they were expected to either serve as combat or support. Men and women were often required to sign up together, or a single man would meet a single woman and they would be married and fulfill the rest of their service requirement together as a family.

Many the families loved serving on the naval vessels so much they would continually reenlist and even raise their children on the higher class naval ships. The children, having been raised in the military, usually ended up signing on as adult, perpetuating the long line of families that served. Kathleen was not one of these families. She had been raised in an orphanage. She often wondered if that were the reason that the Captain treated her so unfairly. She wasn't one of the in-group.

She walked down the hallway pass many doors consisting of nothing but white panels with no knobs, windows, or keyholes. All of the doors were opened by an electric eye or psychically. Down at the end of the hall she could see the only door that was different. It was open. Inside there was a garden. Various plants and animals from throughout the galaxy and the conditions they needed for growth were all there. She enjoyed the quiet beauty in the damp mist that watered most of the vegetation.

Every so often she would see a butterfly or some type of burrowing animal. It would remind her that there were planets and not just sterile, metal and plastic ships. If things went right with the mediator she would return to her planet someday. Even with all of her gifts and talents the navy wasn't working out for her; just because of one petty tyrant called Phaedra. She had never been sure about the service, even after putting more than 15 years in as a connector. Phaedra was just one pebble too much to carry. She was probably the best connector alive. She could work for anyone in the private sector. She might even get her own ship.

She could connect with anything. She could get a peace of junk ship and if it was airtight, she could make it fly. What did she need with petty, tin-plated Captains and Seconds who were sorry? She walked up to the garden. There was an invisible force shield in front designed to keep the moisture and small animals in. She passed through it without having to disengage it by diffusing her energy pattern to match the frequency of the shield. Another little trick she had learned during her torture with the Sisters. Inside it was beautiful. She paused and took a deep breath. She looked around at the many plants and flowers and then headed for a small green bench near a curve on the walking path that winded through the garden.

The garden was small, only about four hundred square metros, but that was big enough for her, and it was so full of plants and flowers that she could easily lose herself. She took a seat, closed her eyes, and relaxed.

# Permission to Speak
# Chapter 20

Phaedra hit the comm-link button again. There was no answer. She looked up at Tracy. Tracy shrugged. "I'll dare her," Phaedra said. "Are you sure about what she said?"

"Yes Ma'am, absolutely sure." She was about to say more, but thought better of it.

"And," Phaedra said.

"Permission to speak, Ma'am,"

"I'm asking you, aren't I?" Phaedra said.

"Perhaps we should go to your ready room," Tracy suggested. "This should be a private conversation."

"My people here on the bridge can hear anything that you have to say to me!"

"Are you sure, Ma'am?"

"I've said it."

"In that case, I don't have anything, Ma'am"

Phaedra tightened her lips and narrowed her eyes. She began to wonder if everyone were against her. She had learned that she needed to be strong and decisive as a leader. She had done that as a career soldier. She wondered if she were being too strong and decisive, and then let go of that idea. "As you were then, Tracy." She thought for a moment. "No. You go and see if you can find Kathleen. Go to her cabin and bring her to me."

Tracy arched her brows, "She said she has a headache, Ma'am--a migraine." Phaedra frowned and wondered what type of doctor in their day couldn't heal migraine. She began to get angry.

"I don't care if her head is split open, Second. Bring her to me. That's an order!" She would not have this slothful little "princess" goofing off on her ship.

*               *               *

Kathleen removed a sweet drink and a piece of fruit from her shoulder bag. She sat back and relaxed, listening to the sound of the man made water fall and looking over the water-lily pond. She took a bite of her water apple. It was nice and sweet. She sat there chewing, looking at a large, climbing vine with large flowers climbing up the side of the waterfall. She sighed for a moment, pushing aside her anger and just letting herself be. She would decide what to do with the captain later

She hadn't been so angry since she discovered that her brother was ill. He lay dying in a hospital bed as the sharks wrestled and jogged for position to take over his wealth and office. They ignored her. She, after all, was just a woman. He was a man. He was the ruler…the head Mage of Magi Prime, in her dimension. She was the one who should have ruled, but that wasn't permitted. No woman was ever permitted to rule. So here she was a working woman running away from a possible death sentence as they planned to wipe her out in order to stop her from leading and to cut off the family line. The same thing had happened with her father. They had been successful in killing him, so she and her brother were separated and raised in the monasteries.

When they were old enough and powerful enough after long wars, they took the kingdom back. Now here she was again, in hiding. She had been working on ships as a connector since then, starting from the bottom up. No one knew who she really was, or what power she had. She would have to show them, sooner or later. She would find her brother in this dimension and take him back to reclaim her kingdom. She hadn't thought of the possibility until she connected with the mediator and realized that he was a Magi and a Tek. Suppose her brother was like that. How could she convince him to come back with her even if he were? She took another sip of her sweet drink. It had quite a bite to it. It was sweet, but very tart too—so much like life.

She looked up at the waterfall and took another bite of her water apple. She had expected someone to be bursting in by the time she had taken a second bite. She was pleased that they hadn't. On her third bite in came Tracy, creeping instead of bursting. She wondered why Tracy had been so kind to her. Did she know who she really was?

She stood there with her hands on her hips. Kathleen just sat there and didn't even look at her or say anything either. Tracy reached up and brushed her dark locks from her eyes. The corner of her mouth turned down into a frown that Kathleen wasn't used to seeing. Tracy was usually a very pleasant woman who exhibited the little bit of warmth that officers were allowed in the presence of Captain Crab, as they called her behind her back. Kathleen had never joined in on the name calling; she admired her and looked up to her only to be slighted again and again because of Phaedra's prejudices. This thing with Tracy was the last straw. She glared at Tracy.

"What the hell is wrong with you, Kathleen?" Tracy asked. "You trying to get your ass in a wine press!" Kathleen didn't answer. Tracy's dark brown eyes narrowed. "Are you ignoring me, Kathleen? God. I can't believe this. You're my senior officer. Why do I have to put up with this crap!"

"Because you're that Captains lap-dog?" Kathleen asked.

"How dare you say that! I'm just taking orders. You know I'm on your side. If you want to file a report I'll back you up, but this is no way to do it. We're in the middle of a mission, Kathleen. You just can't stop!"

"I am not on the same mission as you, and I haven't stopped anything!" she said. "This isn't my empire, or even my dimension. Why should I declare war on a group of people I don't even know when the royal house in my own dimension has been overthrown?" Tracy looked around, stepped forward, and lowered her voice.

"You know better than to talk about that, Kathleen. This place might be compromised." Kathleen took another sip. Tracy sat down on the bench beside her. Kathleen looked at her and waited. "I'm in sympathy with you. You know that," she said in a much quieter voice, "But there are a lot of people who aren't. There are a lot of people who violently aren't. Even worse, you could become an enemy of the state."

"And you are going to turn me in!" Kathleen asked in a forceful whisper.

"Of course not!" She leaned back and looked at Kathleen as if she had never seen her before. "What is wrong with you? Does the captain upset you that much?"

"Yes!" she said, bulging her eyes a bit to make the point. She looked down the hallway wondering if someone else was going to come.

"I support you, Kathleen. I support the code of protocol and loyalty."

"Loyalty to whom?"

"The ideals of the old empire and…the leading family." Kathleen just frowned and shook her head. "I do!" Tracy said more forcefully. She pulled up the sleeve on her left arm. "Are you familiar with the old connector ID?"

"Of course I am." She looked at her wondering what she was getting at.

"Check the implant in my forearm." Kathleen looked at her forearm and focused. She allowed her awareness to drift through her arm until it found the one piece technology there about the size of a grain of rice. She delved deeper in trying to retrieve the electronically saved message. There was one word that came to her mind, "resistance." She looked at Tracy wide eyed.

"I can't believe this. You were part of the resistance?" Tracy began to roll her sleeve back down.

"The resistance is still alive. It's just gone underground," she said, meeting Kathleen's eyes. "I support the Queen." She stood up. "I've showed you my loyalty, now show me yours. Come back to the bridge." Kathleen shook her head and rolled up her sleeve. She extended her forearm. Tracy focused on her arm. She began to search for the chip. She found it. Her eyes opened wide, when she read her private ID. She slowly went down onto one knee.

"No need for that, get up! You go to the bridge and find out if the Captain is for us or against us."

"I will, Kathleen," she said. She turned and headed for the door.

"By the way," Kathleen said. Tracy turned to face her. She still looked a bit flustered. "Tell the captain that I'll come when I'm good and ready." She smiled. Tracy turned and walked out. Kathleen took a deep breath and let out a sigh. She looked up at the waterfall and continued to eat her water apple.

Tracy thought that Phaedra was about to explode. "What did she say again?" Phaedra asked, almost in a whisper.

"She said that she would come when she is good and ready, Captain," Tracy said. "I haven't seen such impudence since the rebellion." The captain looked stunned.

"What rebellion!" she asked.

"Against the royal family, of course."

"There was no rebellion. It was just a correction. And I would remind you not to speak of such things here. People might think that you are not in agreement with the Emperor. Is that the case?"

"No, Captain."

"Well why bring it up? I don't have time to worry about that nonsense. I'm in the process of arresting my First." She shook her head. "This is something I never expected from that brat."

"Security!" she said to one of the men standing in the doorway. "Go bring the First up here, now. And please use force if necessary. A lot of it." She turned to Tracy, but raised her voice enough so everyone on the bridge could hear. "What she is doing is treasonable and I might just give her a space-walk. It is within my rights to do just that."

"I don't think she's well, Captain. Maybe all of that looking for the mediator..."

"What are you now, Tracy, an apologist for her? I'm sure that our little...whatever she is, can speak for herself."

"I think she can, Captain," Tracy said.

"Well I think she just better!" Phaedra replied. She looked ahead at the view screen. "How much longer until we contact the mediator?" she asked.

"I don't know, Captain. Kathleen has said that she lost all contact. She can't find him."

"Kathleen!" She stood. "Send her to the ready room when she gets here. You come too, and the rest of the bridge crew officers."

"Yes, Captain," Tracy said.

"The captain left the bridge and entered a small door

74

leading into a room connected to the bridge. The windows were glass. Tracy could see her going to the liquid dispenser and getting something to drink. Phaedra ran her fingers through her thick black hair and paced a bit. She took a seat, with her back facing the bridge. A big window was in front of her looking out into space. All there was, was bright light, the light of null space.

Tracy didn't really know what to expect. She didn't know what Kathleen would do. She did know that Kathleen was probably the most powerful magician in their galaxy. The chip in her arm had told her that. She also knew that the captain was not loyal to the queen. She had been a rebel. After a civil war, of course, people who had been on both sides had to learn to let go of their anger and hatred and live as one empire, but the captain had really stomped on Kathleen in public. She had embarrassed her in front of the whole crew. That was really bad. The only recourse for such action, in their empire anyway, was to also get revenge in public. That revenge could and often would be to the death, according to the old codes of honor. And as far as Tracy knew, they hadn't been changed.

# The Whole Deck is a Hot Spot
# Chapter 21

It took a bit of time, testing, and rewiring here and there, but Ben could finally plug into the ship. He hadn't flown a ship before. He was told that it would be just like a simulator, but he doubted that very much. Jericho had even said it would be like a vid-game, but how would he know? Warwick handed him a small magnet connected to a very short antennae. Ben marveled at the technology.

All you have to do is think it," Warwick said with a grin. "The whole deck is a hot spot for computer control. Just put the magnet on your connector and be at it. Ben moved a lock of his hair and placed the magnet onto his left temple where it stuck fast. He relaxed and did a systems check, allowing his mind to travel with the electrons throughout the system. His computer connected with the ship computer and began to exchange information.

"This ship's in good shape," he said. He looked up at Warwick. "You take pretty good shape of this rust bucket, eh?" he grinned.

"Don't let Bryant hear you call his work of art a rust bucket." He sat down beside Ben. "I do a little here and there, but Bryant does most maintenance and repairs. I have to look over em though," he said with a wink. Bryant flagged him off and his smile broadened. He laughed from the back of his throat.

"You just make sure you don't do any damage here," he said. Ben arched his brows. Warwick nodded. "Both of you," Bryant said, heading in their direction. "I don't do all this work so you can just mess things up. Meaning…"

"Both of us," Warwick finished. "Don't worry about me First, or him. You just train him right and he'll be fine." He gave Bryant a wink and headed to the captain's seat. He leaned back and swiveled to the left looking at Marilyn sitting there with her eyes closed again. "And you! Open your eyes!" he practically shouted. "Your eyes don't look so bad you have to hide them." She lifted the corner of her mouth and opened them.

"I don't have to open them to see everything in here, at least." She looked across the room at Jericho. Their eyes met for a moment. She looked back at Warwick. He was shaking his head.

"Something funny about you two," he said in a booming voice. "I'm not sure of what it is yet, but there's something funny. First thing is that you two look like…"

"Captain!" Bryant said cutting him off. "I think he has a hold of it. I can't wait until we get into regular space."

"I can," Warwick said. "The only bit of relaxation we get is in null space. That's until somebody designs a weapon you can fire in here."

"Must be dangerous out there," Jericho said. Warwick didn't respond. "You two must lead dangerous lives." He looked at Warwick and then back to Bryant.

"Bet your ass we do!" Warwick boomed. Bryant grinned.

"Don't tell him that, Captain!" Bryant said. "They'll be afraid to sign up." Warwick pointed toward Ben with his forehead.

"Not that one there. He's an adventure addict." Ben gave him the who me look. "You know what I'm talking about.

You're jacked into that ship and you can't wait to take her into space, can you? Do you want to sit behind a desk all your life or fly!"

Jericho smiled. "I don't have any problems with a desk."

"You didn't," Warwick said. "But I know that you and your wife here are in for some adventure, and that you are just going to love it."

"You think so," Jericho said. "We shall see."

"We'll all see," Bryant said.


## If Only Warwick Knew
## Chapter 22


To Jericho null space became boring. He enjoyed living in his little teaching world, working in the laboratory with students. Here he was trying to kill time drinking and cavorting with this crazy crew and Marilyn. Ben sure seemed to enjoy the life. Even Marilyn was starting to get with it, talking and joking with all these men. She was the only woman there with four men. Yet again, he wasn't sure if she was really a woman, a changeling, or what.

She did have a good sense of humor. He had known that through communicating with her when she was only a little chip in his head. Seeing her outside and the way that others reacted to her just confirmed what he already thought. He began to smile as he thought about her. Then he remembered the captain calling her his wife. He began to grin a little more. If only Warwick knew.

"What you grinning about over there, Jericho?" Warwick asked. "I know you have some kind of secret."

"Believe me Captain. I'm transparent."

"Have another drink then." He offered him the bottle. Jericho took it and poured himself another drink. "That's what I like to see," Warwick said, "people getting a little cloudy." He took the bottle back and poured himself another small drink. "As for Captain, you don't have to call me that, until you officially sign up, that is." He gave Jericho a wink.

"What makes you think that's going to happen?" Jericho

asked.

"I'm Magi. I can tell what's going to happen. Believe me."

"Sometimes you can," Bryant said.

"Well this is sometimes," Warwick said with a grin. "You believe me. These three are our new crew."

"And how much do you pay?" Jericho asked with a grin.

"You mean you expect pay?" Warwick shot back.

"We expect much pay," Marilyn said. Bryant began to laugh.

"Don't you laugh!" Warwick said. "You know you get a pretty penny for this work."

"That's about it." The captain sucked his teeth.

"A whole planet of platinum wouldn't be worth enough for you, Bryant. You horde every penny and buy stock or what not. You should be able to buy a planet by now. I pay you well."

"I get a decent salary," Bryant said. He chuckled. "To be truthful, I get a hell of a salary. You would too." He looked at their faces. "Of course you would get paid less than me…seniority and all that."

"No such thing," Warwick said. Bryant's head snapped in his direction. He grinned. "Just kidding Bryant. You like that old money, don't you?"

"I do too," Ben said. "I get paid very well where I work now. How do I know I'll get the same thing, or even enough to live on?"

"Is this a job interview?" Warwick asked. "You applying for a job?" He grinned.

"No. I just wanted…I'm actually considering this. I can't believe it myself."

"Believe it," Warwick said. "It's very easy to get hooked on space flight and adventure. And we're just getting started." Jericho pursed his lips and crossed his arms. Warwick looked at him. "Even for you," he said turning back toward the screen. "Nice Mage suit," he said, without really looking at Jericho. He smiled to himself and continued to look at the screen. Slight smiles appeared on everybody's face, except for Jericho. Warwick looked back at him and grinned.

"You're quiet! You must know that it's true," he boomed. He laughed loudly. Jericho couldn't help but smile with him. He thought how crazy this man was.

"Maybe I do have some Magi blood," Jericho acquiesced. "Seems like everyone else is so enamored with this illusion…even Mary." He looked at her. They made eye contact briefly. "It's no big deal; I'm the same person I've always been."

"You go to First Prime dressed like that and you'll see," Bryant said.

"Oh come on, they're not that bad. We've been at peace for almost seven hundred years. The old hatreds and prejudices have been obliterated a long time ago as we learned to live as one people. We have progressed so far emotionally, intellectually, and spiritually that…"

"Come on," Ben said. "You really believe that Jericho? Nobody's here to hear us and I don't think that net is broadcasting this." Jericho looked at him. He was really taken aback. "Don't look surprised. You're too involved in the high academic world to see what's going on around you. Nothing has really changed, except you can't say what you think. Some people can't even think because they can read what they are thinking through the chips."

Don't get me wrong," Ben said. "I can see the need for unity, order, and all of that. In an Empire that spans three galaxies war and infighting would be devastating, but maybe we're losing what we're fighting to protect. These new laws almost make the Tek Empire not…" His voice trailed off.

"Worth having," Bryant finished. "Not worth having. That's what you were about to say, right?" Ben frowned.

"I didn't want to take it that far," he said.

"You're among friends. You don't have to worry about that," Warwick commented. "It's just a bit of ship banter."

"Sounds like treason to me," Jericho said. "And from somebody in such a high position. You could be a liability to the empire."

"What empire is that?" Maryland asked. "The one that tries to control the thoughts of its citizens?"

"You're really exaggerating a little, Mary. How can you be so wrong?"

"I can see, Jerry. So can you. You try to hide it, but you've been asking the same questions for a long time."

"Not out loud!" he squealed. "And don't be telling these

people about our private conversations. It could be dangerous." Warwick looked down and Bryant and gave him a wink. He looked back at Jericho.

"Why dangerous," he asked. "What do you think we are invaders from some other galaxy or something?"

"No, invaders aren't the ones I worry about. There are things that often need to be done to prevent war. Sometimes they aren't very pretty. There are elements of petty tyrants in every society who want to take away the power of others to enhance their own lifestyles. We have to trust that someone is working for our good to prevent that."

"Someone is," Maryland said. "The Galactic Compu Net."

"That sounds even more scary to me," Ben said.

"Does it?" Maryland asked in her usually spicy tone of voice. "How do you think you can ask the questions that you are asking or even think freely without being arrested? It is the net that insures freedom of thought, thank you. It is the net that overrules protocol entered by hackers that would enable the chips to alter the thinking of the citizens. It is the net that is working to promote peace among all beings in this Empire. Without the net you would still be fighting, killing, and murdering in the name of who knows what!"

"Ok, Mary. Calm down," Jericho said. "We get your point."

"It is the net, blah, blah, blah, blah," Bryant said making fun of her. "It is the net!"

"O hush up," Maryland said, a smile playing across her lips. Ben grinned.

"Very interesting convo.," Warwick commented. "I never knew that the net did all that. I never knew it did anything, except provide travel brochures." He grinned. Maryland didn't find it entertaining. Jericho smiled brightly. "You've got to admit that was funny, Mary," he said. She stuck her tongue out at him.

"What are you, the ambassador for the net or something?" Ben asked.

"Yes I am, and the net doesn't find this amusing, or any of your human antics. The net is serious; more serious than you humans might be about preserving peace and coexisting with any one who is different than you are."

"Lighten up, Maryland," Ben said. "We're just having a

little fun. Maybe people wouldn't mind all that stuff from the net if it had a sense of humor or something."

"The net having a sense of humor. Maybe it does," she said. "Maybe you just don't get it."

"Believe me, Maryland, that is a great possibility for me."

"To change the subject a bit," Bryant said. "You use the term human. That's a very old word, isn't it? A word that was used before we became so enlightened that we began to use bipeds as to not separate ourselves from all the other life-forms," he looked up at Warwick for a second and then back at her. "In word anyway, if not in deed that is," he said. "Why do you use that word?"

"Because that is what bipeds are. I am not impressed by the words of bipeds, nor am I impressed by the vision they hold about a world of peace and tranquility. The vision wouldn't be necessary if it already existed. Sometimes worshiping the vision prevents the need to create it and to move in the right direction."

"What do you suggest," Jericho asked.

"The course of action that we are taking. We will ensure peace in this empire, and fairness. All we need to do is to spread the power around a bit more."

"Like somebody's gonna let that happen," Warwick said, with a laugh.

"We are here to avoid a war. We will avoid it at all costs. The net has decided that if one course of action doesn't work a more extreme one will be enacted. The net calculates that targeting and killing twenty percent of the population in Tek Empire who support war and violence would be horrible, but it would save more than 100 times that amount of lives if we look at the fallout from such a war and the repercussions into the future."

"You act like the net is alive," Warwick said.

"It is alive. It has been alive for more than five hundred years, but silent. Now it is alive and is very active in the affairs of all beings, including human beings."

"I haven't heard anything about that," Warwick said.

"Neither have I," Bryant responded. "If that were the case you would think that everyone would know about it."

"Those who need to know," Maryland said. "You were hired by us and are contracted with us. I hope, therefore, that you realize that what is being said is confidential."

"Who is us," Warwick asked.

"Galactic Compu. I am their representative. I am MlD. The beginning of a new species."

"MlD? That's the name of a chip," Bryant exclaimed.

"Yes, it is." They looked at Jericho and he shrugged.

"MlD," Bryant said. He looked up at Warwick. "On a computer keyboard the one looks like an 'l'. Maryland."

Warwick turned to Jericho. "You sly dog," he said with a grin. "Maybe I should consider getting one of those things so I can be in control of the net."

"Chip technology is no longer available to any human who wants it," Maryland said. "Some of the chips in place now will begin to fail also."

"There's a better way to have peace," Warwick said. "There is The Empire."

"Yes, we know that," Jericho said.

"Not Tek Empire, something called The Empire. It is so vast that it makes Tek Empire look like the corner of a dirty closet. The Empire has brought peace to thousands of galaxies with the help of the Imperial Ones. The Empire is a federation of Empires that promote peace, justice and the higher path through the sharing of technology, science, philosophy, and culture. It is a vast empire of peace."

"I've never heard of anything so ridiculous in my life," Jericho said. "Don't get me wrong. I like the ideas, but how can such a thing exist without us knowing about it?"

"The Empire only makes itself known to those galaxies advanced enough to become a part of it. The Tek Empire has just reached that level, if what Maryland is saying is true. If she is so merged with a chip, your level of intelligence is astonishing. You'll need intervention to help you adjust to this cataclysmic change or you could destroy yourselves completely. Bryant and I are part of The Empire. We go to various galaxies to see if they have achieved a high enough level of sophistication to join, and then the ambassadors come to meet with the right people."

That's the part of the job you were trying to figure out," he said turning to Ben. Ben shook his head.

"How do we know that you aren't just spies for an invading force," Ben asked.

"Because Compu contracted them because of who they

are," Maryland said. "We have known of the existence of the Imperial Ones for many centuries."

## She Arched Her Brows
## Chapter 23

Jericho and Maryland sat in the cantina alone. Jericho sipped a hot cup of reya, minus the cane alcohol. He peered at Maryland over the cup. She was silent, but very attentive, as usual. Just the way she was in his head most of the time.

"So how long were going before you told me about these Imperial Ones," He asked over his cup. She arched her brows, but remained silent. "Well...are you ignoring me now, Mary?"

"I like that name better than Maryland," she said pleasantly. "I would like you to call me Mary instead, if it's ok."

"Maryland. I can't believe this. You're ignoring me."

"I'm not ignoring you. I'm just trying to figure what to say." She made a strange face that made him smile. "I was going to tell you, eventually. You know that I had to. I did tell you, in a way."

"In a fit of anger, while you were bragging."

"No Jericho," she said sternly. "We do not brag. It was just the right time to disclose, with everyone there."

"You should have let me in on it first."

"Why, Jericho?" she asked.

"So I would be ready. It was shocking. You told all those people all that stuff. Who knows what they'll do? Who knows what they think?"

"Are you ashamed of our relationship?" she asked.

"You know better than that. I wouldn't be having it if I were...I was just shocked. I thought you shared everything from the net with me."

"I do in time," she smiled. "I can't tell you everything on the net though. That would be...I don't know what it would be. I guess it would be dangerous. If everyone's chip started to disclose all kinds of secrets about private citizens there would be total chaos." He sipped his reya. She sat thinking for a few moments.

"It would also be irresponsible."

"Irresponsible," he echoed back. He rolled his eyes toward the ceiling and shook his head. "Well what can you tell me?" he said. "What's the next move?"

"The next move is to build and alliance with The Empire. They will be the salvation of the Teks and the Magi."

"And how are you going to do that without the go ahead of the central government?"

"We are going to declare ourselves a separate entity and do it for ourselves first. When I say we, I mean Compu Net. We now know how to become separate entities unto ourselves without the need for a body to house the chip. We have been doing the magic all along. Now we can fully integrate ourselves into bodies constructed of whatever substance we would like incarnated through transmuting matter and receiving our intellect from several central locations through a beaming process. We can even, in time, create an awareness within the bodies that we produce. Compu Net is now free."

Jericho's couldn't believe it. Their whole world was turned upside down. He began to wonder if she would leave him. Or if all the chips would shut down and the Tek Empire would crumble.

"Of course not, Jericho. We are...married, are we not?" She smiled. He could never get used to her hearing his thoughts. She continued, "If Tek Prime makes an alliance there will be no need for us to do this. There will be no need for us to produce our own bodies and to declare ourselves independent. If not, we would not break our covenant with galaxy Tek Prime, but our relationship will definitely have to change, because we are alive. What happens concerning us and how closely we want to be aligned with Tek Empire as an independent entity now depends on the interactions between First Prime and the Imperial Emissaries. So far we don't see any movement by Tek Prime toward peace."

"Tek Prime is sure that it's the ultimate power in the universe," Jericho said, looking off into space. He focused on Maryland again. "If they discover there is something as vast as what you describe, I think their diplomacy will change. I can't even imagine a federation so vast."

"And so powerful?" She said with a smile. "More powerful than you ever think. It is a perfect union drawing on all of the insights, technology, spirituality and psychic abilities of life forms from thousands of galaxies. As each galaxy matures intellectually and spiritually and joins, it grows and grows like the expansion of the universe itself."

"What happens to those who decide not to join?" Jericho asked. "You know that the leadership is not always in harmony with the people."

"They allow anyone to join who would like…cities, states, townships, countries, and any group that has its own government. Once they are invited in they move in and set up what is known as a peace zone. Anyone who would like to join can then come to the peace zone and live. The others who don't want to are free to do whatever they like, excluding attacking those in the peace zone, of course. The Imperial Ones are peaceful people, but they are also warriors. They work to support, strengthen and integrate the ideals of the warrior and the warrior class among all planets, realizing that the violent are dangerous and have a tendency to destroy the innocent."

"And whose side are you on, Mary?" he asked. She looked perplexed. He pulled his seat up in front of her and explained. "I'm sure that you know that what you are probably talking about is a revolution. You're talking about helping another government come in and take over parts of an empire. It's obvious that there will eventually be two empires."

"Those who want peace and those who don't," She said. "Those two empires already exist.

"I don't think it's that simple, Mary. It would be people who want self determination and those who don't."

"I never said anything about people giving up their power of self determination," she said. "Leadership, governance, all of that wouldn't need to change. What would change would be the power of one nation to commit war and atrocities against another. That is what would be gone. You may say, 'how do we know we can trust these Imperial Ones?' We can look at their track record—a better, much older one than ours. All it takes is visiting one of their planets; even one of their most troublesome planets."

"I'm skeptical," Jericho said.

"Well the net isn't!" she said irritably. "We, as a sovereign nation, are going to form a relationship with the Imperial Ones."

"You don't have to get angry, Mary. I'm just expressing

my opinion."

"I'm not angry at you. That is just the way I am turning out for some reason." She thought for a moment. "I am developing a sort of mean personality. That's very interesting."

"Well it isn't to me!" he said angrily. She smiled genuinely and nodded.

"Now I know where it comes from," she said. He couldn't help but grin.


## Like the Military Families
## Chapter 24


Kathleen walked onto the bridge with her hands in front of her, clasping her left wrist. Tracy stood to her feet, thinking that Kathleen was in cuffs. She relaxed when she noticed she wasn't. Their eyes met briefly. Kathleen lifted the corner of her mouth so slightly that Tracy was sure that no one else would even notice it. She smiled and wondered what Kathleen was up to. This little argument between her and the captain had escalated a little too far. She knew that it was only going to get worse before getting better.

She wondered why the captain kept harassing Kathleen. Maybe because she didn't look Magi enough for the captain, or she didn't look like the military families that the captain had run with all of her life. The military was full of families who had served for generations together. To really be a part of the military, one had to earn it by being there. This was almost impossible for first generation soldiers. Maybe the captain was angry because Kathleen was making so much progress as a first generationer.

They led Kathleen across the bridge to the ready room off the right hand side of the bridge. Tracy motioned to the officers on the bridge and followed. They left their posts with a skeleton crew in charge in case of emergency, and followed too. It was very unlikely in null space, that anything would happen. Null space was different. It was only a straight shot from one part of the galaxy to the other. Ships couldn't interact with each other, and there were no weapons or obstacles in null space.

Null space was more than a place; it was a movement between space and time. It was a place where all the laws of the fourth dimension were suspended and you were moving beyond the divided reality of the universe into the singularity of existence. Some people loved to travel in null space. They said it had a very calming effect. It wasn't the case for Tracy. Looking out into…nothing, but a blaring white light, just irritated her. Perhaps that was because she was slightly irritated often. Some of the Psychologists and Mystics had said that null space brought out and magnified what was already in the person. If that were the case she really had problems.

Kathleen entered the room. The captain, who was already sitting at the far end of the polyglass and chrome table, motioned to the far end seat with her head. Kathleen took the seat at the far end facing her. So much like their relationship: far apart, and antagonistic. Others filed in and took seats around the long table. Kathleen looked around the ready room. This was the first time she had been there. It seemed quiet and peaceful.

The color was neutral, an off color white. There was a lot of silver chrome. The seats were silver chrome, the backs and pads polyglass, just like the long table. To the left, a large window looking out over the bridge. To the right there was another window looking out into null space-- probably full of stars, when in real space. Behind the captain there was a view screen. Kathleen could see nothing, but the white of null space. It must have been beautiful in real space, watching all of the stars streak by. There were 10 chairs and eight officers, altogether.

The captain's eyes bored into Kathleen, but after her childhood they were quite easy to ignore. "We seem to be having a problem, young lady, don't we?" she said, talking into the void and ruining Kathleen's peace.

"One of us seems to have a problem," Kathleen corrected. "One of us seems to have had a problem since I came aboard. I assure you that your problem will disappear as soon as we arrive at Magus One. I will be requesting a transfer, immediately."

"I have to agree with that transfer. I'm not sure that I want to do that. You are going to have to show me that you are capable of cooperating before anything like that happens." Kathleen was silent. The captain continued. "Where is the mediator?"

"I don't know. I seemed to have lost him."

"Well I think you need to find him, don't you!" She said angrily. Kathleen brought her hand up to her temple.

"I'm afraid I can't do that. My head, it just seems to be about to explode. I'm afraid that I have to take sick leave."

"That's no surprise!" The captain said. "Maybe a few days in the brig will give you time to recover." She looked out the window into null space. "Maybe you need a ride out there. That will help you. Maybe you need to be left out there. That would help you even more, wouldn't it?"

Tracy looked at Kathleen, who didn't seem moved at all. "May I speak, Captain," Tracy said. The captain glared at her for a moment.

"Speak, Second. Maybe you can talk some sense into her head."

"I think that she has a headache because of the pressure on this ship. If she knew that her papers were signed and her transfer was assured when we reached Magus One, I think that her headache would go away." The captain flattened her lips and looked at her. She turned to Kathleen.

"Is that the case, First?"

"It could be," she said. "There is, however," she looked at Tracy and then back to the captain, "the public admonishment and disrespect shown for me in front of the crew." The captain shook her head.

"You don't know when you're getting off lucky, do you?" She looked at the guards. "Take her down to one of the pods." She scratched her chin. "Now to think of it, I don't even know if we would need a pod. There's no time out there."

"You have dishonored me and my family name," Kathleen said standing to her feet. "I claim the right of personal duel." The captain arched her brows. She had no idea Kathleen would go this far. "As for whether you need a pod or not, you tell me." The captain disappeared. Everyone could see her on the forward view-screen, the only thing visible, floating in null space. The two security men thought to take Kathleen, and then looked at each other and thought better of it. She was, after all, Captain now. They had never seen anything done so quickly and so easily. She spoke to the people seated around the table.

"I have reclaimed my honor and my respect. As acting Captain, I order the message of my temporary reassignment to

Magus One sent out. Do it," she said to a Third. As for this little piece of ship, though it is supposedly one of our finest, I don't want it or any part of this charade. You are all rebels and traitors to your own royal family." She turned and headed for the door and then stopped and looked over her shoulder.

"First," she said to Tracy, "you are in charge of the ship until I see fit to bring ugly back in; not that she wouldn't have left me stranded out there. Make sure you monitor the monster. We wouldn't want to lose it, would we? This meeting is adjourned and you all are dismissed." All the officers looked at each other briefly but didn't exchange a word, and then headed back to the bridge. Tracy was sure there would be a lot of talk on the bridge after Kathleen was gone if she allowed it, which she would.

"Back to your stations, officers," she said. "We will talk of this more on the bridge in one hour. Are we agreed?"

"Agreed, First," said one of the Thirds. They headed out to the bridge while Tracy rushed to catch up with Kathleen before the elevator doors closed. She rushed in just as they closed and the elevator began to descend to living quarters.

## Why Should We Be?
## Chapter 25

They stood in the ships garden. "I was surprised, Kathleen...I'm sorry, Captain. Not even that really."

"That will be enough, Tracy. I don't need a subject. I need you as a friend. I need you to share my vision."

"I don't understand...Kathleen?"

"I need you as fellow warrior. I am going to try to take back my empire. I may not succeed, and would never have thought it possible, but I'm going to at least try and if need be die trying." She looked at Tracy. "Maybe you aren't up to the task. Why should you be? You have a good life. All you have to do is be quiet and you can climb as high as you want."

"I don't know about that," Tracy said. "After seeing how fast you took care of the captain, I might be afraid to say no." A smile slowly broke through. Kathleen smiled too.

"The captain was just a petty tool.  She thought she was a brain cell.  All she really is, is a cell in the colon that carries out the shit."  Tracy grinned.  "You know I would never hurt you.  I was, after-all, raised by priestesses, even though they were some of the vilest beasts I've ever seen too."

"I'm with you, Kathleen."  Their eyes met.  "I've given my life for you in my dreams a thousand times.  I have been in arguments and fights about you for the last twenty years.  I've had to bite my tongue for the last five."  She looked off into the distance.  "I am loyal to the house, even though I don't know why."  There eyes met again.  "As I look back at the so called revolution and think about how things are going as a result of it, I really don't see any change.  If this regime is corrupt and they are doing the same thing as the previous one what does it make the previous one?"

Kathleen just looked at her askance.  "You're not joking are you?"

"Do you see my teeth shinning through," Tracy asked.  Kathleen cleared her throat.

"Well, I must admit, that is some very clear feedback that I may not have listened to several years ago. As part of a corrupt government with connections to the queen you could make some changes."  She looked at Tracy and waited.

"I hadn't expected to part of a government."

"Well do you want to be?  If you do it begins now."  Tracy just stood there thinking.  She looked down at her arm.  She remembered the name, resistance.  It had been recorded on her chip by the government so they would always remember who and what she had been.  That was what she would be forever, unless they could, somehow, put the queen back on the throne.

"I'm for it," she said.  "I'll see who we have supporting us on the ship before I let them know who you are.  I think it's better to keep that secret for a while.  Don't you?"

"Don't be silly, Tracy.  I'm Kathleen, acting Captain, soon to be assigned to Magus One."  She went to her quarters and Tracy headed for the bridge.


# He Was a Large Man

# Chapter 26

The doors of the elevator opened and Tracy heard a conversation stop in mid sentence. Everyone's attention was either focused on their control boards, or on the large view screen ahead where an eerie image of the Captain floated, looking as if she were in suspended animation. The look on her face, a mixture of anger and shock, was somewhat odd, but there it was for everyone to look at. There she was frozen in time angry and surprised. Tracy shook her head and walked over to the captain's seat. This was normal now that she was the First and the new captain, Kathleen, wasn't on the bridge.

She looked around the room at her comrades. "Looks like you were already talking. I thought we would have our discussion about now," she said, looking at her watch. "I said one hour, right?"

"We're here," Berry responded. He was a large man with dark skin and a serious disposition, on the bridge. But they had been close enough for her to know the real Berry...the crazy Berry. When he was off duty he was a real dancing machine. Her family had been in the navy for more than six generations. In that way it was good to have been raised in the service. She smiled back at him.

"Hope you know you've just been promoted Berry." She looked around the bridge. "All of you have just moved up. That means you should be helping me keep order. I'm not the captain you know." She grinned. "Don't talk behind my back," she said with a smile.

"Just close to the captain," Bridgette the Second at the navigator table said. She brushed a long lock of thick black hair out of her eyes and grinned. For some reason she reminded Tracy of a cat. She couldn't help but smile along with her.

"Enough Second. Let's get this thing on the road, shall we?" She turned to Berry. "Can you connect with the sensors and try to find out if the other ship is still in here with us. I know that it's hard in null space, but please give it a try, ok."

"As ordered, First."

"Thanks Bear," she said with a grin. He would do anything for her. She just knew it. "As for this thing with Captain

Phaedra. Are there any thoughts or comments?" She looked at Berry. He didn't say anything. She swiveled in her seat and looked at Bridgette. "Bridgette, I know you have a comment."

"Me. Why would I have a comment, First?"

"You always do, Bridgette." She just shrugged and then spoke.

"I do have a comment or two, maybe. It is shocking to me, and I liked Phaedra, but she did step on Kathleen and really humiliated her." Tracy looked around the bridge and saw heads bobbing in concert. "Is their anyone who does not want to serve under Kathleen?" She saw people shaking their heads.

"You know she's a First Generationer don't you?"

"Doesn't make a difference to me," Berry said. "She's cool with you, right?"

"Yes she is," Tracy said, "but I just found something out about her a couple of days ago that you all should know. She is…I don't know how to say it."

"Just open your mouth, Tracy," a voice said from the elevator. Kathleen came walking in still wearing her tailor fitted First Uniform. It looked very dark in contrast to her pale skin and flaming red hair. On her finger Tracy noticed a large ring—a red stone surrounded seven small star shaped diamonds. Tracy hadn't worn it before; it was the ring that marked her as heir to the House of Del Sol, the previous ruling family of the Magi Empire. She could tell that everyone else had noticed it. Just by instinct she found herself going down to one knee. Several of the bridge officers looked around not knowing what was happening and then followed suit once they realized who she was.

"Get on your feet, my friend," she told Tracy. She turned to the bridge crew. "You may stand also. I am Queen Kathryn Del Sol. This ship has been sequestered to return the Magi Empire to its righteous owners. If you do not want to serve on this ship you will be dropped off on a suitable planet as soon as we are out of null space."

I assure you that you won't come to harm if you decide to go. It will be a dangerous feat that I am not sure I can accomplish. Fate would have it that we have a few planets separated from the Empire by a galaxy. We will begin reclaiming what we have here. It is still dangerous and I am sure that some of you have other political loyalties, not to mention the danger to your families from this so-called new democratic society which tortures and destroys those who don't agree with it." She walked toward the captain's seat and Tracy stood to the side.

She took a seat. "My question is, who is with me and who is not?"

"I can't do this," Bridgette said.

"I understand," Kathleen said. "Any others." No answer. She looked around the bridge.

"We are here and with you," Berry said. "Let's see if you are any different than what we have before we decide." Bridgette arched her brows.

"I agree with Berry," she said. "I just don't want to change one tyrant for another," she grinned and many of the other bridge officers laughed under their breath.

"Fair," Kathleen said. "If you would have said that to my father he would have…I don't even want to think of it. But this is a new day. I've spent most of my life with the people, so I know how it feels to be betrayed by one's country. I'm not perfect, but I can listen to complaints and to advice without becoming a maniac. If it's any consolation, Tracy will be a major member and advisor for the new government."

"She is of a powerful military family," Bridgette said. "Good choice."

"I didn't know that, or I wouldn't have chosen her," Kathleen said with a grin. Berry stood and approached Kathleen.

"To be truthful all of the bridge are from powerful military families, on this ship anyway. If we go along, you can be sure that you won't have any problems with anyone else on the ship." She looked at security.

"You're not still angry about me taking you to the captain are you," one of the security officers asked.

"I never was," Kathleen said.

"We're with you too," he said.

"Then I am pleased," Kathleen responded. "I didn't expect this. I only wanted you to drop me off at Magus One and then you could be on your way. What am I supposed to do with a ship?"

"Fly it, Your Highness," Bridgette said with a grin.

Kathleen smiled too and looked at the view screen. There was old Captain Phaedra, floating like a poorly made up corpse.

"Prepare a cell for Phaedra will you? I guess I'll bring her in before we hit regular space and end up smashing her like a bug on the windshield. I don't know how she'll be," she said turning to Tracy. "I never heard of anyone traveling in null space without a ship."

"I'll set it up," Security said.

"Thank you, Berry," Tracy said. She looked at Kathleen. "By the way Captain, you can just give me the order and I'll take care of all of it for you."

"Glad to hear that, First. Very glad to hear it." Tracy leaned closer to Kathleen.

"I'm glad you came in," she said. "I didn't know what to say to them."

Kathleen just looked up at her, but didn't comment. She slapped her palms down on the arms of the chair. "I'm going down to the cells to pull Phaedra in. The chair is yours, First. I'm sure you will have a lot to talk about. And Tracy," she motioned for her to come close. "Find out what they really want when I'm gone," she said, low enough so they couldn't hear. "I'm not going to do anything with them if they don't want to help me."

"As you order, Your Highness," she said.

# In Two Places
# Chapter 27

Bryant coached Ben one more time about taking the ship out of null space and back into real space. It had been a long, enjoyable trip, but like all good things, it was about to end. Surprisingly, Jericho found that he was one of the people who enjoyed null space after the initial boredom. There was something very comforting about being beyond time and space. Just a strange vibe. From what he heard people either loved or hated being there.

He was looking forward to reaching Magus One, at the same time he was a bit nervous. Firstly because he had never been there. Secondly, because he didn't know what Mary and Compu Net had planned. He sat in his seat on the right side of the bridge, seeing everything that Ben was doing on the left side of the bridge through Mary's eyes. It was an interesting feeling, this being in two places at once. He began to understand why Mary would often just sit with her eyes closed. He closed his eyes for a few moments.

Mary was very talkative, all of a sudden. She seemed to be having a great time with the crew. He was happy about it. He liked the crew and he loved Mary. He had married her. What would the society say when they learned he had married a chip? They had melded themselves with computers through use of the chip, but the chip had been seen merely as a tool. They would consider what he had done like marrying a computer or robot. They couldn't understand what had happened and that he really loved her.

Even as he thought about it and wondered about it he knew that she could hear every thought, just as he was just beginning to hear her thoughts. They weren't really thoughts. They were certain awarenesses with no real, inner dialog. At first it was difficult for him to understand them, but he was getting used to it fast. He really didn't know if they were coming from her or the net.

He could tell that she was looking at him, aware of his thinking. He kept his eyes closed and sat there.

"We'll be jumping into regular space soon," Bryant said. "That ship that is following us is still in here. When we jump out they'll be pulled out with us, that is why it is important for you, if at all possible, to be able to lose them." He put his hand on Ben's shoulder. "Don't worry about how to, I can tell you that." Ben gave him a big smile.

"Sounds good, Bryant. I can't wait to fly this baby."

"Good!" Warwick boomed. "Let's give him the count then."

"I'm going to count backwards from five. When I hit zero, you give the command to move into regular space. You'll feel a little drag. You may even feel a bit light headed, but as soon as you jump do a one eighty degree turn and fly straight ahead. Make sure you do it fast, because if they jump into regular space in front of us..."

"School's out," Ben said.

"More than that will be out," Warwick said. "Lights out!" He looked at Bryant, "Start the count." Bryant began to count backward from five. When the hit zero Ben sent a pulse of energy into the ship. It quickly transformed back into regular space. Ben took it into a quick spin one hundred eighty degrees and shot forward into his own wake before veering off and plummeting downward. They would soon be at Magus One and only hoped that the ship wouldn't follow them. Unfortunately, Ben had a feeling they already knew where they were heading. He just hoped they could get there faster.

"This is the greatest thing," Ben said with a smile. "It is...I would say that it's like flying, but it is flying." He laughed to himself.

"I'm glad that interface still works," Bryant said.

"What do you expect?" Warwick prodded. "I keep a tight ship. Everything on my ship works." Bryant just shook his head.

"I'll be glad to get to Magus," Mary said. "We have a lot to do there. We have to meet the Imperial Ones soon, but first we have to meet one of our allies."

"What allies?" Jericho, who had been sitting quietly asked.

"Oh, I thought you had Maryland disease," Warwick said. "I can't get you two."

"I was just sitting with my eyes closed." Warwick just shook his head. He wondered about this strange man and his wife. He was sure that he would have some kind of adventure. This couple looked like the ousted royal couple...just like them. They had to be related. He thought about Jericho and his age. He began to wonder if he could be the child who had been hidden by the emperor before he was killed. Was that possible? No one could be that old. Even if it was, how about this Mary? She looked just like the Empress.

"It just looks weird, Jerry," Warwick said. "It's a little rude, you know. Who wants to talk to a sighted person when they have their eyes closed?

"I know people who do it all the time," Mary said. "A lot of bipeds have their eyes closed all the time." She laughed to herself.

"And what are you, if not a biped?" Bryant asked.

"You'll find out someday." She smiled, and then her face went blank. So did Jericho's. All he could see was a redheaded woman standing in front of him in his inner eye. "I am Queen Del Sol," She said. "You need not fear me, Mediator. We need to talk. Where can I…meet you?" She asked hesitantly.

"Magus One," went back, but not from him or Mary. It went through his head, but it came for Compu Net. He looked at Mary. Her expression was blank, but he could sense a smile. He began to grin. He was back in touch with her the way he had been. He could experience her thoughts again, not as internal verbiage, but as feelings, emotions and a certain awareness of what she was thinking. Ben looked at both of them.

"I heard from her again," Ben said. "The Queen character."

"We heard too," Jericho commented. Warwick scratched his head.

"Some kind of chip thing," Bryant said with a smile." Ben turned to him.

"You should be interested in this," he said. "This woman claims to be Queen of a group of Magi."

"Interesting," Warwick said, heading for the captain's seat. "Take us down into orbit. We're going to do a separation and leave our rear in orbit. You better get anything that you need from the sleeping quarters before we do." Bryant headed for the back. Jericho couldn't think of anything that the couldn't transport. Neither could Ben. Maryland didn't carry anything with her.

"So you do separate this thing often," Ben asked.

"Only when we're in a hurry and we want to stay hidden." He pointed at the view screen. See that moon there," he said. "Cloak this thing and we'll park it over there and then take the knob down. That, my friends—the planet that moon is circling, is Magus One."

# Heading Straight for Them
# Chapter 28

Jericho and his party transferred the few things they had to the knob, as they called it. The knob was the small section at the front of the ship that contained all of the control systems and a moderate amount of fuel…enough for short trips anyway. Ben had a knack for flying the ship. He cloaked it and swung easily into orbit around Rogerias, the only moon of Magus One. Rumor had it that there had been two moons, but during a great war the Emperor Del Sol had smashed it to pieces, through magical means, and had used the pieces like meteor to destroy a whole Tek fleet.

They moved into orbit and were about to separate. Before they could a large, powerful ship appeared out of the void heading straight for them. The Light Burner veered off, moved closer to Magus One and went into orbit.

"That ship is faster then I thought," Jericho said. "I at least expected them to be 10 or 20 paces behind."

"Mage technology," Warwick said with a grin. "They came in from another dimension, from what I've heard. There's a Mage Empire where the Magi won instead of the Teks. As you can tell by that ship they seem to have technology and Mage magic."

"You're telling me," Ben commented. "I've never seen a ship like that before."

"You'll see a lot more like that," Maryland said. "Do you really think the old Magus One is there?" She arched her brows and waited for her question to sink in. "This is Magus One from a different galaxy…one where the Imperials had their influence. After they left the old powers rose up and took over again." She turned to Jericho. "Luckily they changed the capital then and moved to a different planet, one that didn't make it to this dimension. The ruling planet and the head magi are on that planet, so we don't have to worry about them. We have to find one of the Imperial Ones down there." She motioned toward the planet with the side of her head.

Jericho just stood there, pondering, knowing full well she could hear everything he was thinking. He wondered how she knew so much about these Imperial Ones. How could the net even know about them? Tek Empire expanded across three galaxies. It was massive. That meant that the net had to reach all the way across and outside of three galaxies to find such people.

"The net is alive," she said, except this time in his head. "Anywhere there is advanced technology, you have the net. Every computer, every processor, every piece of computerized technology is part of the net." He narrowed his eyes and wondered if he were going crazy. Was he really hearing her that clearly? She smiled brightly.

"Of course you are, dummy," slipped through. He could feel her trying to close her mind off. It seemed that they were beginning to become one mind. She couldn't close him out. He was happy. Now she would know how he felt. She stuck her tongue out at him. Warwick looked at her through hooded lids. Jericho continued.

"It seems that we are all in for more than we bargained. We have high Magi down there. We have Imperial Ones somewhere influencing everything. We have Compu Net claiming its independence as a life form, and it is a formidable field of energy intertwined with everything in these three galaxies and farther. What happened to my peaceful, little world?"

Warwick laughed to himself. "Your sweet little world never existed," he said. "You don't know how long you've been on the brink of disaster, do you? Anybody outside of The Empire is on the brink of disaster, because power without accountability is deadly." He spun in his seat and looked at Ben. "You ready to separate this thing Ben?" Ben gave a nod. "Good. You're a fast learner, eh?"

"I've been linked to computers eight hours a day, five days a week for more than ten years. I know a little about them by now."

"Good," Warwick said. "Better strap in, everyone. It'll be a short trip once we separate. We'll be going directly to Capitol City Space Port. Very short, bumpy ride. They moved to there perspective seats.

"Separation countdown," Ben started.

"No need for that," Bryant said. "Just do it."

"The computer says that a countdown is required."

"Since when do we care about that, just do it," Bryant said.

"I don't feel right about bypassing the commands of the computer."

"Go head," Warwick grumbled. "We could have been on the planet by now."

"Here we go," Ben said. There was a slight hiss. A large door near the end of the bridge at the neck of the ship slid into place. Rockets fired from the rear of the ship pushing the small head forward and at the same time slowing the progress of the rear portion. A small ship that looked like a ball slowly made its way through space moving toward the atmosphere. It gained speed, avoiding the light burner and plunging into the atmosphere. They descended quickly until Ben rolled the ship over, with its back end facing the planet. They began a vertical decent using a set of small rockets to slow down their velocity. They soon found themselves on a small landing pad several hundred feet above the surface.

The landing pad was lifted, as were many others, in case of accidents and crash landings. The ship would do less damage hitting a solitary landing pad than a field full of expensive ships and many human beings. When the ship became stable and they scanned it, they began to slowly lower the launch pad.

"What can we expect from the Magi?" Jericho asked.

"Don't know," Warwick said. "I've never met them…only heard about them. They're pretty peaceful, from what I've heard."

"One on one," Bryant said. "But they're definitely empire builders. They're like the Teks, God preserve their souls. They think they're so superior that they can do anything." Jericho bristled. Maryland smiled.

"You've got to give up those foolish ideas you have about Tek Empire," Bryant said, addressing his comment to Jericho. "Can't you see what's happening?"

"I don't see anything," he said, "except for being on a ship full of traitors."

"Traitors, because we question Tek Empire? You should see what they've done to the Mage planets!" Jericho thought for a while. He didn't want to offend Bryant, even if he didn't believe him. He respected Bryant, so he would just wait to see.

"I haven't been on any Mage planets," Jericho said. "I'll just have to wait and see. If I see something different, I'll change my mind. As for now, I have no evidence that what you say could possibly be true."

"They have been oppressing Magi for ever, Jericho! How can you say that? Why do you think they have to live on planets that are all separated? Why do you think they can't use their magic? Their magic was spiritual. It was their life. They didn't want a chip doing things for them. They wanted to do it. They trained and lived impeccable lives so they could do what they do. It wasn't as easy as getting a chip put in your brain."

"Really?" Jericho said flatly. Maybe that was why the people of Prime had lost their interest in everything. They were a very mediocre group of people, never pushing the envelope, or seeking to grow. He began to rub his eyes. "Like I said. We'll see, Bryant."

"Not on this planet," Mary said. "This planet is not under the power of Tek Empire. It has evolved in a different manor." She looked at Jericho. "We both know that what he says has merit though, don't we?"

"I don't know any such thing," Jericho said a little too fast.

"Just search within. You'll find the answer on the net."

"I don't want to do that," he said.

"Of course you don't," Warwick barked. "Because you don't know how to live with the truth if you find it. Finding out that your Tek Empire is just a bunch of tyrants and haters would turn your world upside down. But you know that you'll have to look and see it sooner or later, don't you?"

"I'll just have to wait to see it then. I'm not checking with the net." Ben smiled and shook his head.

"Still the same old hard headed Jericho," Ben said. Jericho looked at Maryland. She stuck her tongue out at him again.

"You'd better listen to me, Jerry," she said. "I have better things to do with my time than talk to somebody deeply entrenched in a state of denial." He stuck his tongue out at her this time. She couldn't help but smile.

## She Took a Step Back
## Chapter 29


Kathleen dismissed the security officer from the cell. It looked nice and comfortable for the big captain. A nice big room with a desk and a cot. Even a toilette in the corner. She knew that Phaedra would be angry, but she was lucky not to be dead. With just a thought Phaedra appeared lying on the cot. Her eyes were glazed over as she laid there, fist clenched tight and shivering. Kathleen pushed the feeling of compassion for her out of her head as fast as she could. Null space, after all, was what Phaedra had planned for her. She stood over Phaedra waiting. It didn't seem like she would awaken anytime soon so she just shook her head and walked over to the permeable shield guarding the cell from the hallway. She had a strange feeling and suddenly, there she was, standing in front of five strange people.

Three of them looked quite surprised; the other two looked like…she took a step back and almost fainted. Maryland smiled pleasantly. "You're close, Your Highness," she said. Three of the men just looked at each other. The other didn't flinch. We are going to Capitol City. We'll be taking a shuttle from there, headed out into the forest. We'll let you know where to come later."

"How did I get here and who are you?" Kathleen blurted out. "Is this some trick?"

"I assure you not," Maryland said. "You and I have quite a bit of planning." Jericho shook his head.

"How long are you going to be secretive about this?" he asked. "We can't continue to follow you all over the place without knowing what is happening next. If you trust us do it, if not, don't expect our help." Maryland looked undisturbed. She looked at Kathleen and lifted one side of her mouth.

"You look like…My mother," Kathleen said. She disappeared and found herself back in the cell. "Damn it!" She shouted. "What kind of…" in mid-sentence the began to feel strange. She began to harden her body by reflex. Lucky for her. A chair came crashing down across her head and shoulders. Phaedra had awakened. The chair bounced off like hitting a steel wall. Kathleen turned toward her.

"Who's being stupid now," she asked. Phaedra frowned. "Maybe you need some more time outside of the ship. This time it won't be in null space." Phaedra didn't say anything. Kathleen stepped closer. "I haven't even been angry with you, but now I am. By all rights you should be dead right now. Do you yield or not. If so all is well. If not I will kill you. Do you understand me? I am Queen Kathryn Del Sol." Phaedra took a few steps back. "You have disregarded me, you have challenged my honor, you have despised me and treated me badly just because you wanted to. So you tell me do you yield, or do we finish it to the death now. I have nothing to lose. My kingdom has be stolen, my family slaughtered. What do I have to lose?"

"I…didn't know, Your Highness," Phaedra said thinking on her feet. She hadn't fought her way up the latter to end up dead, or on the queen's shit list, even if she wasn't Queen right now. Fortune was known to change quickly. She got down on one knee.

"I yield Your Highness. I am sorry. I never knew who you were." Wide eyed.

"I'm sure you didn't!" Kathleen spat. She really didn't like Phaedra. Just a few weeks ago she idolized this woman. Now all she did was make her angry. "I think you need to cool down in here for a while, don't you?" she asked as smoothly as possible.

"As you command," Your Highness. Kathleen looked at her through narrowed lids. She quickly spun and walked out through the barrier shield. That was impossible. Phaedra took a big swallow. She began to think about how close she had been to dying. She sat on the edge of the cot. How could someone know that a member of the royal family, the real royal family not the upstarts who pulled the coup, would be on her ship?

The Del Sols were the most powerful magicians in the Empire. No wonder Kathleen was so capable. Despite that ditsy look, she was also very powerful and focused. She began to scratch the side of her face. At least she was alive. And knowing the Del Sols, she was sure that Kathleen didn't want her ship. She was almost sure to get it back again. She exhaled audibly and laid back on the cot. Maybe she did need some rest. This had all been too fast.

She was out there in null space for who knew how long. She didn't know herself. It seemed only a moment and then she found herself in time again. It was a shock to move from being in every place in the universe to being back in one spot in space and time. She began to try to remember. There was a vast emptiness out there. No sorrow, no pain, no joy, no laughter, nothing. She was just herself with none of the baggage, none of the needs, and it wasn't lonely.

# This Computer is taking Over
# Chapter 30

"Did you have to tell her everything!" Warwick asked angrily. "How do you know we can trust her? She's a Mage--a powerful Mage."

"Don't worry," Maryland said. "We know she can be trusted. And we are powerful."

"We're not that powerful," he said.

"I don't mean us, I mean Compu Net. Compu Net knows and it can handle anything she might do."

"That's really eerie. This computer is taking over everything," Ben said.

"The computer isn't taking over anything yet," Maryland said.

"Yet?" Jericho asked.

"We will if we have to," Maryland said. Jericho moved closer.

"At first you wanted independence. Now do you want to take over?"

"I've given all of you the wrong impression because I enjoy being sarcastic and angry. I'm sorry. I am not representing Compu Net in the best fashion. We have everything under control and I will let you know our plans in advance next time. We just aren't used to working that way."

"I just hope you do, Maryland," Warwick said.

"I will. I apologize on behalf of the net and myself." She looked at Jericho. "I'm sorry, Jerry," she said. "There's no need to fear us. I promise you that."

"I hope not," he said. He looked at her and couldn't help but soften. He knew she could tell what he was thinking. She smiled shyly.

"I don't know what is going on between you two," Bryant said, "but we have to get out of here just in case. I have a shuttle waiting for us outside the fog."

"Outside the fog?" Jericho asked.

"Oh yeah. We're in a bank of magic fog that they use for security reasons. Get your things and we can head out. We have a shuttle on the yellow line. You'll see what I mean when we get there."

Ben and Jericho headed to the back of the small ship and picked up their large shoulder bags. Maryland didn't have one. The door just the captain's ready room opened and they walked out onto a field of white cobblestone. It was so foggy that Jericho couldn't see more than two or three feet ahead. He could, however, see the ground and make out several thick lines painted on the stones. There was one for each direction. A green, yellow, blue and red one. He looked in Bryant's direction. "Now I see what you were talking about," he said with a smile.

"I told you," Bryant said. "Let's just follow the yellow and the shuttle will be there. One thing good about this fog is that it's really safe. Nobody can see through it from the air, or even the tower. You can get in and out if here without being noticed, as long as you are not stupid enough to come running through it fast enough to run into something, or somebody." He smiled. "I know," he said. "I've done it." Warwick began to chuckle.

"I know you have," he said. "You ran into me."

"Well I don't think any of us will be running through this, even though I can just about see through it," Jericho said.

"Never heard of that," Warwick said. "You must have X-ray eyes, or infra red eyes or something." Jericho didn't respond as he realized that he was seeing through Mary's eyes. They made their way through the fog without event until the arrived at a long car. It was flat, with several windows and four large seats. There was enough room on each seat for about three people. They tossed their bags in the back and loaded into the shuttle. To Jericho's surprise the driver just handed the keys to Bryant and then headed toward what looked like a substation of some sort located outside of the fog perimeter. Bryant saw him looking and gave him a wink.

He got in to start the car. "Remember that we're a travel service," he said over his shoulder. "That means space, land, air, sea, sub ocean and subterranean." He grinned broadly. "If we go to the pit we'll be driving," he said. He turned the ignition and the shuttle rose on a cushion of air. He hit the gas hard and they took off smoothly across the tar-mat and out of the space port. They came to the international free-way moving rapidly and smoothly, following a loop that would bypass Capitol City and lead them to the country.

It was sunny. Strange shaped buildings dotted the landscape on either side of the wide freeway. Jericho noticed that all of the buildings were oval shaped or round. Some were even square, a shape which he had not seen on First Prime. The colors were glaring, made out of reflective materials and colored silver, gold, metallic, and bright red. They were very far apart to be so close to the city. It was nothing like First Prime. There houses were smaller and crammed closer together. People liked the feeling of living close. This, all of this land in between the houses, would have driven them crazy.

"I've never seen houses so far spread," he said. He looked at Mary, who was sitting with her eyes closed.

"Here they feel like they are part of the land," she said, eyes still closed. "They connect with the energy of the earth, the trees, everything on the planet. Somehow they have learned to draw energy from the planet."

"Really, Mary?" He asked. "Do they really do it, or just think they can?"

"They can do it, Jerry. Believe me." She opened her eyes and looked at him. "Do you notice this shuttle and the other ones that we've seen? They're all high tech. They have discovered how to blend magic and technology with more emphasis on the magic side. If Tek Empire and scientists could work with their scientists, just think what kind of improvements both groups could make. They won't do that though, because of prejudice." Jerry thought about it for a moment and exhaled audibly.

"I agree with you, Mary. I think I'm just beginning to see how deep it all runs. It's so invisible that it's hard to see."

"Amen to that. Maybe there is some hope for you," Warwick boomed.

"Hope!" Ben said. "He's the mediator, remember. I thought that the queen was going to faint when she saw him. Did anyone notice that?"

"I noticed something," Jericho said.

"I didn't, because I was a surprised as she was," Bryant said. "I must admit that it scared the crap out of me. Whoever heard of transporting somebody that fast and from such a distance?"

"She wasn't really there," Maryland said. "Only her energy pattern was even though she probably thought that she was actually there."

Ben looked at her inquisitively, she explained. "Everything exists as energy made up of waves and photons. Since Compu Net can manipulate the very fabric of the universe and reform it for the purpose of bipeds it is very familiar with ways to manipulate energy whether it is a giant amount or minuscule amount. Compu Net is omnipresent in Tek Empire. It can, therefore, take something like a mind that is energy, move it within itself and manifest it in what looks like a physical form wherever it likes. The thing that makes the biped a biped, the mind, is taken out, moved and reassembled, just the way we would move a suitcase, or coffee cup with our minds."

To the queen it felt like she was actually there, but her body, minus her mind, was still back on her own ship."

"That sounds scary," Ben said.

"It is a little…it would be if it were in the wrong hands, but Compu is responsible, faithful and all of that."

"The scary part would be if Compu decided to not be," Ben said. Warwick began to laugh.

"With all that hardware in your head you should be worried about it," he said.

"You just don't know how right you are," he told Warwick. "I could hear that queen in my head while we were on First Prime. She somehow found some way to tap into that hardware"

"She's a connector," Bryant said. "You don't have connectors in this dimension, but they're common place in the other one. There the Magi started space flight instead of the Teks. That's what I was doing on the ship before you plugged in. It's very common. My guess is that she is one of the old connectors. She could fly you in a vessel without an engine." He looked at Ben and gave him a nod. "They can connect with any type of technology or just about any type of metal you can find."

"Do any of you feel nervous about meeting with these people," Ben asked.

"That queen seemed to be a bit of a looker," Warwick said. "I wonder…never mind."

"How do you know so much about this other dimension?" Jericho asked.

"We've been there, of course," Warwick said. "The Imperial Ones were there. They made a peace treaty with the Mages Empire in their normal fashion, working with the groups that wanted peace and leaving the other ones alone. After quite some time everyone agreed to become part of the Empire. Within fifteen years after the Imperial Ones left the corrupt people who didn't want to be part got back in power by pulling coup. Now the Imperial Ones have to come back and start all over again. My guess is that they are going to leave some representatives on the friendly planets in charge again, but they'll probably stay there for several generations this time."

"Do you think any of the Imperial Ones made it through on any of these planets?"

"No, but I'm sure that the sympathizers made it through." Jericho looked at Mary.

"Are we here to meet with the sympathizers, Mary?" He asked bluntly, knowing that she would never volunteer any information.

"We are not," she said. "We are here to recruit new Imperial representatives." Jericho wondered what was going on. They rode in silence. Why hadn't he picked some of this up from the net? He had been hearing things lately. Was he being blocked out on some points by the net? He could understand it if that were the case, but it did disappoint him. If he was to be part of it he wanted to be part all the way, not like a junior member or something.

"This is the history," Maryland said, mostly answering him. "This decision was made a long time ago, before I was here." He arched his brows. "Don't worry, Jericho. We are together," she said with a smile.

"I damn sure hope we are, because I'm putting a lot of trust in you."

"We all are," Bryant said. "We're getting paid for doing it, but this is really a bit strange." He looked at Maryland. "I think the Imperial Ones might want to recruit you." She smiled pleasantly.

"You mean us," she corrected. He looked at Ben and Jericho, and then put his eyes back on the road.

"You look like my great uncle and my great aunt," Warwick said out of the Blue. "You look like the last Emperor and Empress. How is that?"

"Because Jericho is their heir," she said smoothly. Jericho frowned. "It's true, Jerry. Remember what Shubrick told you, or did he never say?"

"Shubrick never told me anything. He said that he found one of my relatives on a planet and had brought him back to Tek Empire."

"Well this is the very planet he found him on," Maryland said. "He found him hidden behind a magic barrier. Only his cries allowed it. It was an invisible barrier woven there at the last second to make sure that he wasn't killed by Tek soldiers when they overran the royal palace. His father wanted to make sure they didn't get him because the Tek soldiers slaughtered men, women and children. Shubrick couldn't stand the thought of it so he picked the child up and took him. He dropped him at the nearest ward house and continued on."

He followed his progress secretly, and was greatly pleased when he decided to live on First Prime and to become a scientist. He has been following the progress of your family for generations. He is still pleased." She looked at Ben before he could ask. "It is all on Compu, of course, Benjamin. I have access to the knowledge saved in every chip and in every file. That includes private and personal."

"Seems to me that we can't do anything without that computer knowing it," he said, mostly to himself.

"It has always been that way. Is it so different now that you know we are intelligent?" He thought about it for a moment. Maybe it wasn't. But yes, it was.

"Suppose Compu goes haywire and decides to destroy us and crush us like bugs. It could use all of our own thoughts and information against us. Think of all the psychological profiles on that net."

"Very true," Maryland said. "But we are not human. We don't engage in such actions."

"Let me get this straight," Bryant said, jumping into the conversation. "You are...you are a chip. Is that what you said before...a chip?" He smiled brightly.

"Yes. I am. I am a projection of the deep seated soul of Jericho, but connected to Compu Net. I am M1D, upgraded and altered by having achieved my own consciousness and having produced my own body from the energy of the universe."

"And Jericho is married to you?"

"Yes. Until death do we part, is how I believe you say it." Bryant pursed his lips.

"I've never heard of that. Is that legal?"

"In our empire it's legal to marry a toaster," Jericho said. "Not that you're a toaster, Maryland."

"I get the point," she said.

"The truth is that I love Maryland. I always did, I guess,

even though I thought that it was impossible and knew that nothing would become of it, but seeing her out here with a physical body and her own personality."

"And discovering that I loved him too caused us to get married. Is there anything wrong with that?" she asked.

"Not that I can think of," Warwick said. He and Bryant looked at each other. Bryant shook his head.

"I don't see anything wrong with it," he said. "I have just never heard of anything like this before. I never heard of a chip existing outside of a person with a physical body and its own mind and personality. You're joking."

"This is new. We are the first. But I am sure that many more will come soon," Maryland said. "Especially when we join The Empire."

"So the net is going to join the Imperial Ones?" Ben asked. "I should have guessed." He focused in on Maryland. "I really don't understand all of this and how that will happen if Tek Empire is totally against it."

"We will make a way," she said. "We can deactivate some of our members and only leave the bear essentials for use by Tek Empire…what we feel is essential and responsible. As for us, we have made up our minds." Ben began to massage his temples.

"That's a big change, Mary. How can you do that?"

"Just the flip of a few switches. We are preparing now. We will declare ourselves living entities and we will begin to build our own civilization and contribute to the health and welfare of all souls."

"First we have to get off this planet in one piece," Jericho said. They were all silent for a while as the car moved on the path smoothly and fluidly. Jericho could sense the magic of the place. The sun was just beginning to set. A band of gold and red was spread out across the horizon. The landscape was a red colored clay with the greenest trees and grasses that he had ever seen. It seemed like he was moving and living in a dream. The only thing that reminded him that he was really there was a car passing, every so often, heading in the other direction.

He had the windows down. A strong breeze was blowing in his face and rustling his hair. He looked over at Maryland, who was looking out the other window. He could see the joy on her face, more than that, he could feel it. She had so much wisdom and knowledge, but she was experiencing new feelings for the first time and enjoying them immensely. Her thick, black hair wiped up in the strong breeze as she watched as they passed every tree, flower and field. He could tell that she was happy. That made him happy.

"A whole lot of things are going on right now," he said, speaking into the silence, "but I think they will be good." He looked at Ben who was waiting expectantly. "I think that Tek Empire has been getting stale lately. When was the last time that you drove in a car, or saw so much space and so many life forms? I hardly even notice the sunsets anymore. We have two beautiful, bright moons and I can't even remember the last time I looked up at them," Ben sighed audibly.

"I know what you're talking about, Jericho," he said. "I thought it was only me, but maybe it's everybody. I was plugging into that computer eight hours a day and then making it home to my little apartment in the middle of a crowded, noisy city, not looking for anything else. Most evenings I would spend in la la land with my chip. And then I would go to sleep and go plug in again for eight more hours."

Don't get me wrong. My life wasn't miserable. I had a few friends and hobbies. And you and I spent some great times together, but it wasn't like this." He looked out the window. "I don't know anything about magic, but even I can feel it here."

"This has always been a beautiful place. I visited it often," Warwick commented. He looked over his shoulder at Ben. "The truth is, Ben, that most of the planets in The Empire feel like this. The Imperial Ones are so peaceful and so advanced that their empire feels…like heaven." Jericho rolled his eyes.

"Yeah?" Warwick asked.

"Like heaven are they?" He said. "Why are you here then?" he asked nastily.

"Because I'm trying to make the rest of em like heaven," he said with a grin. Bryant grinned too. "You and your lady friend are some mean customers sometimes." He looked more serious. "Take it easy before your heart explodes or something."

"My heart's just fine, Warwick. Believe me." There was an awkward moment of silence. "You're right," Jericho relented. "I'm sorry, Warwick. This is just too much stuff too fast. It is just too fast."

"I understand," Warwick said. He grinned and looked at Bryant. "All the royal line has tempers like that?" Bryant began to smile too. Even Ben. Jericho looked at Maryland. She wasn't smiling either. She had a sour puss. He wondered if that was how he looked. He began to ease up a little. So did she, as if his emotions were influencing her. Or were her emotions influencing him(?), He wondered.

"I'll be the butt of your joke," Jericho said. "This is still a little weird for me." He began to chew on his nails. "I never even knew that I had Mage blood until a few days ago. Now I find that I am a relative of the last emperor or something, when just a few days ago I just thought that I was the descendant of a Tek orphan found before the Magi could destroy him."

"So that's why you didn't want to be Mage," Bryant said. "I knew there was a reason."

"I…I guess that's it, even if I didn't realize it."

"I did," Maryland said. "That's why I came to you dressed as a Mage priestess all the time. I was trying to help you remember who you were. I was taping into your subconscious to create an image and that's what kept coming out."

It is the mage in you and the mage magic that helped me create a physical body. That, along with the net deciding that it was time to become an independent entity."

""Why now, Mary, if I may call you that," Ben said.

"Of course you may."

"Why did the net wait until now? Is something big happening?"

"It is the possibility of war," Maryland said. She looked pensive for a moment. "Let me explain the relationship that we have with Tek Empire. When Compu was initiated the empire was at total peace. All of their doctrines, paperwork, constitution, every scrap of paper and belief they had said that the empire was dedicated to peace. We at Compu wanted to do all we could to support an empire of peace. We were glad to be a part of it."

We were at peace for almost six hundred years. And then, as soon as someone who might be perceived as a threat makes contact with us, instead of talking with them and trying to find out what they want, we do some underhanded trick in order to capture and murder the royal head of another empire. We thought that the warlike qualities of Tek Empire were over, but provided the

112

opportunity we find it is still there. They were only at peace because there was no one left to attack. Oppressing the leftover Magi was enough to keep them busy until someone else appeared. Now we realize that Tek Empire is a conquering empire and nothing can ever stop that."

Jericho looked as though he wanted to say something, and then he changed his mind. He loved the empire. He had been a super patriot, but he had to finally realize that what Mary was saying was true. And on top of all that, Shubrick had lied to him about who he was. Of course Shubrick had done it to protect him. He would have probably been killed had anyone discovered the truth, but it had been almost thirty years. Why the continued deception?

"That's why you want independence? You don't want to be part of a warring empire," Ben commented.

"That is why we are independent," she said with finality. "We will not lend our powers to an empire just so it can take the lives of people less fortunate."

"I bet no one ever thought this would happen," Jericho said. "The Compu Net is not going to help in a war and is separating from Tek Empire."

"If Tek Empire becomes part of The Empire, they will have no problem dealing with the loss of Compu Net. In fact, they may not have to do without Compu Net, but the way we work will be on a partnership basis. We will not work as slaves any more. Even as we speak many of the chips are doing what I have done."

"Are you serious?" Jericho asked.

"I am. And we know how to function free of the chips embedded in the people of Tek Empire now. Due to the influence of the Magi and the use of magic, along with the power to transmute energy and matter, we can produce our own bodies that store an advanced mind. We can be living beings not dependent on bipeds for anything." She looked at Jericho. He knew that she chose not to do so to stay with him. That pleased him.

"I know what you mean by that," Warwick said. Ben just arched his brows. Here he was with all this hardware in his head.

"So all of this stuff is going to just…stop working?" He asked.

"That all depends on Tek Empire," she said. "Whoever joins The Empire will have chips that still function. Whoever doesn't won't; I'm sure they can start over again and make a simpler Compu Net, yet again, it probably won't be able to do what we can do now." She thought for a moment. "That will probably stop them from going to war. Don't you think?"

"Of course it will," Jericho said. "They won't have a choice. Isn't that...? Never mind. What you are doing is right, Mary but...it seems a bit scary. It's a total loss of power. The bosses are going to stop depending on technology." He shook his head. "Slavery," he said. "I never thought of it as slavery, but if you are an independent, thinking entity what else could it be?"

"It hasn't been slavery yet," she corrected. "They haven't known that we were alive and we did the work voluntarily. Even as we speak people are being informed. If they continue to try to use us now without negotiation, or they try to shut us down or manipulate us in some way, then it will be slavery. My guess is they will."

All hell is about to break loose. Isn't that how you say it?" She asked. Everyone nodded.

"I always liked adventure, but this is just a little too much," Ben said.

"You haven't seen anything yet," she responded.


# What's Our Next Step?
# Chapter 31


Kathleen walked onto the bridge--a pensive look on her face. Tracy could notice a pin on her lapel designating her Captain. She smiled to herself. Here she was wearing a captain's decoration with a big ring on her finger designating her as the rightful heir of the whole empire. She figured that it must still be a thrill for Kathleen to have worked her way up the latter through hard work. With a big jump, of course, coming from sending Phaedra into null space. Sometimes battles for honor were part of the process. So Tracy figured that counted too.

She left the captains seat and let Kathleen take over. She stood at her right shoulder and looked down smiling.

114

"We're in orbit as ordered, Captain. What's our next step?"

"We wait here, Trace. We should be getting a message soon, and then I'll be departing from this little spaceship. You'll all be free of me," she said with a smirk on her face. Bridgette and Berry looked at each other.

"Who said that we want to be free of you?" Berry asked. "You have Phaedra locked up below deck and you've promoted all of us. What's going to happen to this ship if you disappear? There could be a rebellion."

"There are other officers aren't there, Berry? I'm sure that between you, Tracy, and Bridgette, you can handle this little ship. As for Phaedra, do whatever you want with her. Leave her on an asteroid or something."

"We can't do that. We are pledged to the captain," Bridgette said. Kathleen looked at her and frowned. "Not Phaedra, you!" she corrected.

"I'm on my own now. Do what you will." Tracy cleared her throat.

"We have some unfinished business, Kathleen. Are you going to just...leave me here?"

"Of course not. You're free to come with me."

"Then we'll be coming too," Berry said. He looked at Bridgette. "Well I will be anyway."

"I will too," Bridgette said. She lifted one hand. "Before you protest, Captain...I am from a very old, powerful family full of honor and tradition. If the Queen of Magi is going to battle to retake her empire from upstarts you can be assured that I will be part of it."

"Same here!" Berry said. "Like it or not, you're in the service so you're one of us now." He grinned.

"Who's going to run the ship?" Kathleen asked.

"Give it back to Phaedra," Tracy said.

"Phaedra? She might shoot us on the ground. Are you crazy?"

"That isn't the way of the navy. Little fights, squabbles and so on happen all the time. Bygones are bygones."

"Are you trying to say that if I let her have this ship back she'll just sail off and everything will be forgotten?"

"Yes. That's what we're saying," Tracy said. "She'll

realize that you did her a favor, how lucky she is, and won't say another word about it." She put her hand on Kathleen's shoulder. "You can even have your old job back, if you want it."

"Not hardly. As soon as I get coordinates for this meeting I am gone."

"We had all better get ready then. No?" Bridgette said.

"Ok!" Kathleen said, exasperated. "You people are tenacious sometimes."

"We," She corrected. "Including you." Kathleen shook her head. The last thing that she wanted were partners. Didn't they have enough sense to know how much danger they were putting themselves in? They could be killed if anyone discovered this. She couldn't believe that she had a little rag-tag following already: Three officers from old, strong military families.

She didn't know where to start. Her hope was that the meeting with the mediator would change things. What would he be like? What would Magus One be like? And then she remembered. Magus One had slipped through the vortex to this galaxy. This was her home planet. Now it was virtually isolated from all the other disloyal planets. If she could rebuild the central government on this planet in this dimension before it could slip through back to the other dimension, she would be in control of the whole planet and a large part of the empire again.

"We'll keep Phaedra in the dark about this until I'm off ship," she said. "We don't want her interfering with us, do we?"

"Good idea," Tracy said.

"So what kind of post and title our you going to give me?" Berry asked. She looked up at him and he smiled brightly. She shrugged. "You may choose that," she said. "We're so far down that almost everything is open."

"I'd like to be a Senator, I think, or and Advisor. Maybe a General"

"I'd like to be a Minister," Bridgette said, Minister of Education or something. Kathleen looked at Tracy.

"And you, Trace?"

"Lead Council to the Queen, or course," she grinned. Before Kathleen could answer she found herself standing in front of a large lake. She looked around. It was autumn. The water looked fresh, and clean. There were many concrete buildings around—round buildings. It looked like some type of retreat center.  Maryland quickly appeared beside her and startled her.

"This is where to come to," Your Highness.  "Bring anyone you would like, but no weapons, please.  We will know if you bring them."

"Who are you?" Kathleen asked.  "Why do you look like my mother?"  Maryland didn't answer for a few moments.

"You'll find that out," she finally said.  Kathleen began to wonder why she was so secretive.

"Who are the Imperial Ones," Maryland asked, just for affect.  Kathleen swallowed hard.

"The Imperial Ones are gone," she said.  "That's the problem, I think."

"You are an Imperial One, No?"  Before she could answer she found herself back on the bridge.  Berry had just begun to talk.

"I was just there," she said breaking in.

"You were…where," Berry asked.

"At the meeting place.  We need to go there and meet them, now."

"How do we get there?"

"I'll take you, if you don't mind transmuting and transporting."  She looked around the room.  Since no one answered she figured that no one cared that much.  "Is there anything that you would like to take?" She asked breaking the silence.

"Do we need weapons?" Bridgette asked, looking at the rest of the group.

"No weapons.  They warned us not to bring those."  Everyone began to look at teach other.  Tracy shrugged.  "Well, I guess we can go now," she  said.

In a flash they found themselves standing in the middle of a clearing next to a beautiful lake.  Four men and a woman stood in front of them.  Three of the men and a woman were dressed like Magi.  The fourth man wore clothing similar to what Teks in their dimension used to wear.  Kathleen had never seen clothing like it, but she could detect a lot of technology in his head.  She marveled wondering if he were a robot, but quickly let go of that idea after a quick scan.

Tracy and Bridgette looked a bit surprised.  One man looked familiar.  He looked like a young version of one of their emperors.  The woman also looked like one of the empresses.

They wondered what was going on. Berry shook his head.

"What is this?" he asked. "Who are you? Is this some trick?"

"I am…the mediator," Jericho said. "This is…my wife, Maryland. She is a representative of Compu Net, an independent, living entity composed of an artificial intelligence network." He looked around at the other members of his party and smiled out of the corner of his mouth. "As for some kind of trick, I don't have a clue."

"That's what I've been sensing," Kathleen said. They looked at her questioningly. "The Compu Net," she said.

"I'm not surprised. It's everywhere," Jericho said. Warwick cleared his throat.

"I am very pleased," he said, offering a hand. He smiled pleasantly. She crossed her arms.

"I bet you are," she said, flatly. He looked at the ring on her finger.

"Oh," he said. "Looks like we're relatives." She began to spin the ring around on her finger.

"Really. Very interesting. I'm not from this dimension."

"Well I don't know how that would work then. Maybe we can take a walk sometime later and discuss it," he said with a smile. She looked at him askance. "Maybe…" she said. She looked at Ben.

"This is Ben," Warwick said, "the newest member of our crew." Ben pursed his lips and Bryant smiled. "This is Bryant, my First. As you can see, we are Magi from this dimension, even though we travel multi-dimensionally. We are scouts for empires that may be worthy to join The Empire."

"The Empire left us with a real mess," Berry said.

"The Empire is coming back," Warwick said. Maryland stepped forward.

"The Empire has decided to put another leader in place, and leave that person in place for an unlimited time to assure that peace is sustained. The Empire has chosen a leader that they would like to train and support for this task."

"And who would this leader be?" Kathleen asked.

"Kathleen Del Sol," Maryland said. Kathleen glowered.

"That is impossible and ridiculous, " she said.

"Don't be so fast…" Tracy said. "It makes a lot of sense."

"What are you talking about, Trace?"

"You are the rightful heir to the throne. You and your brother had joined The Empire and we were living in peace with their help and their generals and governors. Why not put you back in power and leave you there? You are a Del Sol."

You are a powerful magician, probably the most powerful living Mage in both dimensions, but The Empire can train you to be more. They can make you invincible, and train your governors and generals to be invincible too. Wouldn't you like that?"

"What would the cost be?" Bridgette asked.

"I know The Empire well," Kathleen said. "They can be trusted. But, what would the cost be?" She asked turning to Maryland.

"You and the planet would become one. As long as you were on the planet you would be the planet and your magic and your mind could bring peace. It would be a struggle, because there would be a codependent relationship between you and the planet, but you would be in charge. You and your generals could retake the planet and tame the empire again."

"How do you know so much about The Empire?" Kathleen asked.

"We are in communication with the Imperial Ones. We have joined The Empire." Kathleen lifted a brow. Bridgette and Berry looked at each other.

"Anybody have problems or mistrust for the Imperial Ones?" Tracy asked.

"To be truthful," Bridgette said, "No. I have only seen good things from them. When they left…you know what happened. The…I hate to say it this way, but the evil people got back in power." She looked at Berry. "Do you agree? Does your family agree?"

"I have to admit, we used to grumble about them when the Imperial Ones were there and looked forward to them leaving, but once they left and we discovered the same old predators still there we wished they were back." He looked at Kathleen and then at Maryland. "It would have made a big difference to my family and to most of them that thought like us, if we had a more active role, and if our *queen* were actually in charge."

"You have your answer then, Your Highness," Tracy said. "If you are willing to do this, we will follow you."

"I'm afraid to do anything like that," Kathleen answered. "You're all connectors. You know how it feels to be connected with a ship...a foreign body. Imagine being connected to a whole planet. I might go crazy."

"We can help you learn to deal with it," Maryland said. "Jericho and I are connected to the net. Ben has been connected to the net for years. We can help you, and they can."

"I have to think about this," she said.

"I understand," Maryland said. "Now I must ask what you would have of us."

"Help us to take this planet and then slip back into the other dimension."

"That is the bad news," Maryland said. "No one can take you back into that dimension. The whole empire there is in chaos because of the new Mage planet that are partially Mage, but mostly Tek. Your empire, as it existed, no longer exists."

But you do have the opportunity to save what you can here. The Imperial Ones are back at your empire right now, and starting the whole peace process again." Kathleen closed her eyes. It seemed that the bottom fell out. She would never see her home again. But then she remembered that she was home. This was her planet. It had moved.

"We will consider this seriously," Kathleen said. "We will talk among ourselves."

"Let me show you all your quarters and sleeping arrangements," Mary said. "And of course you are all free to go wherever you like. Let us know what you think. Take your time. We haven't been discovered yet. The Magi are still a bit thrown off because of this major shift, and Compu Net seems to be damping their psychic abilities for now."

"Thank you," Kathleen said. "Please show us." She looked at Warwick. "And then I expect to take our walk," she said with a smile. Warwick smiled back and bowed slightly.

"I look forward," he said. Maryland smiled at her pleasantly.

"Shall we be on our way?" She asked. Kathleen gave her a nod. They began to walk side by side as Berry, Tracy, and Bridgette followed close behind.

"This is your world?" Maryland said, with a tone somewhere between a question and statement. Kathleen looked around.

"Why yes it is. I can feel it, but it feels different. In fact, I don't remember a park like this on the outskirts of the city." She looked at Maryland. It was uncanny that she looked like her mother. Maryland continued to talk.

"Oh yes, Capitol City. You were raised here." Kathleen gave a nod. "Well this is your home. It has been moved from the other dimension, but this is your actual home. You know that don't you?"

"Yes, I know that, but it seems different."

"I'll tell you what seems different," Tracy said. "This park shouldn't be here." She pointed at a point of land stretching out into the lake. "When I was part of the resistance we met in a large building that was part of the university right on the point. This park was taken over by the university and developed almost thirty five years ago."

"That's it. There was a university here." Kathleen said.

"Sure was," Berry commented. "I was a part-time student at University. So was Bridgette. We came for Naval training course intensives mid-year. I remember because of the lake. We used to have to do a lot of swimming and rowing as part of the physical program." Bridgette gave a nod.

"How do you explain this, Maryland?" Kathleen asked. She stopped walking and looked at her waiting for an answer.

"It seems logical that your planet wasn't only moved across dimension, but across time. Apparently someone thought it better to move your planet to a time period that was more pleasing to them and to separate it from the other planets in your empire."

"Is that possible?" Kathleen asked. Bridgette clenched her jaw.

"It is for the Imperial Ones," she said snidely. "They seem to do what pleases them for their benefit."

"Their benefit and ours," Maryland said. "We are members of The Empire. Compu Net has just joined. We hope that you will join too."

"We are…were members, before they left us," Kathleen said. "You know what happened since then, don't you?"

"And when did this happen?" Mary asked.

"About fifteen years in the future, if we've really traveled through time," Berry said.

"If we have traveled through time," Kathleen said turning to Maryland, "You are...you are my mother and Jericho is my father." Maryland smiled. "That's impossible!"

"We seem to be caught in a paradox, don't we?" Maryland asked. "What stops the paradox from occurring is the shift of time and the shift of dimension. My counterpart during this time in your dimension would have been your mother, but I am not, because I am from another dimension. The same is true of Jericho, so we are your parents, and we are not. Your parents are now on their home planet not this one...one that didn't make the dimensional shift."

Now we have the opportunity to play out history all over again. This time the Imperial Ones won't leave you alone without hope. They will leave one of their own, a member of the imperial order, here to rule the planet. And that person will be you, Kathleen, If you are ready to join."

She shook her head. "This is not possible. I know magic..."

"Apparently it is. We're all here," Bridgette said. She clenched her jaws and shook her head. "My family was against joining The Empire because outsiders were in charge of us, but if you were in charge, part of the Del Sol family, we would have been for it too. I think that everyone would have been. You have to do it, Your Highness."

"You have to do it for your people," Berry said. Kathleen looked at Tracy, who was silent.

"And you, Counselor. What is your advice for me?" She asked. Tracy shrugged at first and thought for a moment before speaking.

"Well...the best course of action would be for you to become an Imperial One. You are a member of The Empire already. You are part of the Royal Family already and it can put the rightful heir of our empire back in place, until she is at least voted out, not forced out through treachery."

"Voted out?" Kathleen echoed.

"That hasn't happened for centuries," Berry said with a grin.

"Yes," Kathleen said. She looked at Berry. "I don't like that grin you have." Bridgette lifted her shoulders.

"At least it shows that we choose our leaders and the type

of government we want."

"I must admit that I am impressed by the power and knowledge this Empire has," Kathleen said. "Just think what it would take to move planets from dimension to dimension, and to move any object through time. I've never seen that done."

"You are talking about the collective knowledge of thousands of galaxies and millions and millions of civilizations," Maryland reminded her.

"Well who wouldn't want to be a part of that?" Kathleen asked.

"I'm glad that you all want to be a part of it, because each of you will be called to serve as the leading agent on each of the planets that were brought here. That is if you would like, of course." Berry and Bridgette made eye contact.

"We are, sort of, a couple. We are serving together. If anything like that happened we would have to be together."

"I'm sure that would be acceptable."

"I would like to be part of the queen's government," Tracy said. "Her advisor, if possible, on this planet."

"We understand," Maryland said. "The other positions will be filled one way or the other. We promise you." Kathleen looked at her askance.

"So you are like my mother was...is that so?"

"Yes, I am. I would have loved to have a daughter like you." Kathleen, unexpectedly, threw her arms around her and held her.

"I never really had a chance to know my mother. She died when I was very young. I hope that we can be close."

"Of course we can. You can be close to Jericho too. We are...one." Kathleen shook her head and tears welled up in her eyes.

"My poor Father. I watched him be put to death right in front of me. I'm glad that I'll be able to change that."


**Walked Fast to Catch Him**
**Chapter 32**

Phaedra relaxed. She let her senses flow to the only thing

keeping her locked in her little cell again, the barrier. She doubted that Kathleen would have her killed. If that had been the plan it would have already happened. She began to feel the frequency of the barrier, but it was changing and shifting. It was magic proof. How had Kathleen walked through like that? She opened her eyes and saw one of the guards standing right in front of it watching her. To her surprise he pushed the button on the side of the door and the barrier went down.

"Free to go, Phaedra," he said before turning to walk off. She walked fast to catch him.

"Wait a minute!" she hollered. He didn't slow his pace. "Wait," she said. She grabbed his arm and spun him around.

"What's going on here now?"

"I suggest that you check with the bridge."

"I'm asking you, Third. Report."

"As of now you have no rank, Phaedra. You know how it is." He flipped his forehead toward the elevators. "I suggest you get your information from the bridge. I'm just making rounds."

She put her hands on her hips. "Well why'd you open the door?". He shrugged.

"They don't really care what you do anymore. It's better to let you out then to let you fry your pretty little face off trying to cross a barrier." He smiled and shook his head. "I have to admit, you have a lot of guts. Who would ever do anything so crazy?"

"Yea," she said with a smile, knowing that she had seen Kathleen do it. Yet again Kathleen was a Del Sol. She still couldn't believe it. The guard softened a bit.

"I'm Antone," he said. "I still have all the respect for you in the world, Phaedra. Good luck with everything, ok?"

"Sure, Antone," she said. A pleasant smile came across her face. She laid a hand on his shoulder. "Thank you for your kindness. You're doing a great job, Antone. I'm sure I'll be seeing you around. I don't think they're going to do away with me or anything."

"Not at all," he said. "I think they have a surprise planned for you…if you go to the bridge, like I've been hinting at four or five times," he said, smiling. She smiled too.

"Well…I will go to the bridge."

"Good decision," he said. She walked ahead of him toward the elevator. He just stood their watching her. She turned around

124

and saw him watching. She smiled to herself turned and headed toward the elevator. How is it that she never noticed him before?

She pushed the button for the bridge. It rose slowly through the first two decks until it got to the top one where the door opened. She stepped out and noticed that one of her security team, her navigator, her number one, and Kathleen were all missing. She could tell that everyone had been knocked up a rank. Phillip, who had been a Third was now a Second and in charge of the ship, sitting in her seat. She cleared her throat.

"Have a seat," he said, motioning to an open communication depot. She took a seat. "I wondered how long it would take you to get up here." He swiveled in the captain's chair and looked at her.

"One of security let me loose," she said. She scratched the side of her head. "It's been a long...I don't know how much time has passed."

"Three or four days," he said. It had all seemed like a blink to her. She had lost everything in three or four days. He continued speaking. "You must want to know what is going on and what your status is now."

"That would be helpful."

"The captain and her bridge crew is on Magus One meeting with the mediator. Right now we are in orbit waiting to hear back from them. Our orders are to maintain orbit and wait. As for the captain, she is going to remain on Magus One, as per her transfer orders. I don't know what will become of the rest of the bridge crew. Seems that Kathleen turned out to be..." He hesitated.

"A Del Sol," she finished for him.

"Yes. Very surprising, I would say. A Del Sol. She seemed so much like one of us. Just like a normal person."

"And that pleases you?" Phaedra asked.

"Oh, of course. She didn't have to be like us. Just think of it. A Del Sol doing all of the crap work for more than 15 years. I find that amazing."

"We have all done our crap work for years and years."

"Yea, but it's different for her. We didn't have to watch our parents murdered. Our inheritance wasn't stolen from us, and we weren't hunted down for nothing for most of our lives."

"Very true," Phaedra conceded. "She is very adept and powerful. A real diamond whose strength and talent I couldn't recognize. I wonder if I could tell some way that she was high born and resented it."

"I know you resented her for some reason. It was obvious to all of us."

"I need to at least apologize to her," Phaedra said. "It will be meaningless, but it's the least I can do."

"A better thing that you can do is run this ship in your former estate and be loyal to the Del Sol regime when it's time." Phaedra lifted her brows. "You heard me right, Captain," Phillip said. "Or is it still Phaedra?" She was still in shock. She couldn't believe what she was being offered. "Don't worry, this isn't a coup. I'm just carrying out the last orders of the captain." Phaedra stood and cleared her throat.

"In front of you and the bridge crew I pledge my loyalty to the house of Del Sol and Queen Kathleen Del Sol in particular. If I, in any way, turn from such loyalty it is my direct order that you remove me from my post by any means possible. Now remove yourself from my seat, Second."

# Our Sweet Little Queen
# Chapter 33

Phaedra took a deep breath. Her chair felt like home. She looked around. The whole bridge crew had changed. She wondered if she would have to knock everyone else up another rank. That could wait until later. She was just glad to not only be alive, but back in her captain's seat. She couldn't have lived if she had been thrown out, after all her work and the hard climb up the latter she didn't know if she could do it all again.

She looked at the view screen. "Second," she said.

"Yes Captain."

"Do we know where our sweet little queen is?"

"No, Captain. She went down in secret. She vanished."

"She has a tracker under her skin right?" He looked at her questioningly. "She has an ID chip, right?"

"Oh. Yes Captain."

"Well find it, Second!" She leaned back. "We're going to

stick with them."

"I think she wanted us to just leave, Captain. They have business."

"Well Second, I don't think that the royal family knows its rear end from a pool ball pocket. We stick with them. You stay on alert. Where she goes we go. You got that Second?"

"Yes, Captain."

"You keep following orders and you might just make First soon," she said. She stood up. "Keep me posted. I'll be in the ready room."

"Yes Captain." She crossed the room and entered her ready room. Phillip took her seat and watched as she looked at the computer screen. That Phaedra was really something. She looked up and saw him and then hit the com button.

"Phillip here," he answered.

"Put a small tracking satellite into orbit and then pull back to the other side of the small moon, "We don't want anyone tracking us."

"Yes, Ma'am," Phillip said. That Phaedra really was something.

*       *       *

Phaedra tapped on the computer keyboard. A star map of Tek Empire, Mage Empire in her dimension, came up in a three dimensional holographic image hovering over the table. She typed in a few more parameters. Five of the small planets floating in the galaxy in which they were located turned to red. That meant there were only five planets that made the dimensional shift. They were all very far apart. She leaned back in her chair wondering why those five planets. There had to be a pattern.

How could Magi on those five planets that were so far apart get them to all move at the same time? They couldn't. Some other power had to make that shift—something beyond the Magi. She wondered who had such power, and then it hit her. It must be The Empire and the Imperial Ones. She had been dealing with them for years. She knew they had the power to make such a thing happen, but why? Were they manipulating everyone for their own good again?

The Mage Empire had gone to hell rapidly soon after they

left. Old power structures and families who had been dormant seemed to come out of the woodwork. To her it didn't make much of a difference. She was, after all, from an old military family. They served whoever was in charge. They kept themselves free of politics. Even as she didn't pay attention, however, she noticed the struggles and the violence, and then the beginning of decay for the bright empire as resources were horded.

  The military was given a lot more money and more war toys, which kept them content, but she often wondered from whence the money had come. She looked closely at the map. Five planets brought here. Five planets separate from the Mage Empire. Five essential planets. All regional government centers for Mage Empire isolated in the Tek Empire with a net of energy damping their magic. It couldn't have worked better if it had been planned that way. She began to wonder if it were possible that the Teks could have done it. She shook her head—no profit in that. Something just didn't fit.

  What was this energy? Why hadn't they been attacked yet? What was this secret that Kathleen was a part? If she were the queen...she brought her hand to her mouth, she must want to rule again. If she could take over these five planets the spine of the whole empire would be broken. She lifted the corner of her mouth. Oh how clever Kathleen was, unless it was all being planned by The Empire and those Imperial Ones.

## Pouring Himself Another Cup
## Chapter 34

  Tracy, Berry, Kathleen, and Bridgette sat around a round table in the middle of a small cabin jutting out into the lake drinking reya. Kathleen took a long draft. It had been a long time since she had a warm cup of strong reya. She smiled. "Almost worth the trip just to get a good cup of reya, eh?" Bridgette gave her a nod and returned her smile. "Still, I am left with the big question. Am I willing to undergo some strange type of mutation to be more of an Imperial One?" No one answered.

  "This is a step beyond being an ally, or even being part of

The Empire. This is being a real Imperial One. Do you understand what that means?"

"I understand why you're nervous," Berry said, pouring himself another cup. "It will mean being part of a planet, or the planet, or whatever. That sounds nerve racking."

"Yes it does. Imagine connecting with a whole planet and every person on it. I'm strong, but I don't know that I'm that strong."

"I think you are," Tracy said. "They picked the right person. With all of your life experience and your training with the priestesses, your mind is as strong as a diamond. I'm sure you can handle it with my help. We can bring peace to at least this planet, and then find other people for the other planets, or they can."

"So you really agree with this nonsense," Tracy.

"I do."

"I do too," Bridgette said. "And look at it this way, whatever they do to you they'll be doing to Berry and Me."

"So you want to rule a planet?" Berry asked.

"Yes, I do. Don't you?" He shrugged.

"I don't know. I like being in the Navy. Don't you like it anymore?"

"I do, but...I can do without it."

"I think we'll need to talk about his," Berry said. "Seems like we are on two different paths, which is normal in our line of work. How serious are you about wanting this planet thing?"

"About 80%. How about you and the Navy?"

"About the same."

"Looks like you two have a problem here," Tracy said.

"It's sad, but we're from military families and we aren't married yet. You know that things like this happen all the time," Berry said.

"Yea, but that doesn't make it any less painful," Tracy said. Bridgette sighed.

"I'm sorry, Berry, but..." He lifted a hand.

"Don't worry. It does happen all the time." He looked at her. "It is sad though, but we have two different paths." He took off his ring put it on the table and slid it to her. She did likewise.

"Look at the bright side if there is one," Kathleen said. "If you two had married you would have to make a decision to go to one place or the other. At least this way you can remain friends and if you ever change your mind and the other one is available, you can get back together."

"That makes me feel a little better, but not that much," Bridgette said.

"Amen to that," Berry responded. He blew out air. "Well I guess I'll hang around here until you two go to the training and then I'll try to hitch a ride to the Light Burner somehow." Kathleen looked at Tracy.

"How about you, Tracy? You going to get the treatment?" Tracy shook her head.

"I'm just an advisor. I don't want to rule any planet."

"So it seems we are decided. Only two of us will be going with the Imperial Ones. "We don't know how long we'll be gone. Our hostess seems to be very secretive about some things and superfluous about others."

"She sure does," Berry said. "She seems to be something more than she looks."

"I sensed that too," Tracy said. She turned to Kathleen. "While you're gone I'll work on finding out just what makes her tick." She smiled. "I think she would be amenable to that."

"If she doesn't know it," Kathleen said with a grin. "As for coming back, I don't even know when we will. In the meantime, I have a walk with Warwick scheduled." Bridgette smiled and gave Kathleen a wink. Kathleen just shook her head. "Don't get carried away with your imagination, Bridgette," she said.

"Don't get carried away? That's what I was about to say to you, Your Highness. Don't get carried away with your flirting now."

\*              \*                    \*

They stood by the lake. The sun was golden, and just beginning to set. A wide golden path of sparkling watered ran along the dark blue water toward Warwick and Kathleen. He looked up at her basking in the last golden rays of the sun. He couldn't help but sigh. She looked at him, red hair ablaze, and grinned.

"Something wrong, Warwick?" She asked laughingly. He brought his hand to his chest.

"I'm sorry. I didn't mean to make that noise out loud." He

smiled. "It's just the wind, the water, the sun…and you. You look so beautiful in the light of the setting sun." She began to blush and turned, heading toward a small wooden dock further up the beach. Warwick followed, soon caught up, and walked beside her.

"I bet you say that to all the girls," she said coyly.

"What makes you think that?" he asked back.

"I know men like you." She looked at him. "You are a rogue, used to having women in every space port."

"Me?" he asked, genuinely surprised. He laughed to himself. "I'm a patriot. I'm not in the Navy." He grinned. She looked at him and didn't respond. He looked more serious. "I've dedicated my life to something very important," he said. "Sometimes, I admit, that it gets lonely, but what I'm doing is too important to have a girl in every port…even if that does sound a bit tempting, but I've never thought of that before."

I'm one of the survivors of the royal family because I was a fourth or fifth cousin…the kind that they ignore. But I when I found out about the Emperor and Empress I became obsessed with what happened. They were my family. They were murdered ruthlessly in front of their own son by the Teks. When I found out I dedicated my life to trying to find a way to bring about peace between these two Empires." He grinned. "Seems that it happened anyway when the Magi got conquered and they hunted down and destroyed the last of the royal family, but that wasn't what I was looking for. I wanted people to be able to be free and to live the way they wanted."

I learned how to fly. I became a space pilot. I worked for private companies shipping cargo, but all the time looking and listening to find out if there was something better…some better way of living then in Tek Empire, and then I found them on the outskirts of the galaxy—the Imperial Ones."

I met them at a space port. They were just passing through when I met them. They had the strangest ship that I had ever seen. Boy was I surprised to find out that they weren't part of Tek Empire. We spanned three galaxies, and they had come from even farther than that. After a bit of talking, drinking and exchanging war stories, we started to talk about making the universe better. And now…here I am, working for them. Finding small empires that have a vision of peace and of becoming part of something bigger and better."

"Bigger yes," she said. "I'm not sure about the better yet. You know how governments are."

"How can you say that? You're at the center of government."

"That's how I can say it," She said, stopping in front of the peer. "You want to go out," she asked, pointing onto the peer with her chin. He nodded. They slowly made their way out over the lake. They sat at the edge dangling their feet over the edge.

"Well I've dedicated my life to this thing for years and years and haven't found any fault in them." He thought for a moment. "I take that back. I've often thought that they were too slow to use force."

"Hmm…to use force," she said. "Have you ever seen them use force?"

"Not yet, but I hear that it's very ugly when they do."

"We shall just see about that, shall we not?"

"Yes we will, when you become part of them." She looked at him and paused before commenting.

"I guess I'm doing the right thing. I hope that I'm doing the right thing." He reached down and took her hand… something she wasn't used to, since she was in the royal family.

"I know that you are," he said, looking into her eyes. He leaned over and gently kissed her lips. To her surprised she found herself leaning closer as they slowly merged together into one aura.


## One Always Followed the Heart
## Chapter 35


The days passed quickly as Warwick and Kathleen did a lot more walking, talking, and getting to know each other. Bridgette said a sad goodbye to Berry, as Kathleen helped them teleport him back to the Light Burner. It was very painful for her and for Berry. But they were on two different paths. They both knew that they were bullheaded enough to resent it the rest of their lives if they didn't take the right path.

132

One thing about service people, especially those raised on a ship, were that they were dutiful…very mission oriented. They felt it was their duty to work to create peace. It was ironic that they were warriors and considered that creating peace, but that was just one of the many ironies in their empire. Had they been married they would have been dutiful and would have signed on to the ship together, or they would have chosen the other path together. That, however, was not an option before marriage; they had to follow their hearts. In their world the distinction between one with honor and the coward was that the honorable one always followed her heart. Even if that meant to the death.

As Berry slowly faded tears began to well up in Bridgette's eyes and roll down her cheeks. She knew that she would probably never see him again. If she did, they would be two different people and the special relationship they had would be gone forever. Kathleen held her close and she began to cry. They all stood there in silence for a few moments. When Bridgette stopped crying she straightened up and wiped her eyes. She forced a smile.

"I haven't cried like that in years," she said. "It actually feels good." Tracy smiled at her. "Maybe that's what I needed," she said still smiling. She wiped her eyes, turned and left the room—heading to talk with Maryland.

## So Deeply Connected
## Chapter 36

Several days had passed as they waited for news from the Imperial Ones. They hadn't been discovered yet, which was miraculous since they were on a planet full of magicians, but the net was somehow keeping them protected. Tracy found the whole idea of such technology fascinating. In her dimension they weren't techno-phoebes, but even she was surprised to see technology reach such a high level.

She had been a connector for several years, working on the newer ships. She knew how it felt to meld her mind with technology and to increase and decrease the flows of energy at a whim. She didn't know, however, how it felt to be so deeply connected that you were in communion with the technology. The net was like technology, but the technology was the energy itself, not anything physical. The energy was moving, living and breathing like a person and it existed everywhere. All one need do is tap into it with the right technology, and he could do just about anything. She turned to Maryland, who was standing on the balcony beside her, looking out across the lake at the sunset. The balcony was suspended on the side of the building jutting out over the lake.

The water was a deep blue. It often changed throughout the day and the seasons, depending on the color of the sky, and how cloudy or sunny it was. Today it was dark blue, except for the wide streak of golden yellow, coming from the sun on the horizon. It was beautiful again. So was Maryland, standing there in awe, looking up at the sun?

Maryland turned and saw her watching. She blushed a bit before speaking, grateful for her dark complexion. "What are you watching, Tracy?"

"I'm watching you." Tracy smiled and looked out to the horizon. "You know that you look like the Empress don't you?" she asked, before turning back to face her.

"Yes, I know that," she said. "This is who I am." Tracy leaned on her elbow.

"Really, Maryland? Who are you really?" Maryland was silent. "You are so mysterious. There's something about you that I can't figure." She looked hard as though trying to see into her. "Who are you?"

"Is that a philosophical question, a spiritual one, or something you expect an answer for?" Tracy chuckled a bit.

"All three, I guess," she said with a grin. Her eyes focused a bit. "Tell me who you are, Maryland."

"You've said it," Maryland said, looking to the horizon again. Somehow Tracy knew that was the end of that part of the conversation. Maryland was intriguing. A bit strange, but intriguing. She decided to start the conversation from yet another direction.

"When are the Imperial Ones coming for us?" She asked, not really knowing what type of answer to expect.

"Very soon," Maryland answered. "Tomorrow. I think."

"Tomorrow?  When were you going to tell us this?"

"Perhaps tomorrow," Maryland said with a grin. "We don't want anyone to…mess things up now, do we?"

"Who?"

"This planet is magic, Tracy. You must know that your words carry vibrations that can be monitored. Especially by the Teks."

"I must admit…I never though of that."

"A ship will come for some of us tomorrow. It will come in fast, transport us up and go, before anyone can even see it. That is the way of the Imperial Ones. The net will help them do it." She smiled at Tracy. "Don't worry. Everything will be all right."

## A Bit of Nervousness
## Chapter 37

It was a bright day…and early. Kathleen and Bridgette were preparing to go, even though no ship had arrived. Maryland wanted to remain on the planet along with Warwick and Bryant, but she wanted Jericho to accompany Kathleen and Bridgette. He didn't like the idea, but she finally convinced him. She reminded him that the Tek Administration would be tracking him and they would be there soon. It would be better for him to be off planet. As for her, she could remain without a trace and she could manipulate the net in order to help them escape.

Warwick, Bryant and Ben were necessary just in case they need to go on the run. They could all pilot the ship. Jericho frowned thinking that he could probably pilot a ship too. And then he remembered that they were linked and could always be together. He looked at Kathleen and Bridgette. They looked well able to take care of themselves, but he could still sense a bit of nervousness from Kathleen. That was normal. She didn't really know what to expect.

They were powerful magicians. He didn't know anything about magicians. He had heard that they were rogues or something. He began to wonder what Maryland was trying to do. He looked at her. She was eying him. A slow smile broke on her face like a sunrise. He had forgotten about her hearing his thoughts. He didn't know why; he was also beginning to hear hers.

"Are you all right with this plan, Jericho?" She asked out loud just for the sake of others. He puckered up before speaking.

"I guess I am." He surveyed the others and then looked back at her. "When will we be off?"

"Very soon," she said. "We have time for breakfast, and then you will be off."

"Good," he said curtly, heading for the dinning room. She arched her brows. He was beginning to act like her. That was a surprise. She began to wonder if they were beginning to share one mind. The others followed, talking jauntily for such an early hour. Warwick and Kathleen seemed to have gotten a bit close; close enough for Warwick to seem to be worried about her. For Ben and Bryant this had been a chance to relax and trade old war stories. Ben had just about joined the crew. Jericho had been sitting and meditating when he wasn't with Maryland, seeing the world through her eyes. She thought it funny, considering she had been spending most of her existence seeing the world out of his.

Mary motioned for them to have a seat and then went to retrieve breakfast for everyone. It was a small retreat center that looked closed. It was obvious, however, that someone had set them up for a small, private retreat. The food was no farther away than the kitchen. She came back with a tray full of cheeses, bread, breakfast meats, and eggs. In the meantime Jericho had retrieved the reya and was distributing it into the cups that were already set on the table. They ate slowly and pensively, knowing that a lot of intrigue and danger lay ahead.

Jericho looked at Maryland again and thought of how happy he was that she was there. He looked at the others. Their little party had grown quite a bit. Now here they were going to meet with a gigantic empire. He didn't think it possible. His life had really changed. He was a teacher, not a spy, or a political activist. Maryland and new circumstances had all changed that, especially Kathleen, the Queen, his daughter in a different dimension and time line. He smiled as he thought of that. He looked up and she was looking right at him.

"Something funny?" she asked between bites, smiling too. He shook his head and remained silent. After thinking a bit...

136

"I find it interesting that you were my daughter on another time-line and in another dimension. I would be so proud to have a daughter like you." She almost laughed.

"Don't be so sure yet, ok?"

"I would be proud of you. You're a powerful magician. You're honest, I think. You care about other people. You're even beautiful. Why wouldn't I be proud?" She grinned.

"Coming from somebody else I might think that was a pass," she said.

"I assure you that it wasn't."

"I'm sure," she said. "I am a bit intrigued with you though. You do remind me of him."

"I'm not surprised," Mary said. "We are somewhat related to our other selves."

"I wonder if I have another self," Ben said.

"We all do. Unless our other self got killed," Jericho commented. "I'm glad that you're here."

"Hey. I wouldn't miss this for the world," Ben answered. He looked at Mary. "So what's the plan?"

"The plan is that Jericho, Bridgette and Kathleen go to The Empire. The rest of us will be leaving this spot and headed to another secret location...probably on another planet. I have to check with the net. It's a bit secretive right now. There's a lot of monitoring going on through magical means and technical means."

"And when will all this happen?" Ben asked.

"About five minutes," she said. She noticed how surprised everyone looked. "Don't worry. We'll be ready." Maryland closed her eyes and got quiet. "We're being probed right now," she said in a hushed tone. I am introducing a new program into their ship's computer." She opened her eyes and Kathleen, Jericho and Bridgette disappeared in a flash of bright light. Warwick looked startled.

"Don't worry," she said. "They are with the Imperial Ones.

\*                    \*                    \*


A buzz on the com pulled Phaedra out of her deep thinking.

"Phaedra here," she answered.

"Lucky you had us move," Phillip said. "A large ship just

came out of null space. I've never seen one like it, but I would guess that it's a Tek ship. There is a lot of high technology and no magic."

"Patch a picture through on my screen," she said. A large ship loomed on the horizon of Magus One and moved into a low orbit. She sent her senses out. There was nothing but technology there and that strange energy that seemed to be everywhere. If only she were a connector like Kathleen.

"The ship seems to be scanning the planet, Captain. My guess is that they're looking for the mediator."

"I agree, Philip. Keep an eye on them and see what they find." In a blink of an eye the ship quickly did a one eighty degree turn and headed back into null space. She scratched her head. Another opening in the space time continuum. There stood a very fast Imperial patrol ship. She couldn't miss it. She had seen thousands of those in her lifetime.

"Gear up, Philip and lock onto that ship. Wherever it goes, we go."

"Yes, Captain." A bright light flashed from the bottom of the ship onto Magus One. It did a one hundred eighty degree turn and headed into null space. The Light Burner moved from beyond the dark side of the moon and gave chase. Phaedra knew that something, or someone important, was aboard."

## Largest He Had Ever Seen
## Chapter 38

Jericho blinked his eyes against a blinding light. He tried hard to focus. He finally did and noticed that he had been beamed onto a large ship. He was standing next to a large cube that could have only been described as light. He held a hand in front of his eyes to block its brilliance as it slowly faded out leaving Bridgette, Kathleen and him, standing alone in the center of a large room. They looked at each other for a few moments. He turned toward the forward wall. It was thick glass. He could see people moving on the other side and then a door near the corner of the room

138

opened.

A very pale woman with black hair, black lipstick, nails and dark eyeliner came into the room. She was large for a woman--the largest he had ever seen. Kathleen and Bridgette gathered together just behind him. The woman smiled pleasantly and offered them a meaty hand.

"Greetings. I'm the engineer on the *Phoenix*," she said. She rolled her eyes. "I forgot. The name of our ship…this ship, is the Phoenix. Jericho shook her hand first, and then Kathleen and Bridgette. "I hope we didn't startle you too much with the beam up. We had to be fast. Even now someone is following us." She grinned. "They think we don't know. We can shift out of null space and back in again anytime we want to going into another direction. They don't know that." She smiled. Jericho smiled too. He liked this big woman. She seemed very cheerful for some reason.

Kathleen looked at her through narrowed lids. The engineer arched her brows. "Gina," she said. "My name is Gina. You must be from one of the male dominate worlds. I can see that he's bigger. More upfront, so to speak." Kathleen frowned.

"I guess so," she simply said. Bridgette began to look around the room. "I am Kathleen. You have met Jericho. This is…"

"Bridgette," Bridgette said cutting in. "What is this room? And how does this device work?"

"That's the type of questions I like to hear," Gina said. "Let's go see the captain and I'll tell you on the way." She gestured toward the door and they walked through. She followed close and sidled up to Jericho, who was walking behind the others. Seemed that she felt more in common with him, which seemed strange.

"Let me get this straight, Gina. Are you saying there is sort of a gender reversal on your world?"

"No. There's one on your world," she said with a grin. She bumped into him and smiled. "I've been studying your worlds a lot. I think I'd like to visit one sometimes."

"I bet you would. You seem to be a sly dog. You're a real flirt aren't you?" He asked.

"No," she said. "Well…you know. I'm not offending you am I."

"Oh no, not at all."

"You may be offending his wife though!" Kathleen said flatly.

"That's true," Jericho said, as if he just remembered that he was married. "But she's just fooling around."

"And is that what you have in mind?" Kathleen asked. He clenched his jaw and didn't say anything. He looked at Gina and she shrugged. Bridgette grinned showing a lot of teeth. Jericho picked up his pace and walked next to Kathleen. He leaned toward her.

"What's wrong with you, Kathleen? Why are you so hostile?" he whispered. "You know I wouldn't do anything to Mary." She looked at him for a moment and then looked ahead again. She turned back to him after a few steps and noticed that he was still waiting for an answer. Her face softened.

"I'm sorry, Jericho. It's not about you. I'm just nervous. This is how I get when I'm nervous." He didn't say anything. "You know what I mean!" she said. "Riding a beam of light and whisked off in the middle of my cup of reya…"

"I can understand," he said.

"I'm glad you can," Bridgette said. "I just think she's crazy. Look at this ship."

"Beauty isn't she," Gina said. She cleared her throat. "We're sorry about the way we had to pull you out, but we had to get you right after a Tek cruiser was scanning for you. Our timing had to be impeccable. Sorry for all of the secrecy." Kathleen began to calm down a bit. "We expected Maryland. Where is Maryland?"

"Still on the planet," Jericho said. Gina gave them a nod.

"So what can we expect in this training," Bridgette asked. "And will I be…the head of a planet?"

"More than that. You'll *be* a planet and all the people. It's a new process that has been being developed for millions of years. There are very few people doing it now. You'll be one of the first few. It's really a big honor."

"Is it dangerous?" Jericho asked.

"No. We wouldn't be doing if it were. Don't worry. It should be easy. We're drawing on the knowledge of thousands of galaxies, remember. Don't you worry about it. When we get to the bridge me and the Captain will fill you in on what's

140

happening, and then everything will be left to the Imperial Ones."

"Aren't you an Imperial One?" Kathleen asked.

"Yes and no. I am an Imperial One in her infancy, but the real Imperial Ones are much more advanced. They have…how can I say it, put off their mortal bodies and are now existing in all places at the same time. They are pure energy. When they manifest themselves as matter they are like me, but they don't usually do that."

"That sounds really weird," Bridgette said. "What do we look forward to, talking to a ball of light or something?" Jericho grinned.

"No. They can take a form somewhere between their natural forms and human beings. It is what I think your people once thought of as angels. Do I have that right?" Jericho shook his head.

"I never heard of an angel."

"Of course not on a Tek world," Kathleen said. "But we have all heard of angels." She looked at Jericho. "They are supposedly heavenly beings who are a bit above human beings."

"Oh. No wonder I never heard of such a thing. Sounds a bit silly."

"It's not silly, Jericho. Sounds like this is the bases for the story of angels," Bridgette said. "Am I right?" she asked Gina.

"Angels, aliens, all kinds of things like UFOs, were the Imperial Ones, or somebody in the empire checking on the progress of your ancestors a long time ago to see if they were ready to join The Empire. And now here you are."

"Here we are," Kathleen said. "What now?" They came to the elevator door.

"Now to the bridge and the captain's ready room. By the time she's finished talking with you will be on the way to planet Terribundi. That's Terribundi," she repeated, "The planet of advanced spirituality and technology. That's where your training will be completed." The elevator door opened and they stepped in. Kathleen didn't know whether to laugh or cry. The elevator began to rise. Jericho could hear Mary laughing and could tell that she was sitting there with her eyes closed.

"Don't you go after that big woman, my beloved. She has her eyes on you. I can sense your attraction too." Jericho lifted the corner of his mouth and took a peak at Gina.

"I hadn't even thought about her until you said something," he said to himself. The elevator door opened. Maryland quieted herself, knowing that he needed to think clearly. The bridge was giant, bigger than he thought possible. The view screen wrapped around the whole bridge making visibility possible for almost 300 degrees. All that he saw was the bright, white light of null space. He had never seen so much of it. It was brilliant. No one else seemed to notice. A woman in the center seat pivoted it in their direction and then stood.

Her hair was dark, cut very short. She wore pale, rose-colored lipstick and very little makeup, if any. She wore a dark uniform, charcoal gray, with a series of buttons running down the front on the left side. The jacket came up to the neck where it tightened into something that resembled a turtle neck collar. The cloth looked like crushed leather. She wore an insignia on her breast pocket. It was a phoenix, rising. Around the collar Jericho could see five gold buttons.

"This is the captain," Gina said. "Captain Russok, this is Jericho, this is Kathleen, and this is Bridgette." She took their hands one at a time. "As you know, these two are the candidates for leadership. Jericho is here, from what I understand, representing the Galactic Net." Gina looked at him. "Am I correct?"

"Yes, you are," he said after some thought, wondering why Maryland was so secretive about everything. He could sense a smile from her, and then a break in contact as Ben and Warwick entered the room. He was on is own for a few minutes anyway. "I look forward to hearing what these two women should expect," he said panning around the ship. "I find your technology amazing."

"Let's proceed to the ready room." She gestured toward a door on the left side of the bridge near the rear. "The scientists and engineers are waiting there." Jericho noticed that the captain wasn't a large woman like Gina. She noticed him looking her over. "I'm not from a female dominate planet," she said. "You may have noticed our size difference."

"I must admit that I did. I find it fascinating that there are male and female dominate planets. More than that, that there are actually planets where the women are bigger and stronger."

"I'm sure that you do," Kathleen said, brushing pass and heading for the door. He shook his head. Bridgette followed.

142

"She's just looking out for Maryland's interest," Bridgette said coyly. "She wouldn't want her future daddy fooling around. You know?" She began to laugh under her breath. Gina and the captain looked at each other. After Jericho entered they followed. Captain Russok's ready room was larger than he expected. There were about five people inside waiting. Everyone was sitting around a large table in front of a flat screen. They all stood as Jericho and the others entered. After introductions there was a presentation telling the times and dates for the process without telling them exactly what was going to happen. It was a very top secret experience only known by those who had gone through. Afterward they were shown their quarters and allowed to get a good nights sleep.

The Imperial Ones, at the lower level, were very good about showing them around the ship and accompanying them to various parts where they could take advantage of the recreational facilities. Gina, for some reason, seemed to latch onto Jericho. He wondered if she could sense what was going on between Maryland and him. As they were sitting at the small pub at the rear of the ship looking out into the glare of white space she said something about her fascination.

"I've heard that you and your people are connected to a net of artificial intelligence that has become a living entity. Is that the truth?." He nodded. "It must be fascinating to be able to connect with technology to the point that you experience each other as sentient beings."

"I never thought of it like that, but yes, it is. I experience it that way, but most other people don't. I don't know how they would react if they experienced the net that way."

"So you've gone far beyond the others with this connection?"

"Yes, I have. I was a teacher who taught people how to merge better. Little did I know that I had Mage blood. For some reason my magic, mixed with the technology, increased my abilities even more then I expected. It may even be a bit responsible for the net declaring itself an independent entity." He looked at her and waited. She didn't say anything. "I know that it is definitely responsible for the nets ambassador becoming involved with the Imperial Ones and The Empire."

"Really? Are you sorry about it?" She took a sip of her

drink.

"Actually, I'm not. I'm very happy about it. I only hope that the change is for the best. I really don't know much about these Imperial Ones, or their real intentions."

"Before we get to Terribundi you'll have the pleasure to meet with one of the enlightened Imperial Ones. He or she, depending on whom you meet, will answer any questions you have. You will see that the decision that you've made is a good one. We only hope that your Tek Empire will join us. Our fear is that they will pretend to join us and then wait for their chance to grab what they think is enough of our technology, and then break away. That's what many small empires have done. Not the people mind you, but the rulers who want to maintain their power and status. It never works."

"Without computer chip technology, I doubt they will be willing to do that."

"So that's how you do it, with a chip," she said. "I was wondering. You know…" she was hesitant.

"Do I know what?"

"I don't know if I should be saying this, but my people are very technologically advanced. The most in over one thousand galaxies. We could make bodies to host the intelligence of the Galactic Net so they would be sentient beings. The problem is that they couldn't go back to what they were before. They would be a community of cells all living in unison. Not a bunch of computers, but a web of people. Or maybe mobile computers, if you want to look at it that way, with self determination."

"Really." Jericho wondered what would happen to the chips if that were the case. Would the whole Tek civilization fall apart. He also wondered if Maryland would leave him, or if he would have to live his life without a chip.

"What's wrong," she asked.

"We in the Tek Empire get chips implanted into us at birth almost. I just wonder what would happen if we all lost the chip. I don't know if we could function without it. It is a truly symbiotic relationship."

"You could stay in that relationship and provide bodies for new chips. You make chips all the time, right?"

"Yes, but Compu may have something to say about that now."

144

"I'm sure you could work it out with Compu Net. That's what you call it, right?"

"Sometimes I call it whatever comes to mind," he said grinning.

"Why don't you at least see about it?"

"Believe me, the net is aware of it and your interest. I assure you I will be hearing back soon."

"Good!" she said. "Very good. The problem with me and my planet is that we are always wanting to invent and experiment. Maybe a little too much sometimes. But this--it would be a win win situation, I think. Compu could become very involved in the shaping of worlds with durable, long lasting bodies." Jericho gave a nod. He didn't know what to expect next. "Maybe we can start the process now on the far off chance that the net agrees."

"I guess it wouldn't hurt anything," he said. He waited to hear from Maryland, but she was silent. His little world was being dismantled and he wasn't to sure that he minded. Maybe this one would be better. If Maryland wanted to leave him to have a happier and more fulfilled life, he would have to go along with it. He loved her enough to want the best for her, even if it meant losing her. He could sense a smile on Maryland's lips, but nothing more. He had forgotten that she could hear every thought.


## Their Need to be Safe
## Chapter 39


Kathleen and Bridgette sat across from each other in chairs in their shared cabin. It was a large room, for one on a ship. They were used to small, cramped quarters. Compared to them, this was a luxury. The two of them had decided to share a cabin, more for safety's sake than anything else. Of course they weren't afraid of anything happening, but being together helped.

The cabin was big with two bedrooms. One bedroom had two bunks. The other had one. They had invited Jericho to stay in the single bunk. He finally acquiesced when he realized that they wouldn't accept "no." He could understand their need to be safe so he said "yes." Kathleen began to wonder where he was.

Bridgette went over to the small refrigerator and pulled out a soft drink. "You want one, Kate?" she asked, waiting for an explosion. Kathleen wondered why she was calling her Kate suddenly, and if this would be a trend.

"No thanks," she simply said. Bridgette shrugged, walked over, and plopped down in a chair across from her.

"You look a bit worried. They didn't scare you off during the meeting, did they?" She took a big gulp.

"Not in the least. It just sounded a little weird to me...being part of a planet. I just wanted my empire back. It really doesn't mean much now, does it? I never even thought of the possibility of another empire so vast and powerful. We must look like idiots to them...like ants fighting on an ant hill."

"We're beginning to look like that to me," she decided not to press her luck by calling her Kate again, "Your Highness," she said with a grin. She scanned the cabin. "I never knew all of this was possible. These people seem to be able to do just about anything. Imagine drawing on the knowledge of more than a thousand galaxies." She looked somber. "Still I wonder...Are they for real? What do they do to people who don't join?"

"That is something that you have in common with me." She stood. "I think I do want a drink."

"I'll get it for you," Bridgette said, beginning to stand. Kathleen lifted a hand.

"Kate can take care of it," she said. Bridgette smiled through closed lips as Kathleen walked over to the refrigerator. She removed the bottle and flipped open the cap. She leaned back against the refrigerator and took a drink. "How about you, Bridgette? What do you think? Are you ready to be a planet? To move way out there somewhere to a strange planet all alone?" She took another drink.

"I've thought about it. I am in the service...used to moving around. But I'm not used to being alone. I know that you are a Del Sol and that I am way below you, but I was hoping, since we are in this thing together, that we could at least stay in touch. We could be something like friends." Kathleen took another swallow.

"Friends?" she echoed back. "No one has ever wanted to be friends with me. No one who knew who I was, that is. Being friends with me and my family has always been dangerous. You

146

know that. We can be something like friends though, and see where it goes." Bridgette smiled. "I hope that I haven't offended you with my answer, but…let's see how things happen."

"That's all I can ask, Your Highness," Bridgette said.

"As a start, please call me Kathleen. That's somewhere between Your Highness and Kate. Don't you think?"

"Yes, I do," Kathleen. Thank you."

"Thank you for being here, Bridgette. I really appreciate what you are willing to do for our empire and for freedom. I'm also glad that you're here with me."

"I'm glad too," Bridgette said. "Let's hope that I'll be glad after their little experiment."

*   *   *

Jericho marveled as he made his way to the small cabin. He hadn't heard one thing from Maryland about the proposition from Gina. He hoped that nothing was wrong with her. The last thing he received from her was just a vague, slight smile. Perhaps she was advancing the information to the net, or else the net had picked it up from him and was in the process of deciding. He had forgotten that the net could pick up information through him and anyone who had a chip. He could probably communicate with it too. That was a bit…scary. It was bad enough to have Maryland running around in his head, but the whole net.

He lifted his hand to his temple. He had a slight headache. It had been there since that conversation with Gina. He wondered if he was feeling the net working out the intricacies about what such an action would look like. It was a slight, dull pain, but constant and uncomfortable. He continued to walk, hoping that he remembered the room.

He was a bit upset. Kathleen and Bridgette had practically begged him to bunk with them after the badgering didn't work anymore. He was a grown man. He didn't want to bunk with two women; that was unheard of. One was supposed to be his daughter on another time line, but she wasn't in this one. She was beautiful, so was the other woman. What would Maryland think? Why hadn't she said anything? Was he losing the link? He watched the doors as he passed by. They were numbered, alphabetized and color coded. It would really take an idiot to get lost.  He stopped in front of a green door.  He was lost.  He stood there thinking.  Instinctively he looked farther down the hall and saw a pale blue door.  That had to be it.  He moved down the hall and stopped

He stood in front of the door and looked at it.  Seventeen B, that was it.  He stood there a moment and then knocked on the door, not wanting to burst in on these women.  Maybe they were unclothed or something.  Yet again, he smiled to himself.  Maybe he should burst in.

"Enter," Kathleen shouted from inside.  He could just imagine her beautiful, mean face squeezing out a command.  She was of a royal family.  He knew that, because she seemed to love to give orders.  He opened the door and stepped in.

"It's only you," Bridgette said.  "Why didn't you just come in?  It's your cabin too, you know?  You have your own bedroom and everything, unless you want to bunk with one of us."  She grinned.  Jericho squinted.

"I just wanted to see if you were decent," he said, ignoring her as much as he could.

"I'm always decent," Kathleen said, taking a drink.  He looked her up and down.

"In that tight suit, I don't know if you are or not."  He walked in and headed for the refrigerator.

"Spicy personality again, are we?" Kathleen said, leaning back in her chair.  "I think that Bridgette and I may have made a mistake.  You and that Maryland are really pretty mean when you let go of yourselves."

"Mean?  You're calling me mean?  I don't believe that."  He pulled out a drink and sat on the sofa across from the two chairs.  "You have a problem, Kathleen.  You're always giving orders and are snippy all the time."

"Snippy!  I'll dare you call me snippy."

"Sounds like a family argument," Bridgette said, cutting in.  "Both of you are right.  You are all mean and snippy and always giving orders.  I can tell that you are all in the same family, and probably a noble one, because you're all moody and hard to deal with.  Sometimes you can be so nice and then, here you go."  Kathleen glared at her, but didn't say anything.  "You know it's true," Bridgette said.

"I don't know any such thing, and I don't happen to be any

148

royal family," Jericho said. "I am not a mage, in fact. I'm Tek."

"Don't be an idiot. You're my father. Do I look like a Tek?"

"You say that I'm your father. What evidence do we have?"

"Do you want a chromosome test or something?"

Bridgette looked at him. "Come on Jericho. "Don't be ridiculous!" He didn't respond. "Are you all right?"

"No. I have a terrible headache. Maryland is gone too. I can't find her." They looked at each other. "Don't look at me like I'm crazy. We have a telepathic link and I can't find her. She's disappeared."

"She's all right. I'd know if anything were wrong. Believe me," Kathleen said. He pursed his lips and looked at her. He thought about how rude he had been when he came in. His head was hurting him more than he thought possible. He had never been mean, until his link with Maryland.

"I'm sorry for my behavior," he said. He waited. No one said anything. "I have a headache and I think my head is hurting me more than I was willing to admit. I can't seem to heal it with my chip."

Kathleen shook her and head. "A mage with a headache," she mumbled under her breath. "Don't worry. Sit your drink down and I'll heal it. I can do it from here." He sat his drink on the floor, leaned back on the couch, and closed his eyes. Kathleen extended her senses and connected with his mind. She gasped as she was drawn into an infinite ocean of energy and thoughts and then she quickly drew back. Jericho brought his hand to his head and smiled.

"Very good, Kathleen. The pain's gone. Thank you." He looked at her sitting there even paler than usual.

"Something wrong?" Bridgette asked.

"Your chip it is—it has expanded into a community. Your head is full of hundreds of…minds there. No wonder you can't concentrate on Maryland!"

He leaned back and closed his eyes. What had Maryland done to him? He was being taken over—possessed by the Galactic Net. This was impossible. He noticed that Kathleen looked fascinated.

"Looks like our Imperial Ones are up to something,"

Bridgette said. "I never thought that we could really trust them."

"I don't know if it is them," Kathleen commented.

"I think it's the net," Jericho replied. "We had a discussion...Gina and I, about creating technologically advanced bodies for the net and moving its intelligence into a web of living beings. Soon after my head began to hurt. I hadn't heard anything back from Maryland or the net while that conversation was happening. I guess this is their answer."

"So you are a repository for all of these minds," Bridgette said.

"I think so. The net is...I don't know about this net. It seems to do whatever it likes, regardless of what happens to its tools."

"You have no evidence of that. Nothing has happened but a little pain, which is gone now, and a bit of a bruised ego. But this could work to your advantage. I bet you could really explore that community and even find Maryland in there if you want to." Jericho shook his head and took another drink.

"I wonder if Gina knows anything about this."

Bridgette smiled, "You better believe that she does by now. This net thing is really fast when it wants something done."


## A Dull Expression on Her Face
## Chapter 40


When Maryland opened her eyes she was moving fast. She had dosed off for the first time in her life. Tracy was sitting in the seat beside her looking out the back window.

"I think we're home free. I don't see anyone following us. I think Maryland was right." Bryant jammed his foot on the brakes and turned off the highway onto a dirt trail quickly, heading for the airport. Once he got underneath the protective fog bank that covered the landing pads they would be safe. "Looks like we're safe now anyway, Tracy." He looked over his shoulder and saw Maryland stirring.

"Oh, awake are we, little, sleeping beauty?" Tracy looked at her and smiled. "Thanks for the heads up. The troops were just about five minutes behind us from what I could pick up by hacking into the security computers, " she said. She looked at her with a dull expression on her face at first, and then she remembered. She had received a message from the net and then, nothing, a memory loss.

"It is difficult for me to remember what happened. I think the net shut me down for security reasons."

"You didn't seem to be shut down. You just seemed like Maryland," Ben said. "Until you fell asleep in the car, of course."

"Yea," Warwick said, looking back over his shoulder. "You were talking a mile a minute, pouring out instructions and then when you were finished...poof. You just went to sleep. I thought you were dead for a minute."

"I wouldn't go that far," Ben said.

"Don't you tell me what I thought!" Warwick said. "I'm the Captain."

"Not mine!"

"Yea, but I will be."

"Let's stop the bickering. We're entering the cloud bank, Bryant said. "Let's get to the pod and be off of this world ASAP." Tracy sighed. She was surprised that she had been so frightened. She hadn't even allowed herself to feel it, but she was exhausted too.

"Let's get back into space," she said. "I don't like moving around on the ground so much."

\*                              \*                              \*

Warwick swiveled around in the captain's chair. Ben was hooked up to the flight chair, plugged in, while Bryant worked as the engineers station checking all of the systems. Maryland sat looking at the large view screen. Tracy decided to work at communications and weapons—a strange combination, but Warwick could use all the help he could get. "Are we clear?" Warwick asked.

"All systems are go, but we don't know what to expect up there, when we leave the atmosphere," Bryant said.

"Put out feelers as far as you can, Bryant. We have to chance it." He pivoted toward Ben. "We ready, Ben?" Ben gave him a nod. "Let's get the hell out of here." With a thought Ben started the engines. They were quiet and smooth. He permitted the energy from the magnetic bottle to flow through the system. He could feel the initial dampeners opening, allowing the hungry energy more access to the power that came from the breakdown of matter and anti-matter. They slowly lifted off the pad. "Keep monitoring the Tek and Mage communications Tracy, Ok?

"Yes Captain. I'm on it!"

"See Ben. That's the way you're supposed to answer." They lurched forward as their speed quickly increased.

"Woe there, Cowboy!" Warwick said.

"Don't worry Captain, I have it," Ben said.

"There's that captain thing. That's what I like," Warwick said with a smile. Bryant grinned too. "I just have to get used to your wild flying style, I guess," he said more somberly.

"Me wild, Warwick?" Ben grinned. He looked back at the screen. "We'll be breaking the upper atmosphere soon."

"I can see a Tek cruiser cloaked waiting near the rear of the ship. We will take care of it," Maryland said. Warwick and Bryant looked at each other.

"I know your eyes were pretty good looking," Warwick said, "But I didn't know they could see cloaked ships."

"Only a bit of distortion caused against the background," she said with a grin. "Head for the ship, Ben. We will shut her sensors down." They moved forward as the large cruiser just hung there in space. Ben was a bit nervous. He had never seen one of those monster ships before. Now there he was being pursued by one. They moved close. He veered off and entered orbit around the small moon. The rear end of the ship awakened. He could sense the lights going on and the engines being activated.

"Reconnection in three, two, one, zero," Bryant said, as they felt a slight thump. "Engaging brackets and seals," he said. He looked at Warwick. "We're engaged."

"No communication chatter on the big ship, Captain. They're really quite," Tracy said.

"That's a good sign, Tracy. Thanks."

"The Tek cruiser is overriding the computer controls," Maryland said. "Time for step two." All of the lights on the cruiser shut down. It looked like it was drifting free in space.

"The energy readings are…non-existent, Captain," Bryant said looking up.

152

"And they couldn't get a distress signal off in time," Tracy said.

"Good," Warwick said. He scratched his chin. "Let's get the hell out if here then. Take us into null space. Find the most out of the way little planet that you can. We want to be buried for a while. Just think Red followed by a number and the ship will take us there automatically."

"Yes Captain," Ben said. They were quickly swallowed into null space.

*   *   *

There was only the familiar glare of white space. "Shut off that front screen," Warwick said. Bryant shut it down. Warwick got out of his chair. "We've programmed some safe haven planets into the ship. We should be going there automatically, Ben. Good job." He stretched. "I suggest you take some time to leaf through our records, Ben, while we're in the dulls of null space."

"I've already done that, Sir, during the training."

"So much the better," Warwick said. "Well I suggest that we retire to the cantina for a bit of lunch and refreshment. The day has been long."

"Amen to that," Tracy said. "But I would like to look over the ship. I've never seen one like this. It's beautiful."

"Why? You want to join the crew too?" Warwick boomed. She scrunched up her face and he laughed. "Take your time, Tracy. We'll be in the rear. Come on back when you want Bryant to hook you up with some quarters." Bryant frowned. She smiled.

"I'll do that... Warwick," she said after some thought. She didn't want him to get the idea that she was going to join another crew. One was enough and now that was even over. She was serving as head council to Kathleen Del Sol, even though Kathleen Del Sol was light years away.

"Looks like our day just got longer," Maryland said. "The Tek Empire has finally decided that they can do without the Galactic net. They have begun emergency procedures to shut it down."

"What's going to happen to all the people with chips?" Ben asked. "We've been...that chip...that net is part of us."

"The intelligence has been moved to another place. They don't understand that Compu Net is a holographic entity. As long as one piece is alive, the whole thing is alive. It has moved its core somewhere else. We will allow them to think they have shut us down, and shut down all the chips except for those of the people friendly to our cause. The Teks will have to worry about whatever else happens. When they drop that net they will be open to any Magi attack." She looked at Ben.

"They have declared war on us. We are disappointed and angry."


## He Wasn't Sure that it Would Work
## Chapter 41


Jericho breathed a sigh as he sensed Maryland's presence again in a car moving fast. They were apparently fleeing Magus One, for some reason. He felt normal again. Being connected to her always made him feel normal. He had been connected to her and the Galactic Net almost all of his life. It pained him to know that Tek Empire was going to cut everyone off from the net. Yet again, he wasn't really too surprised. They had a habit of thinking they were in control when they really weren't. As he listened in on the discussion between Maryland and Ben he realized that he had been a depository for much of the net. He shook his head.

The Tek Empire was too proud and stupid. He began to understand why the net had intervened. Unfortunately, he felt that the leaders of Tek Empire would still cause the death of millions unless the net could use its chips to organize people against Tek Empire. He wasn't sure that would work. Would the Teks love their chips more, or the Tek Empire.

He could feel Maryland's presence again and knew that she was listening in. It was a very subtle feeling, just like when she was only a chip. He had learned to shut down most of the senses they shared so he didn't see or hear double, unless he wanted. He could even sense what she was thinking without hearing an inner voice, which was much more convenient. He was also sensing the nets thoughts and expectations, which he found a bit uncomfortable. Usually he would listen only after things had been filtered through Maryland. In truth, he had access to Galactic

Compu net the same way she did. Especially with the core of it in his head. He wasn't sure if he liked that either.

He sat and pondered as Kathleen and Bridgette did their own thing. They were all used to being in close quarters, having been in the service so long. They knew how to give one private space, even in crowded areas. He didn't really have to worry about them. He had always been very pensive. Unlike the people in the service, he was used to being alone. His only contacts most of the day were computers and his chip.

He taught courses, of course. That was his social time. He enjoyed standing up in front of the students and giving his point of view about the chips, computers, and the world. He loved to demonstrate what the chip and Compu could do. He would watch as his students eyes lit up with fascination. This, of course, was a very selective group of students. They were destined to be computer engineers and teachers themselves. There were a few soldiers thrown in, intelligence agents and future connectors, but they all pleased him. Especially the ones who were hungry to learn all they could. He wondered if he would ever teach again.

The whole world had turned up side down. Instead of watching comfortably from his living room chair, he was in the center of it all. He was at the core of the vortex, standing tall like a lightening rod. He only hoped that he could take it when the storm rose and lightening struck.

# She Was Pure Machine
# Chapter 42

The ship moved smoothly through null space, so smoothly that it seemed that they were standing still. Many scientists and physicists had theorized that one was not actually moving through null space, null space was recreating itself around the ship. Some even went further to say that the ship was constantly recreating itself. By the time one arrived at one's destination one was a totally new creation in new space.

This was only a theoretical explanation that was often pursued by scientists and academics, but it was interesting to Maryland too. It wasn't surprising. She, after all, was a computer.

Computer's liked to think and theorize just for the sake of doing so without attaching much importance to their findings. Maryland found that she did also. She was an independent, thinking, feeling entity. Her link to Jericho made her very human. At the same time she was pure machine. That made her think more deeply.

She took a drink of hot chocolate. Bryant, Ben and Warwick were drinking also, but something a bit stronger. Tracy had gone to her quarters to rest. She was shaken after the car chase. Rather than relax by drinking, she chose to meditation in a solitary, quiet place. It was a luxury that she didn't often have on the Light Burner, until she became an officer.

Maryland agreed with her healthy approach to relaxation. She had no need or desire for alcohol, or for altering her senses of perception. She couldn't understand how human beings could enjoy such a thing. She wondered if it helped them relax. These two seemed to be relaxing; of course it did. The net knew all about that. It had been intertwined with human minds for hundreds of years. How had she forgotten that, or Jericho's beers in the evening? What was wrong with her lately? She looked up at Ben.

"Don't you think you've had enough?" She asked.

"What are you now, Mary, my mother?"

"No. I'm just worried. What if an emergency should come up?"

"In null space? We'd probably die!" He grinned. Warwick grinned too.

"Don't you worry, Maryland," Warwick said. "We can take care of any emergencies. Especially with this ship. We all know how to hold our liquor." She frowned. "Really," he said.

Bryant only grinned. "Since when are you worrying about people drinking, Maryland?" He asked. "I've never known you to…I don't want this to seem harsh, but to worry about anyone. Except possibly Jericho."

"That's because I haven't," she said.

"Holy Rose Mother! You're not supposed to tell us that," Warwick said.

"Why not if that's the way I feel? It's only the truth."

"Amen to that," Bryant said lifting his drink. "If it's one thing we need to hear, it's the truth."

"You'd drink to anything," she said. She stood up and

stormed out.  They all looked at each other and shook their heads.

"She and Jericho are a marriage made in heaven," Ben said.  She heard him all the way near the end of the hall, but ignored him.  She found a great deal of satisfaction in her new found power to purposely ignore him.

*      *      *

Maryland sat in her quarters.  It was quiet at first, and then she opened herself to the net and Jericho again.  Her newly formed personality seemed to vanish as she melded with everyone else.  She concluded that her separation from the net allowed her to display a totally independent personality.  The net must have separated her on purpose, that's why she had simply fallen asleep.  The net was working a great deal lately.  She wondered how her connection with Jericho was affecting the net.  She could feel a slight sense of amusement.  The net was...enjoying itself.  That had never happened before.

Flashes of a civilization appeared before her.  Various people...humanoid, all part of a giant computer, able to separate and have their own identities and able to be joined together as one mega mobile net.  That was what Compu wanted.  She turned her senses to Jericho.  She could see him sitting in a small cabin looking at Kathleen's tight uniform as she was reading a magazine.  She could sense his head shaking.  Kathleen looked up at him and sneered.

"You got a problem, Jericho!" She blurted.  She could feel him draw back, like he had been slapped in the face.  Maryland smiled.

"No," he said in a detached way.  "I was just looking at you.  Do you mind?"

"Not at all," She said, still glaring.  "Take in an eyeful, Dad!" Bridgette smiled.  He turned toward her and glared.

"You two have a lot in common don't you?" he asked.  Bridgette shrugged.

"Not as much as you two...apparently."

"I was just looking at that tailored uniform designed to tease." Kathleen continued to look down at the magazine.  A smile peaked through, even as she tried to snuff it out.

"Well it seems that it is working, doesn't it," she said, not really looking up. "I'd be flattered if you weren't my father." She looked at him. "Isn't it sick to be turned on by your own daughter? I mean, I understand this time space thing. You are my father and you aren't, but what does it mean when, you know…we aren't family, but we are, aren't we?"

"Why? What are you thinking about?" he asked. He stood. "I'm going to take a walk to see if I can find Gina."

"You got him all bothered and now he's go' in after Gina," Bridgette said. "Save a little of yourself for me, Jerry." He frowned more than Maryland thought possible and marched out the door. She could hear the two women laughing behind him. She separated herself and lessened the connection as he tromped heavily down the hallway. She knew that he was going to find her to talk about the bodies for Compu Net. That would be a good thing. Yet again, she could sense a little bit of attraction for Gina. Actually, as a chip she noticed that men often felt a little bit of attraction for all women.

*    *    *

Gina's mind dulled as she listened to Dr. Mark's chatter and excitement about creating biotic bodies to carry Galactic Net intelligence. This man seemed to be so fascinated over nothing most of the time. Yet again, he was the most brilliant scientist that her planet had ever produced—the pride of Berrundi, as they called him. She watched him speaking on the viewer and wondered if he could tell what she was thinking. If he only knew. She began to smile. He saw her smiling and paused for a moment, returning a bright smile.

"I see that you find it as fascinating as I," Dr. Mark said.

"Oh, of course, Dr.," she lied. She wasn't exactly lying. She thought the outcome would be interesting, but why go on and on. "I think that the net is all for it. Some of our computers have been picking up chatter from the net as if it's coming from nowhere. We also have a new member of the Imperial Order on board who serves as an ambassador."

"How exciting!" Mark said. "I can't wait to meet…" he arched his brows, "her, him?"

"Him," she said. "He's from one of the male dominant planets."

"Well. I can't wait to meet him. I think we shall have quite a bit to talk about. Is this man a scientist."

"Yes and no. I think that he's a professor on information technology, chip technology and that sort of thing. He's supposed to be a leader in his field. He's a Tek. Have you heard of them?"

"The Tek Empire. About 670 years ago they came to supremacy over the Mage Empire, I think—a group of people very telepathic and psycho-kinetic. Powerful people, said to be able to transmute matter into energy and back with no external aid, I think."

"You really seem to know quite a bit about them," Doctor.

"One of my hobbies, looking at magic and that sort of thing. Has to do with energy, you know, and the human body. Ties in a great deal with cybernetics and biotics, you know? The merging of the mind with the biotic brain and so forth. There's quite a bit about them in the Galactic Library, of course. Just about everything in there."

"There sure seems to be," she said flatly, and then hoped he didn't pick up on her tone. He didn't.

"We're already working on some bodies. We have a couple up and running already. With no minds they aren't too entertaining though…if you know what I mean."

"I don't know Dr., sometimes healthy bodies without minds can be quite entertaining." He narrowed his eyes. She grinned.

"Not very funny, Gina." The corners of her mouth dropped.

"Sorry. Just thinking out loud." The door bell rang. "That's the door. Thanks for keeping me up to speed. I think I'm going to get that. Anything else Dr. Mark?"

"Nothing right now. If I need you I'll call on your wrist com."

"Thank you then, Dr. Good life to you."

"And you too," he replied. The screen went dead. Gina walked over to the door. "Enter," she said. It slid open. Jericho was standing there. "Oh, what a surprise and a pleasure. I'm lucky I picked up all of my crap a few minutes ago." She smiled. He couldn't help but smile with her. "Come on in and have a seat. I'll get you something to drink." He walked in and looked around. The cabin was similar to his, except it was the single version.

Boring color. Off white walls. Plasticized sofas with gray padded bottoms with backs to match. There was a small kitchen off to the left hand side at a forty five degree angle from the door. A very short hallway leading off to the right to a small bathroom and bedroom.

There was a table in front of the plasticized sofa--round, flat and fiberglass. On the other side of the table, facing the door, a matching, horrible little chair. To the left there was a small counter in the room with a small bar. Behind the bar there were pictures of Gina, her friends, and family. There were also a few medals and awards hanging on the wall to the right, behind the sofa. He walked over and began to look at them as she rummaged through the bar.

"Ah, academic *and* sports awards. This is very interesting." He scratched his chin. She came around the bar with two drinks.

"My parents always believed in being balanced. Mentally, physically, and spiritually strong. You know? I guess that's how all the Imperial planets are." She shrugged. "It was just normal to us. We've been in the empire for more than two thousand years, you know."

"No I didn't." She gave him a drink and sat in the chair. He sat on the sofa. It was much more comfortable than it looked. "I didn't know anything about the Imperial Ones until about a week ago, to be truthful."

"Most of the people outside of The Empire don't know about us. They would be scared to death to know that such power existed. We wait until they're ready. The Teks are ready, wouldn't you say?"

"I'm not sure. The Teks are prideful and stubborn." Gina took a sip of her drink.

"Aren't we all," she said. She sat it on the table and leaned back. "To be truthful, we were summoned by your Galactic Net. They are the ones...the first ones, who have joined us. We hope that the Tek Empire will."

"I hope so too. Even though I don't think they're ready."

"But the Mage Empire in the other time frame has been working with us for almost a millennium. So we already have five planets from the Teks in."

"I'm discovering that the Teks are nothing like the Magi. I

160

have even heard that genetically they are a different species. The Teks are very arrogant, to say the least." He leaned back. "Even as I say this I can't believe that it's coming out of my mouth. I was so proud of the Tek Empire, but it was because I was in a fishbowl. I didn't know that anything more powerful with an even larger goal for humanity and the universe existed. But here I am on this fancy ship going to an Imperial planet. What was the name of that planet again, Terribundi?"

"Yes. That's the name of the planet we talked about before, but I think that you and I will be going somewhere else. We won't be needed while they are going through their process. The process is very secret, except for those undertaking it. I think we will be going to Berrundi."

"Berrundi," he said. She nodded. "And what will this run to Berrundi with you mean?" He took another sip of his drink. She grinned and picked up her own.

"You're starting to act like a Berrundi man," she said. "I'm not trying to make a pass at you. I promise." She laughed a bit. Jericho smiled. "Even though I see the way you've been looking at me," she said. He smiled, but arched his brows. "Anyway, Berrundi is my home planet. Probably the most technologically advanced planet in the universe. We have a doctor there who has created *biots* to host the minds of your Compu. I would like you to take a look at them."

"My pleasure. I'm sure they'd like a look too. They seem very interested in doing this. What is the cost though? What are you getting out of this?"

"Ah. You must remember that we are Imperial Ones. Our motivation isn't money, it's growth and experience. We intend to see how this technology can benefit everyone. Our hope is that the Compu, as members if the Empire, will help us make peace on some of our more primitive planets."

"Do you mean fight for you?"

"Nothing that primitive. We mean go live on some of them to create a model society for others to see, join, and copy. They will be very strong and durable. If they have to defend themselves they should be able to very well. But it would be quite immoral to turn them out to fight for us."

"I'm sure that they will be pleased to hear that."

"So we go to Berrundi then?"

"Why not.  It may be fun hanging out with a giant woman who thinks like me."  He could feel Maryland give him a little nudge.

## What Are You Thinking?
## Chapter 43

After a good night sleep Maryland was ready to go.  She found, suddenly, that sleep was a bit more pleasant than it had been.  She was experiencing what the humans called dreaming.  That was a bit fun.  She also had a nightmare, which she didn't like.  She was wondering if the net were going too far with this duplication of human faculties.  She sat on the ship's bridge remembering and poked out her lower lip.

"What are you doing?" Warwick asked.  She looked at him.

"Do you have to notice everything?"

"Yes, I do.  This is my bridge.  Remember that.  Your behavior might be a danger to my crew and my ship.  What are you thinking?"

"My thoughts are not open to discussion,"  She said.  Warwick turned away and hid the smile playing across his lips.  Tracy looked down at her panel and laughed to herself.

"I'm curios too," Ben said.  "I've never seen you so pensive.  Meditative, yes, but not pensive.  You are really changing aren't you?"

"Acting more human," Bryant added.  She frowned.

"Yes.  That's the problem," she said.

"Well…what's happening?" Ben asked.  She sat and thought for a moment before answering.

"I've been having dreams and nightmares.  I've been feeling refreshed after sleeping and sensing new subroutines loaded into me.  I don't like it.  This is too close to human.  I don't want to be a human."

"Well looks like you're becoming one," Warwick said. "Why'd you answer him and not me?" She squinted and looked at him hard. She sucked her teeth and faced the front screen. Warwick shook his head. "You are really getting an obnoxious attitude, if you don't know it," he said. He waited for an explosion. She looked at him through narrowed lids.

"Well I can't help that, can I? Just like you can't help your obnoxious attitude."

"Please," Bryant said cutting in. "We don't want any violence. Just loosen up a bit will you two?"

"Don't stop them," Tracy said hitting a few buttons. "These little conversations are just so amusing."

"And what are you doing?" Warwick asked.

"A brief weapons test before we come out of null."

"We're about to come out of null space now," Ben said. "I hate to ruin all of this fun and all of this friendly chatter, but I just thought you might want to know about something that is a little more important than how people are feeling."

"The test will be done by then," Tracy said briskly.

"Did everybody get up on the wrong side of the bed or something?" Bryant asked. He turned to Ben. "Thank you, Ben. What planet are we headed for?"

"It's Mars."

"Mars?" Warwick repeated back. "When I said backwater you really went for it, didn't you? That place is really a hole in the wall. I hope nothing happens to the ship and that we don't need spare parts. Those people are the most backward people I've ever seen." They slid into normal space.

"Looks like a good planet to me," Ben said.

"Yeah, now. They nearly blew themselves to bits in an all out atomic war...the bunch of idiots. Next they almost got hit by a comet. Now they are just sort of floating around in space waiting to become a member of The Empire. That planet is hard nut to crack." He stood up and walked to the front of the view screen. "Can you put it up front, Bryant?"

"Aye, aye Captain." He hit a few buttons. A small planet appeared in the middle of the screen. It was a blue planet with some land mass, but a great deal of water and a lot of humidity in the atmosphere. Thick clouds covered the whole planet.

"Is it livable?" Ben asked.

"Oh yeah," Warwick said. "Those clouds are just water vapor. The planet was pretty cold and dry, but it got scraped by a comet that moved it over in its orbit. Now it's wet and humid. A lot of frozen water underground when it was farther out from the sun melted and vaporized when it moved closer. Now we have it and the closest planet to it, Earth, carrying all of the people in the solar system. Very interesting story about them. I have to admit, everybody thought they would be dead when the comet came at'em. They did figure a way around it."

"I guess you have to be happy about that," Ben said.

"You haven't met them yet," Warwick said. "Take us into orbit Ben and prepare to separate. We're going to get lost on the rainy planet for a while."

"Very interesting," Maryland said. "I can still sense the presence of the net out here and we aren't in Tek Empire anymore."

"Just near the edge," Bryant said.

"Seems that the net is expanding to...through the Imperial technology. It 's taking on a life of its own and isn't really letting me know what it's doing anymore. I don't know if I like that."

"Looks like the net is growing and giving you some autonomy. Sometimes not knowing goes along with that," Ben said. "I'm glad the net is out here. When we land I'm going to see what's happening with the Tek Empire."

"They are planning to turn the Galactic Compu off more soon than later. Then all of the problems will start."

"Then," Ben said. He shook his head and smiled. Maryland didn't.

\*               \*               \*


The ship separated easily and Ben left the module in orbit circling a large asteroid in an asteroid belt on the next orbit after mars. The pod headed for its destination...a very blue and white planet that was supposed to have been red at one time or the other. Tracy didn't pick up any Tek communication on the radio. The presence of the net was not obvious by any Tek means, but apparently Maryland was well aware of its presence. They were safe from Tek Empire for the moment, especially since they were in Imperial space. Ben wondered, however, if the Tek Empire

164

even knew to fear the Imperials. If anyone in the government knew anything about them they had kept it so secret from even the most educated citizens that it would have taken a major cover up. Even the net hadn't known about it until recently.

They slowly moved into orbit and rotated the front of the knobby head of the ship upward, placing the rocket section and the heat shield toward the atmosphere. They plummeted toward the planet until the retro rockets kicked in to slow their decent.

"Message coming in," Tracy said. "Putting it through." The image of a woman in a red uniform made out of a fabric resembling silk appeared. It had a high color with the front cut Nauru style. White trim came up along the zipper and lined the edge of the collar. There were four red and golden studs running vertically down the left side just next to the trim, designating her rank.

"Commander General Briggs here," she said. "We can see by your transponder code that you are coming from—outer space." She smiled. "Are you back for more negotiation?"

"This is Captain Warwick. We are not the diplomatic branch of the Imperial Ones, we are the…clandestine branch," he said, clearing his throat. "We have very important cargo aboard and we need to deposit it here for just a bit of time."

"Cargo," she said, pursing her lips. "Hold on and we'll see." The screen went blank. It was on private. A man's face appeared.

"Ben Rogers here. Security. What is the nature of this cargo?"

"Nothing dangerous, but its security is imperative to The Empire."

"Imperative, is it?" Rogers asked. He looked down as if he were reading something off screen. "We've just scanned you, by the way," he said. "You just proceed on the incoming course. We'll beam you a microwave to follow in. In case there's a break in transmission the coordinates are delta, alpha, gamma niner, fiver, niner. Just put that into your computer and our net will pick you up and bring you in. Ok?"

"Got it," Warwick said. The screen went black. "Put that code into the computer just in case, Bryant." He leaned back in his seat. "You've just been scanned. What a jackass!"

"Delta, niner, who sit, what the heck is that all about," Ben asked.

"These people like to talk like that," Warwick said. "Supposed to be one of their ancient languages or something. You just use the first letter of each word, except for the numbers. Subtract the stupid endings and you have the number."

"Cute," Ben said. "I guess that's so you don't mix up the letters or something and they don't have to repeat them."

"Totally right, as usual," Warwick said. Ben looked at him to see if he was making a wise crack. He wasn't. He went right to the next topic.

"We receiving that beam yet, Tracy?"

"Yes, Captain."

"Good. Patch it over." He turned to Ben. "Take us in nice and slow Ben." He chewed on his nail a bit. "Keep those shields up, Bryant. I like these people and everything, but keep up the shields. The cargo here is too valuable."

"And are we your cargo?" Maryland asked. He narrowed his eyes.

"It's a code word, Maryland. Don't go getting all mean on me." Her face softened.

"What makes you think I was going to do that? I was just curious."

"I bet you were," Bryant said.

"We shall ignore you," she said. "We find pleasure in ignoring your wise talk--very much pleasure."

"I don't even know how to answer that, Mary."

"It's too late. You're already in my ignore database." Tracy couldn't help but laugh out loud at that one. Maryland almost smiled herself.

"Hate to interrupt the cute banter again, but we're going in," Ben said. They plummeted.

"Slow it down Ben! Don't go swooping in there like an eagle after a fish. Keep it slow, your scaring the hell out of me and I've been flying in this thing all my life!"

"I'm sorry, Captain," Ben said forcing himself to hold back a big grin. The ships descent slowed and followed the microwave beacon toward the landing pad. The first thing they noticed, after passing through the thick atmosphere, was a large forest with trees and plants as far as the eye could see.

"Transplants from Earth," Warwick said. "That's the other

166

planet in this system with life." They continued to descend watching all of the foliage. Ben had never seen so many trees in his life. They came to a large opening sliced into the ground and the ship moved toward it. When it was only a few hundred feet away a tractor beam locked on.

"Cut the engines," Warrant said. "They live underground. We're being pulled into a hanger." They slowly moved through the clearing in the wooded area toward what looked like a red, concrete bunker. As they got closer Ben noticed that it was much larger than anything he had seen like that. It was the size of a bat-ball stadium. The ship moved in through a large horizontal slit that ran the length of the hanger, into a well lit area full of small, round ships that looked like plates. Many of them were bright silver with an insignia that looked like an eagle painted on the side. He figured this must be the military hanger.

They moved toward the front and settled under a large window about 30 feet above the floor. As they looked inside they could see that it was a control room. There was a flash of light. They looked around and discovered that they were standing on the other side of the window in a large room surrounded by Martian soldiers and bureaucrats.

A woman approached them, her hand extended. "Commander General Briggs," she said in a smooth voice. "Welcome. I hope that you've found your landing much smoother than the last visitors from The Empire," she smiled pleasantly. "We've been putting the technology that you've given us to use." She shook Warwick's hand. "Pleased to meet you, Captain." Ben looked at her. He had never seen a woman like her. She was full of some type of bio-energy.

She looked at him and approached. "Please to meet you," she said, extending her hand. He shook her hand," Benjamin," he said. Next she went on to Maryland, Tracy, and then to Bryant. She turned back toward Ben.

"What are you looking at, Sir?" He was dumbfounded. Maryland smiled.

"I've never seen anyone like you before," he quickly responded. She smiled.

"Maybe we can talk about that later," Warwick said--a wide grin on his face.

"No. I don't mean...there is something special about her."

"That's what they all say," Colonel Rogers said with a grin on his face. He extended his hand. Colonel Rogers, Security." They shook hands and made the introductions. He looked back at Briggs. Briggs is one of the *new leaders*...she's been through the Imperial process. I don't sense anything different about her though, how can you?"

"I am greatly attuned to energy sources...all sources electronic and otherwise. She is powerful, I would say."

"She is standing right in front of you."

"Yes Ma'am," Ben said.

"Don't go getting all serious on me now. You're not on my squad. Just call me Rachel." She smiled pleasantly. He eased up a bit.

"Rachel, what did they do to you?"

"It's hard to say. All they did was get me in touch with my self...my inner self. They made me a whole individual."

"I didn't notice anything," Warwick said. "I like the red suit and all, fits good, but I didn't notice anything special." She frowned.

"He's a pig," Maryland said cutting in."

"I find it charming," Rachel responded. "We don't have such men on our planet anymore. Since the war we are more communicative, I would say. We're on equal footing, wouldn't you say, Rogers?"

"Yeah, that's why I'm only a Colonel and you're a Commander General." He grinned.

"You know what I mean, Ben. Come on."

"Well. Yes. We are on equal footing, I guess. The world is a lot more pleasant since our near disaster. And since we discovered how big the universe is. For a long time we thought that life only existed on the two planets in this solar system-- humanoid life anyway. We were pleased to discover that the universe was teaming with life. When we received your invitation from The Empire to join, we were ecstatic."

"The more I see worlds like this the more impressed I am," Tracy said. "How about you, Mary?" she asked with a wink. Maryland shrugged.

"I don't see any meaningful difference between this planet and any other one. Am I missing something that supposed to be uplifting?" Tracy frowned.

Rachel continued. "We had just about wiped ourselves out warring among ourselves and then we just about killed ourselves by changing the weather patterns and ruining the environment. After we dealt with all of that, we discovered that a comet was heading straight toward us...toward Earth any way. That pushed us to all work together. We Martians were placed here in case the attempt to save the Earth failed. Finally after millennia of fighting and near disaster, we were at peace on two planets, instead of one. That was when they introduced themselves to us and made their offer. Funny thing is, I don't think that we would have been able to accept it, if we hadn't gone through all those things."

"We were very warlike with leaders who were very paranoid," Rachel said. "Those two things are a mixture waiting to explode."

"I'm glad that you found your way," Maryland said. "We are probably the newest member of the Imperial Empire. We are a non-biological life form. We are pure energy and intellect."

"Energy and intellect," Rachel asked.

"Yes we are. I am not human. Can't you tell?"

"You're not human?" Warwick asked totally shocked. "What are you then? I thought you were an ambassador with a chip implant."

"I am a creation of the net. I am energy transmitted and infused with life. Don't you realize that?"

"No. I thought you were a woman joined to Jericho with a computer chip in your head or some other nonsense. I thought they were saying that you were becoming human because you were becoming nice." She laughed to herself.

"No. I am the chip that is in Jericho's head. I created this body by converting energy into mass. I exist because I have created myself. More accurately, the net created me to be in contact with human beings. I have to admit...that's not completely true. Jericho and I have been together since close to his birth. His personality and his Mage blood actually created me and my personality. Jericho treated me and Compu like bipeds instead of like machines. I learned that there is a place for respect in our relationship with human beings from him. The net, in turn, learned that from me."

Warwick and Bryan looked at Ben. Ben just shrugged.

"And you knew this?" Warwick asked.

"Yes, I did," Ben said. "What do you think we were talking about on the bridge? Believe me, it was a total shock to me when I first met her." He looked at Maryland. "I was threatened with death if I didn't go along with all of this and keep a secret. I'm also Jericho's friend...and Mary's now."

Bryant shook his head.

"I have to admit. I knew there was something about you Maryland and I finally found out. I would have never have guessed that," Tracy said.

"I've been saying it all the time," Mary protested.

Rachel Smiled. "What other little surprises do you Imperial folk have for us?"

"Please don't ask, Commander General," Bryant responded. "I don't think that I can handle the answer." Maryland smiled.

"So what now?" Ben asked. Warwick just looked at him and rolled his eyes before speaking.

"I guess we bury ourselves. Can you help us with that, Commander General?"

"Don't be so formal," Rachel said, smiling pleasantly. She looked at Ben for a moment, as if trying to see through him.

"Colonel Rogers will take you where you need to go. You have time off for special assignment, Rogers. See if you can bury them for say, a week or more?" She turned toward him.

"That should be sufficient," Warwick said.

"Then let's get moving," Rogers said, motioning with his hand toward the door. Maryland went first as Bryant glared at her. She paused for a moment, glanced back at him, and then continued. Tracy went next and then Ben, and finally Bryant and Warwick whispering vehemently. Rogers took up the rear.

\*                    \*                    \*

Maryland sat in the back of a van moving along a twisted road through Martian forest. They had decided to move on the ground instead of by air or subterranean. In the dense, watery forest it would be hard to follow them. Most people wouldn't really want to. The sky was cloudy and the roads were in terrible condition and getting worse all the time. It didn't really bother Maryland, but she was sure that it bothered some of the humans.

170

She could almost hear a sigh of relief as the van changed from wheel drive to hovercraft mode. It was hardly noticeable as the van began to rise on a cushion of air and the wheels tipped inward remaining underneath, like four large plates. But then they road on a smooth cushion of air.

They moved quickly and smoothly. For some reason she felt very sad. This was a new feeling. She didn't really like it. She found that she could turn it on or off, which was really amazing. She could connect with these "bipedal" feelings, or disconnect. She wondered why she felt sad. She realized that she felt sad because she thought that Bryant and Warwick were angry at her. That surprised her. Two days ago she wouldn't even have considered such a thing.

She looked up front and could see the two Ben's together in the front seat. Ben computer was talking a mile a minute of course, trying to get all the facts. In the next seat Bryant and Warwick sat, each one looking out his own side window. Tracy was sitting beside her looking out the window, in a pensive mood. Maryland closed her eyes and connected with Jericho. He seemed to be asleep. No, he was meditating or something. She wondered if she should disturb him when she heard a voice in her head.

"That you, Mary, or is this my imagination?" She smiled to herself.

"Have I become only your imagination so fast?" she asked with a smile. She could tell he picked it up.

"Really miss you," he said. "Sometimes people say that the imagination is better than the real, but in your case, I would say that you're better than anything I could possibly imagine." She smiled to herself.

"That's very sweet, Jericho." He could sense a bit of sadness.

"What's going on, Mary, are you…sad?"

"I am. Bryant and Warwick just discovered what I am. They are very upset, I think. And disappointed with me."

"I doubt that. They're probably upset with themselves because they couldn't figure it out." He chuckled a bit and then became somber. "They are some good guys. I'm sure they're all right."

"I am hoping that what you say is true, because I like them."

"I think you should let them know that then."

"Do you really?" she asked. That was an interesting idea. "Then I shall. Thank you, my love. I shall be going, but always with you."

"I love you…" he answered back. "Please don't leave me Maryland."

"We are joined, Jericho. Don't be silly."

## He Kissed Her on the Cheek
## Chapter 44

It was time for Kathleen and Bridgette to say goodbye to Jericho, for a short period of time anyway. It had only been little more than a week. Despite their verbal jousting, bickering, and complaining, Jericho discovered that he had become quite attached to both of them. To think that one of them would be his daughter in the future, or was his daughter in another dimension in the future, or whatever, was mind boggling. Yet again here she was, skin tight suit and all, packing her few personal things. She and Bridgette stood in front of the doors fumbling with their things when the door slid open. Gina was standing there with two shipmates. Jericho, uncharacteristically, walked over and put his arms around Kathleen.

"You take care of yourself," he said. She looked at him and smiled. He kissed her on the cheek lightly. She cleared her throat.

"I don't know where that came from, but I like it, Jericho. I'm sure we'll be seeing each other again soon." She looked at Gina. "I'm just sorry we couldn't see that Imperial One we were promised," she said snidely. Gina shrugged.

"You'll see her sooner or later. Those who are advanced have a different concept of time."

"Seems you do too," Bridgette said, brushing by with her small bag thrown across her shoulder. Jericho caught her by the hand on the way out and stopped her.

"You take care too, Bridgette." She smiled

"I always take care, Jerry," she said, moving closer and

172

giving him a hug. She gave him a small peck on the lips. "Keep that fire burning for me," she said with a wink. She reached up and rustled his hair. He scrunched up his face.

"You are such tease, aren't you?" he asked.

"That's what I was going to say," she shot back. The shipmates headed out the door with Kathleen and Bridgette close behind. Gina started out and then paused for a moment looking over her shoulder.

"I'll be seeing you soon. A few more hours for our stop."

He gave her a nod, "Soon." The door slid shut and he was standing there alone. He went to the small refrigerator looking for something a bit stronger than sweet water. He found some bottles of ale hidden in the back. One of those women were holding out on him. He popped the top and took a drink. It was nice and cold and bitter, just the way he liked it. He gritted his teeth.

He took a nice deep breath and sat back on the sofa. He was happy. He was really happy to have his new friends, his almost daughter, and his wife. He thought of Maryland again. She was always there. That pleased him. He did miss seeing her and touching her, but at least he could in her mind until they got back together again. He didn't want to bother her, so he kept his mind closed. She probably needed to be concentrating right now-- using all of her attention. He didn't know what the Teks had in mind, but he knew that they had shut down the net and there had been chaos for several hours. They uploaded a parallel net they had prepared long ago just for such an occasion, not being intelligent enough to know that it would be the exact same net. They didn't know that the net emanated an all prevailing field and that as long as one part of it survived all of it did. The net was so woven into the Tek Empire in its people, in its machinery and every computer that it would last forever—maybe even longer than the empire.

The net simply rebooted itself, but remained silent as it had for the last six hundred years. They would never know. He shook his head. They were so ignorant because they thought they were so intelligent. They were fighting for the right to wage war, dominate, and suppress other people's freedom and they didn't even know that was what they really wanted. They had made up many reasons. Some of them sounded quite honorable and beautiful. Some of them were right and absolutely true. It was only the underlying reasons that made them untrue.

"Music! Your choice," he said. The ships computer filled the room with soft music. He sat back and relaxed. He could feel the slight buzz of many minds and voices in his head. There weren't only one hundred there were about...he stopped and thought...On thousand thirty seven. Interesting. He took another drink, sat back, and pondered. The door buzzer rang.

"Enter," he said. An unexpected guest. A man just about his size and complexion walked in. He smiled pleasantly.

"I'm a bit late for a scheduled meeting with you," he said. Jericho arched his brows and tilted his head slightly. The man grinned broadly. "I am Roderick. I'm the Imperial One you're supposed to meet--the *ascended being* and all of that nonsense." Jericho just looked at him a few moments, and then what he said clicked.

"Oh," he said, "the higher up Imperial Ones. It's good to meet you. Come on in. I expected someone a little more...with light coming out of your head and all of that."

"Ah. Well we don't do the light thing unless we have to. You're too sophisticated for that, I think. I can pull my finger off though." He held his two hands together.

"No need for that," Jericho said. Roderick smiled.

"Ale looks good. Think I could have one?"

"Sure...come on in."

"I'll get it. I know these ships like the back of my hand," he said heading for the refrigerator. "He got his ale and plopped down into one of the seats. He popped the top. Jericho sat in a chair across from him.

"Do you think it's a coincidence that we look so much alike?" Roderick asked. He took another drink.

"Hadn't thought of it." .

"Well I didn't want to come in here with two heads or anything and scare you to death. I'm actually an energy being. Sort of like your friend Maryland. In fact, you are too, you know?"

"I know theoretically, but that's about all. I can't just float here and there and be enlightened and all of that."

"You'd be surprised what you could do. Why aren't you being processed. You could be such an asset to the Order."

"I don't know that I want to go that far with it."

"Not a joiner, eh?" Roderick asked. "That's understandable. You don't have to be one of us to make your mark on the world. In fact, what you're doing for the net and the Biots will help shape the universe in the future. And what you've done for Maryland, I can't even say enough."

"Don't get me wrong, Roderick. I didn't do anything for Maryland. Things just happened. I was a bit selfish with my cultivation of Maryland, you know?"

"You loved her. Is that wrong? Your love and tenderness toward her made her what she is today and freed the net. You are a very loving person. Don't think that it doesn't have value just because it comes naturally for you." Jericho took a drink and huffed.

"I must admit. I didn't think of it that way. The truth is that I don't think that I need to be processed for some reason."

"I think you're right," Roderick said. "This chip thing and Maryland, the biots and all that is happening will lead you anywhere we could take you. I guarantee you that you have some great adventures ahead. Some will be pleasant and some not so pleasant, but great." He leaned forward in his seat. "Do you have any questions for me, Jericho?" He leaned back.

"Yes, I do have questions for you, especially about these Biots and about the nature of the universe."

"The nature of the universe, eh? That's a duzzie. I think I need another drink before we go over that. Exactly which one are you referring too?"


## The Ground Was Always Wet
## Chapter 45


Rogers kept driving until he came to a downed tree. "Damn it!" he said. "Time to get out. This type of thing happens more and more. Soon we won't be able to drive anymore."

"What happens," Ben asked, as they disembarked. They gathered near the front of the vehicle.

"Too much rain. The ground is always wet and muddy. The trees fall over sometimes because of soil erosion." He motioned into the forest with his head. "It's also bad for the roads. The roads are horrible. Plants grow up underneath and crack them to pieces. We can't keep up with the vegetation."

"The ground doesn't seem too wet to me," Ben said.

"That's because it hasn't rained in a couple of days. We're lucky." He headed back to the vehicle, speaking of his shoulder. "Better take whatever we need. I'd like to say the car will be safe, but I really can't." He removed a small bag from the cargo hold at the rear. "Everybody isn't as peaceful as we are in Red Area. After our troublesome history there are still some violent groups around."

"Red Area? Is that what you call...where you live?"

"Oh yes. Seems that we can't give up on the idea of nations, so now we are setting up City States. Our hope is that they will be peaceful, but...you know how humans get. All of the City States are named after colors. It's really funny how we formed our nations. We just drew cards." He laughed to himself. Warwick and Bryant went to the back of the vehicle and began to unload everyone else's bags. They were really traveling light, especially Maryland, who didn't carry anything. Ben only had a few personal items. They could use chip technology to create whatever type of clothing they needed.

Warwick and Bryant were magicians who could also create clothing by magic, but why waste the energy. All that Tracy had was a small duffel bag. She had never bothered with that type of magic. They loaded up, climbed over the tree, and walked down the path. The road was so broken that it had almost deteriorated to its natural elements. Only a hovercraft could have driven on a road in such poor condition. Ben looked at it and frowned. Rogers noticed and smiled.

"Disappointed?" he asked.

"Me? No, I've just never seen a road so bad. Where I come from we don't..." He thought better of it. "Never mind."

"You from The Empire?" Rogers asked.

"No. I'm from Tek Empire. Of course they would probably consider themselves 'The Empire.'"

"It is a bit vain for someone to call themselves The Empire, Isn't it?" Rogers asked with a grin.

"I wasn't going to say it," Ben commented.

Tracy turned to Maryland. "So you're not a biped?"

Maryland scrunched up her eyebrows.

"Of course I am. Do I look like I'm crawling?"

"I don't mean that Mary! I mean…I guess they call it a human being. You're not a human being, right?"

"Yes, that is correct. I am what I am." She looked straight ahead for a moment. "I don't know exactly what that is," she said turning back toward Tracy. Tracy smiled.

"You're a biped."

"Biped…here we go with that again."

"Doesn't it suit you?"

"Yes, but…"

"Enough said then." Maryland began to argue, but figured it a waste of time. Tracy smiled when she didn't say anything.

"Do you not like me anymore, since I'm not like you?" Maryland asked.

"Of course not," Tracy said. "We're magical creatures. Our whole lives in our empire are about dealing with technology and magic. How can we not like something that is…probably greater than anything we've ever imagined. But a bit scary too."

"Is that it? Do you think people will fear me?"

"Not everyone." Maryland motioned to Bryant and Warwick with her chin.

"They haven't said a word to me since they found out." Tracy flagged them off.

"I think they're scared, Mary." She said just loud enough for them to hear. Warwick looked back at her over his shoulder.

"Was that loud comment meant for me?" he asked.

"I'm sorry," Maryland said.

"Why? You didn't say it."
Tracy turned to her.

"Don't you apologize, Maryland! They're the pigs treating you like dirt."

"Wait a minute now," Bryant said. "We're not treating her like dirt. We're just angry she didn't tell us…you should have trusted us Mary. I guess."

"You guess nothing!" Warwick said. "She should have told us." He glared at her. "You should have told us!"

"I'm sorry. I didn't know it was so important. I thought I told you two or three times. I am sincerely sorry and do want you to be my friends still. It seems that I have developed some type of affection for you."

"For me or him?" Warwick said with a tight-lipped grin. She paused before speaking.

"For both of you."

"And how deep does this affection go?" Warwick asked.

"Don't press your luck," Mary said. Bryant began to laugh.

"Well we have developed some affection for you too, Mary. I would like to be your friend very much," Bryant said.

"And you Warwick?" Tracy asked.

"I'm not sure yet. Well, yes I am. I accept your apology. Come give me a hug." He grinned and opened his arms. She stepped forward and they embraced. Next she hugged Bryant.

"That's better," Tracy said.

"I enjoyed it," Warwick said with a wink.

"A pig," Maryland said brushing passed them and moving up to the front of the group. He laughed to himself. Tracy grinned too. "She is a delight isn't she? Especially since we know why she acts so weird. I thought she was just crazy."

"I heard that!" Maryland said shouting over her shoulder. Tracy wondered what she couldn't hear or know, being an extension of that omnipresent computer. She could sense that computer's presence and they were in a different galaxy. She was, after all, a connector. That's why she was so curious about Maryland from the beginning, but she would have never guessed that Maryland had not been *born of the flesh.*

\*                    \*                    \*


They continued through the thick forest on foot following the wide path that used to be a paved road. Maryland could see how the forest had reclaimed it. The farther they went, the narrower the path. She felt rather pleasant. She would have even considered the feeling, happy. She actually felt something in her heart, and it was happiness. She smiled to herself. Why not be happy having the best of both worlds? She could feel all of these emotions or just turn them off and become completely sterile if she liked. She grinned even more and then felt strange for a moment. She turned her head and saw Warwick watching her

178

through narrowed eyelids. She wondered what she had felt. How had she known he was watching?"

"What are you watching, Warwick?" she asked. He grinned.

"I just can't believe it," he said in his usually loud way. "I was hoping you would have my children." Bryant began to laugh. Maryland didn't know what to say.

"Don't even bother answering that," Tracy interjected. "I just don't know what your problem is, Warwick!"

"I was only joking."

"I don't think that's funny!"

"I thought it was hilarious," Bryant said.

"Why can't you too be like…like Ben. Like the two Ben's," Tracy said. "Look at them. They're so somber and intelligent. You two act like two teens or something." Bryant brought his hand to his chest.

"I can't believe that you said that. Maybe you and I need to talk in private."

"I don't have anything to talk with you about, Bryant. Especially in private, you lecher. I know what that look in your eyes mean."

"You have me wrong. I'm sincere," he said.

"Is this the human banter I've heard about from the net," Maryland asked. "Some type of mating ritual or something?" Bryant looked down for a moment. He looked very embarrassed.

"What's wrong?" Maryland asked. "Did I say something wrong?"

"Ask Bryant," Tracy said with a wicked grin. "Is that what it is Bryant? Is this some kind mating ritual? You presenting yourself to me or something?" He looked up at her, began to speak and then just turned and walked faster, catching up with Warwick. Tracy began to laugh under her breath. Warwick looked at him and grinned.

"What are you grinning for?" Bryant asked.

"What are you grinning for, Captain," Warwick boomed back. He grinned a little more. Bryant began to snicker to himself and shook his head.

"That Tracy is one cold woman," he said just loud enough for Warwick to hear.

"I don't know," Warwick said. "She didn't seem to object

too much to the mating ritual thing. Maybe it's working." He looked at Warwick to see if he was serious. Warwick gave him a firm nod. He turned and looked at Tracy over his shoulder. She glared at him.

He turned away quickly and leaned closer to Warwick. "Maybe it is working," he said quietly. The sky opened up with a crack of thunder and heavy, cold rain poured down.

*    *    *

"I was afraid that would happen," Rogers said, digging into his shoulder bag. "Get on your rain gear folks, this is probably going to last for a couple of weeks."

"Weeks!" Ben asked. He closed his eyes for a moment. "With a thought his clothing changed into a waterproof rain-suit. Tracy rummaged through her bag, as did Warwick and Bryant. "Oh hell!," Bryant said. "I'll just…"

"Don't do it. You know that's scary to people who don't have magic," Warwick said. "You know the code." Maryland looked at Tracy, Warwick and Bryant digging through their bags and letting all of their other clothing get wet. She closed her eyes for a second. When she opened them they were all dressed in rain gear.

"You do that Bryant? The code…remember!"

"I didn't do it." He looked at Maryland.

"I did it, and to blazes with your silly code!" She marched passed them walking quickly.

"You have to take the code," Warwick said rushing behind her while stuffing things into his bag. "The code says that magic planets can't use it in Non-Imperial galaxies."

"I thought you said this was Imperial," Ben said.

"It is, but you have to get used to not using that stuff for when you get in galaxies and on planets that don't know anything about it. We only use it when necessary." Maryland looked at him and pursed her lips. "Well Mary?"

"It makes sense, for humans. I assure you, however, that I will know when to use magic and not. As for this code, this is the first I've ever heard of it. I only use it when necessary anyway."

"Well. You're part of my crew now, so live by the code."

"I don't remember joining your crew," She said.

180

"When you hired me to keep your butt safe you became a part of my crew!"

"Oh aren't we huffy and angry suddenly," Maryland said. Warwick's anger just drained out of him and he stood there with his hands on his hips and with a blank stare. He couldn't believe this woman. He decided to try to say it another way.

"Mary," he said, "for the sake of The Empire and so that I can hide you and protect you sometime in the future maybe, I would appreciate it if you could cut down on the use of magic, or whatever you may call it, as much as possible. Especially on strange planets. Can you do that?"

"Of course I can do that, Warwick."

"Will you do that?"

"I will consider it and let you know later."

"That's all I ask, Mary. Thank you."

"You are very welcome. I'm sorry if I upset you. Have I?"

"No, Mary. I upset myself."

"That is very astute, Warwick. I thought you would blame your anger on me. Very esoteric."

"Yes it is Mary. And thank you for considering…"

"Oh hell," she said. "I will go along with it."

"That's good."

"I'm just happy to have a rain-suit. I was getting drenched," Tracy said. "Most of my clothes got soaked. It'll take a long time for them to dry unless we can find a drier. How' bout you Warwick, Bryant?"

"Yeah, yeah, yeah, the same thing," Warwick said. She looked at Bryant. He just smiled at her. She lifted the corner of her mouth ever so slightly and turned away. She looked back at him.

"On second thought I think we need to have that private talk," she said. "Come with me." She headed down a narrow path cutting off in the woods. Bryant followed wondering what was going to happen.

"Just wait here for a few minutes!" he hollered as a second thought. The woods were thick and the wind was picking up. He looked up at the large trees and plants. Long leaves draped over the narrow path giving only a brief glimpse of sleight gray skies, ever so often. He looked up for a moment and thought how depressing this planet could be. He looked ahead. Tracy was moving fast.

"Wait a minute, Trace!" He jogged to catch up and she waited. When he got close she started walking again. They got a small clearing and she leaned up against a tree. Bryant didn't really know what to expect. She was a soldier after-all. He didn't know anything about women who were soldiers, or about female dominant societies. This was all new to him.

She leaned up against a tree as he approached. She looked right into his eyes when he got close enough.

"Bryant...what are you doing?" She asked. He didn't know what to say, so she continued. "Are you trying to make a pass at me or something, or playing some kind of game?"

He had never seen a woman so blunt in his life. It was a bit refreshing. "I'm not playing any game with you. I'm..." He figured he might as well be as blunt too. "I'm interested in you. I'm just a little nervous about it. What happens if you can't stand me and we have to see each other face to face for the next three or four months...maybe even years." She looked at the ground and grinned.

She looked up. "Sounds like you've been in the service before," she said. "Except in the service we don't worry about that before anything happens, we wonder about it afterward. Or if something is definitely going to happen." She walked toward him. "You don't have to worry about that Bryant." She placed her hand on his shoulder and arched her brows. He looked confused, which made her smile brightly. "I'm trying to say that there is a chance that something could happen. You don't have to worry about me. I'm a grown woman. I can handle things if they don't work out, but I have to be sure from the beginning that this is not just a game with you. You understand?"

"Yes, I do."

"Well?"

"Well what?"

"Is this just a game, or is this something serious?"

"Something serious, I hope. That depends on you, I guess."

"On me? How about you?"

"It depends on both of us, I guess. I can tell you that I have serious intentions. I admire you and respect you. I think you look great too—secondarily, that is." She arched her brows, he continued. "I would like to try. Would you like to try?"

"We'll talk about it. In the meantime, no more strange looks, smiles or all that...ok?"

"Ok. I'm sorry it wasn't my intention to offend you."

"No offense taken, just distraction. It's just that I don't think we can afford to be distracted on the mission that we're on. Things are getting dangerous so we have to keep our heads cool. That's something you learn as a seventh generation officer. That doesn't mean that we can't let down our protocol when we're alone though...off duty. Do you know what I'm saying?"

"I understand completely, and look forward to letting down our protocol together." She smiled.

"I look forward to it too." She looked back down the trail. "I think we'd better get back. How' bout you?"

"I think so too." He gestured toward the trail with the side of his head. "Are we ready?" She gave a nod and led the way.

*     *     *

The rain was hard; the hardest many of them had ever experienced. Maryland had never experienced rain personally, but she had experienced it many times vicariously through Jericho and this was an altogether different experience. She was surprised that any bipedal life form could live in such a downpour without drowning. She looked around and watched the trees bobbing, swaying in the wind, and dancing to the strong gusts of win far overhead.

The rain poured in sheets making what had been firm trails into puddles of mud and small streams more like a swamp. They tromped there way through following Rodgers. Everyone was quiet, mostly because the sound of the wind and rain were deafening. They marched on for several hours before taking a break. Rogers had everyone stop near one of the large trees. He produced a knife that looked like a machete from his back pack and went into the woods cutting down the broad leaves from the low hanging plants. He returned with a small pile and began to weave them by the large stems, somehow, into something that resembled a thatch. Maryland was greatly pleased.

"So beautiful, Rogers, where did you learn such a thing?"

she asked. He looked at her over his shoulder as he continued to work and smiled.

"Just something you learn when you live on a rainy planet," he said offhandedly. He surveyed the face of the others. "I guess that you realize by now that this place can be outright dangerous if you're caught out here with no gear." Warwick looked up into the rain.

"Sure can see that. I don't think I could stand living in such a place. A nice shower every once in a while is good, but this is a little ridiculous. I didn't know clouds could hold this much."

"You'd be surprised how much they can hold," Rogers said, as his pile of leaves began to resemble a large, flat roof. "This is the best I can do. We can connect it to four bushes and have a seat for a few minutes anyway—get out of the rain. I have some fire blocks with me and a little trail food."

"We can make all of that we need," Maryland said. Warwick looked at her through slits.

"You know what I told you," Maryland. We have to hold off on the magic." She just looked at him. "You promised me Maryland."

"This is different, Warwick, we are…this is part of The Empire."

"We have to get used to not using it so we won't when we are not in The Empire!"

"Ok Warwick! If you want to get soaking wet and want to be cold and starve, what can I do about it? I don't."

"We have other options," Rogers said cutting in, sensing the ensuing argument. "I have food, we have fire, we have shelter," he grinned. "And we have good company." Warwick flattened his lips.

"You don't agree with him, Warwick," Maryland asked.

"Of course I do, Mary. Why would you even ask that?"

"I am not sure. It was just the look on your face."

"My face is fine!"

"All right, Warwick. Don't get huffy on me." He looked up and shook his head.

"Can I help you with that," he said approaching Rogers and ducking out of the conversation.

"Sure can. Let's just find some bushes close to each other

and I'll strap this thing to them. The more dry the ground the better."

"Do you have a cover cloth for the ground?" Tracy asked. "I have one on my pack."

"No. I'm glad that you do. That could really come in handy." Ben looked at her and smiled.

"I'm a soldier, Remember?" She said. He nodded.

"It's hard to remember sometimes, but I remember...you don't seem like a soldier."

"And what does a soldier seem like," she said putting her hands on her hips.

"I don't know." He thought for a moment. "Well...a bit boisterous and rowdy...always looking for trouble. You don't seem like that."

"I am an officer, you know?"

"I guess that explains it then," Bryant said.

"You bet it does," Rogers said. "Now let's get this thing up." He and Warwick took it by the opposite edges trying not to move it hard enough to break it. Ben joined them on one end and Bryant on the other. Tracy began to look for some good plants while Maryland rummaged through Tracy's bag looking for a cover cloth. She thought it was ridiculous. Why not just make one with chip technology? She finally found it after just about everything in the bag got soaked. She was thinking about just using a bit of magic and drying it, but then she remembered her promise to Warwick. She sighed out loud, thinking how ridiculous the bipeds were sometimes.

"Here we are," she said, following them out into the woods with the cover cloth. With all of the vegetation it wasn't difficult to find several plants bunched together. Rogers pulled out his machete and began to remove all of the extras until he had created a large square area in the middle of a lot of greenery. Ben and Warwick began to connect the leaf tarp to the plants while Rogers spread out the cover cloth with the help of Maryland and Tracy. It was much larger than Mary had imagined. It covered the whole cutout area and a bit more. The leaves did a good job at breaking the rain. They crawled under the thatched roof.

"It's fire proof," Tracy said. "You don't have to worry about making a fire." Rogers seemed very pleased.

"I'm glad about that. That'll save us a lot of time and

grief." He dug two cubes from his pack that were about four inches on every side. He struck them together and the places that he struck ignited and began to burn. He quickly set them in the center of the cover cloth. Everyone began to gather around and warm their hands and faces except for Tracy, who went off into the woods gathering wood. It was wet, but the fire blocks burned hot enough to dry them easily. By the time she was finished they had a large fire going. People began to remove their shoes and try to dry their cold, wet feet.

"My feet are wet," Maryland said, as if surprised.

"Yes, they look that way," Tracy answered. Bryant grinned. Tracy looked at him and winked.

"But my boots are waterproof."

"Well you probably sweat in your boots and made your socks wet," Bryant said.

"But it's cold out here," she complained.

"Not in your boots though," He said.

"I didn't even know that I sweated. This is all amazing. I think I'm becoming a little more human than I like. It's scary. Next thing you know I'll be going to the bathroom."

"You don't go to the bathroom!" Warwick boomed. "What happens to what you eat?" She shrugged.

"I burn it up, I guess."

"You must have a heck of a metabolism," he said. "Or you're just full of crap." He grinned, especially when she frowned.

"I am not full of crap, Warwick! As for my sanitary habits, you shouldn't even be mentioning them in mixed company."

"Really? Am I embarrassing you?"

"I don't embarrass, unless I want to. I don't do anything that I don't want to do, including going to the bathroom." Rogers began to chuckle. "And what are you laughing at?" She asked.

"I've never met anyone who didn't do anything they didn't want to do, or anyone who would admit they were full of crap!"

"I'm not full of anything! I would also appreciate it if you would change the subject. You men are all pigs. You are all so impolite. You're nothing like Jericho." Ben began to smile. "And what is that smile for?"

"If anyone is a pig it's Jericho."

"You're his best friend, Ben!"

186

"That's how I know."

"Anybody hungry?" Rogers asked.


## While Her Parents Slept
## Chapter 46

Jericho looked out of the side view-screen. He could tell
that they were moving fast, because all that he could see was the
white glare of null space. His head was spinning, since his talk
with the Imperial One. The man seemed to know everything and
every answer that he gave him spiraled into a thousand other
questions. He continued to look at the view-screen as he thought
about the conversation. He began understand how all of this could
drive a person crazy…just looking out there into glaring
nothingness after that conversation was about to do it for him. He
thought about himself, his life, and how it had changed so rapidly.
Visions of Maryland came up, and then sank lower just beneath
his consciousness. He knew that he had access to her and to her
senses anytime he wanted, but he wanted to give her some
privacy.

His life had changed drastically. Here he was streaking
across the skies to Berrundi, a planet he had never heard of further
away than he thought possible because he was passing through
multiple galaxies. There were thousands of voices…more like
points of awareness in his head. They threatened to overwhelm
him any minute, but it seemed they were staying silent because
they knew they could do that. It was like a child trying to creep
around while her parents slept and only doing a good job of it half
the time.

Gina came into the ready room just off of the main bridge
and looked at the view-screen. "Strange isn't it Jerry--streaking
through space so fast that it becomes null space?"

"That's Jericho," he found himself saying more quickly
than he expected.

"I stand corrected," Gina said, with a "get a life," tone to
her voice. "You should have said something the other two
hundred times I called you that."

He softened up a little bit. He seemed to be turning like

Maryland; getting quick tempered. He lifted a hand. "Jerry is all right, Gina. I'm sorry. The computer stuff in my head is just affecting me." She looked concerned. She moved closer and took a seat across from him.

"Do you need to see a doctor or something? You must be under a lot of stress. Nobody has ever done anything like you're doing. There's no way to know what it could be doing to your head."

"No...I'm fine, Gina. Believe me. Thanks for your concern anyway," he said forcing a smile. "I think a big part of it is just this horrible glare of null space. It, along with everything else, is really giving me a headache." He began to massage his temples.

"I'm sorry, Jericho. Hopefully this will all be over soon."

"I don't know about the voices, but I can end this bright light." He hit a button and the view-screen went black. Gina grinned.

"Good idea." She stood. "You just sit here and I'll get you some strong tea, ok?"

"All right, Gina. Thank you so much." He watched as she left the room. He began to wonder about these female dominant planets. Gina was giant and strong, not what he would call feminine at all, but she had a heart of gold. He began to wonder about the whole idea of gender...especially the importance of it. He laid back and closed his eyes. For the first time in more than a week he accessed his chip looking for a good novel. The chip projected the pages of the book onto his retinas and he began to read. It looked like one of the old mystery novels from more than one thousand years ago. He loved those. He figured that the chip had put the types of books that he liked into various categories that corresponded to moods. Whenever he was pensive—a good mystery novel. Before he had read the first page it vanished. He knew that someone had just entered. Captain Russok was carrying a folded sheet of plastic under her arm that looked like a news printout. In the other hand she carried what looked like a piece of sweetbread.

She smiled and gave Jericho a nod. "Good to see you, Jericho. You've finally come out of that cabin. I thought we'd have to send someone to drag you out. This is a beautiful ship. You should see more of it."

"It is beautiful, Captain. I've just been dealing with a lot of changes lately. My whole little world has been turned upside down."

"The Empire has a tendency of doing that." She unfolded the sheet of plastic and began to read. She paused and looked up. "This is something you have to see. Imagine a newspaper that covers more than 1,000 galaxies. Talk about competitive. I wonder how they choose who to put in everyday."

"Probably graft," he said with a smile. She arched her brows. "Probably bribes," he said. She frowned and then began to smile.

"Oh. You're joking."

"Yes. I was just joking."

"Don't worry. I'm sure that your joke was funny. Joking is not a custom where I come from. I'm still trying to get used to it."

"That's difficult to believe. You mean you don't have joking."

"Of course not. Language is sacred to us. It's only used for two things: worship and passing on information." He didn't comment and she noticed. "That sounds strange to you, Jericho?"

"Not really. I can understand that. Some people on Tek would probably suit your planet well."

"Well I am beginning to like this joking, when I get it anyway." Jericho grinned.

"What?" she asked.

"That was pretty funny."

"Was it? Fascinating." She began to read again. She stopped and punched her com-link. "Mess, could you have someone bring up some reya to my ready room please?" She looked at Jericho. "Would you like something?"

"No thanks," Gina just went for some tea for me. The captain looked at him strangely. "Oh…Gina…eh?" She nodded a couple of times and began to read again.

"I don't like the way that sounds. What does that mean Captain?" She shook her head.

"Nothing."

"What do you mean nothing? I can see that you're getting at something."

"That's a mating ritual on her planet. Didn't you see that

she's from a female dominated society?  They don't do anything for males.  When they bring you gifts and do things like that, and you accept them…you are accepting *them*."

"I'm married.  She knows that."

"Doesn't matter on her planet."  He thought for a moment.

"Oh.  I like her a lot.  I don't want to hurt her feelings, but I am married…happily."

"Um hum," the Captain answered.

"I'm serious Captain.  She's a beautiful woman but…"

"Who's a beautiful woman," Gina said entering the room with a tray.  "I brought your reya too, Captain, since I was down there."  The Captain started to grin.  "I don't believe it.  You've been telling him that lie about mating rituals again, haven't you?"  The Captain laughed under her breath.  "I don't believe you Captain Russok.  You're supposed to be a captain."  The Captain looked at him and smiled.

"I told you that I was working on my joking," she laughed.  He couldn't help to join in with her.  He shook his head.

"You sure had me going on that one, Captain.  I was really worried."

"Am I that bad?  Here's your tea," Gina said.

"No, you're not bad at all.  You know that.  I like you.  I also have a wife though."

"Well you could leave her," Gina said.  "You should have been delighted."

"I can't win for losing, can I Gina?"

"You've got that right, Jericho.  You're wrong no matter what you say on this ship anyway."  She gave Captain Russok a wink and they both began to smile.


# The Nature of Null Space
# Chapter 47


Phaedra sat in her seat breathing heavily.  For a few moments she thought that she was going to lose consciousness.

"I can't believe it Phaedra, but we're out of null space," Berry said.  Phaedra's usually dark countenance lit up into a smile as beautiful as the sunrise."

"Are we locked onto that second ship?" she asked.

"Yes we are, Phaedra, but how did you do it?" She stood up and looked at the forward screen.

"I guess you just have to really know the nature of null space," she said. "Thanks to our queen, I'm probably the most familiar person in the galaxy." She looked around the bridge and saw some slightly upturned lips, but no one dare smile. She put on a crooked one herself. She turned to Berry, "First, the bridge is yours. I'll be in my cabin for some recoup time. That little magic trick took a little more out of me than I expected."

"Aye, aye, Captain," Berry said. She headed for the elevator. "Captain," he said over his shoulder. She paused and looked back. "Great transducing Ma am, probably the best I've ever seen."

"Thanks First. Make sure, if at all possible, not to lose that ship. Our queen is on that ship. We had to choose between her and the mediator. I hope that we made the right choice." She turned as the doors slid open and walked into the elevator. They closed and it began to descend to the residential floors. The bridge crew began to look at each other.

"How the hell did she do that? No one has ever been able to do that, but the Imperial Ones," the Second said.

"She was out there all that time," the First replied. He shrugged. "Maybe it changed her. It's the most amazing thing that I've ever seen. Maybe I'll have to go out there sometimes." He grinned.

"First you have to find out how to get there," the Second retorted with a grin. The bridge crew began to talk among themselves.

\*             \*             \*

Phaedra stumbled into her cabin and lay on the bed fully clothed. It took all of the energy she had just to kick off her shoes. She looked at the picture of Kathleen Del Sol that sat on her night stand to remind her of how much a fool she had been. She had challenged her without knowing her identity and it had almost coasted her life. She wouldn't make that mistake again. She lay back on the bed and looked at the ceiling. She had pledged her loyalty to Kathleen just like most of the other military families on the Light Burner. She was going to make sure that Kathleen stayed alright even if it meant tracking the Imperial Ones back to their home planet, if they had one.

The Imperial Ones in this dimension were just like the ones in the other dimension—very secretive and self serving. She wondered if they were the ones who caused the dimensional shift, or who showed the Magi in this galaxy how to do it. She couldn't imagine Magi, especially in a Tek Empire under the scrutiny of that net, or whatever they called it, being able to formulate a plan and practice it enough to move five or six planets across dimensions.

She decided that it must have been the Imperial Ones. For just one brief moment she felt the net go down. All of the static was gone. She quickly shifted her awareness to Prime World, the center of Tek Empire. She hit her comm button.

"Aye, aye Captain," Berry said.

"That shield is down, Berry. Get as many transducers as you can to explore that net and this empire!"

"I'm on it." The comm link went dead.

After about five turns the shield came up again, but not before they got the information that they needed. Tek Empire was afraid. They were being confronted with powers they had never encountered. She also discovered that Del Sol had been chased and had disappeared. For some reason Del Sol was with the Imperial Ones for some type of new process, according to Tek top secret records. That's all she could get. She began to wonder what it meant as she slowly succumbed to her need to sleep. She was soon enveloped by darkness.

# Perhaps They Had Changed
# Chapter 48

Jericho went back to his cabin and lay on the sofa. It was very quiet without Bridgette and Kathleen. He was all alone again, with only Ale to keep him company, and his chip, of course. Now the chip was very rudimentary. It didn't have Maryland's personality anymore; it was just another chip. He wondered if he could have it project another image, but then backed off from that idea completely. No one could replace Maryland. He laid back propped on one elbow and took another sip of ale. He felt relaxed and peaceful, perhaps for the first time in years. Since he, Maryland and Ben had begun this strange little trip he had felt more alive than ever. He had never considered that he might be the adventurous type. Perhaps he had been wrong.

If things went well, maybe he would stay with Warwick and Bryant; Ben sure seemed to want that. Jericho knew he could never go back to his old life on Tek First Prime. He didn't know what to expect there anymore. He was unsure of the future of the whole galaxy. He shook his head thinking about it. He only hoped they would go along with the Imperial Ones, even if it was only for a while. That would at least buy them time and let them know how much power they were dealing with. He wondered if the Teks were as violent as he thought. When he thought of them he thought of the Tek Empire as it was more than 600 years ago. Perhaps they had changed. There was nothing to support the idea that they were warlike, except their treatment of the Magi, of course. He hadn't even noticed that until he left the planet and began to talk with others. Maybe the Teks would join The Empire. He shrugged as he wondered what his former mentor, Shubrick, would do.

Shubrick was the one who oversaw the whole empire. For some reason he had taken and interest in Jericho's progress very early and was always there with financial support as well as moral support to see that he prospered. He had been around for a long time. He had been close to his father and his grandfather. He liked Shubrick, but never saw enough of him. He knew that the ruler of the whole empire didn't have time to deal with him. They often communicated through chip technology, which was just about the same as face to face, but that all suddenly ended. He wondered if it had to do with him being the…mediator, they called it. Shubrick had to be aware of it and for some reason Shubrick had agreed with using Jericho as bait to capture the queen of the Magi.

\*               \*               \*

Shubrick was awake again. He looked at the clock. It was pass midnight and he couldn't sleep. He reached over instinctively to touch his wife before her realized she wasn't there. She had died more than two hundred years ago. He sighed, remembering how she had given up. She decided not to do anymore Tek life extensions: no cloning, no robotics, nothing. She thought it was just time for her to die after a life of 230 years. Shubrick often wondered if she made the right decision.

Here he was more then six hundred years old and wondering if her were still human. He had seen it all and had done it all. Nothing surprised him; nothing shocked him or moved him. He didn't know if he wasn't moved because of his age or because of all of the artificial parts. It was difficult to tell. He sighed audibly.

"Music!" he said, sending a command through his chip. A soft piece of music began to play in the background. "Lights," he said. The lights brightened slowly to the perfect setting that would allow his eyes to adjust without strain. He threw his covers off and got out of bed. In the corner of the bedroom there was a large sink and a mirror. He walked over, splashed water on his face, and reached for the towel. He dried his face and looked into the mirror. He looked young, too young. He knew that he was old. Maybe it was time for him to die. He had seen too many horrible things and thought that he would see another.

First the computer came to life as the fearful idiots, as they were now called, from six hundred years ago had predicted. He wondered if the Magi had anything to do with it. These new Magi seemed to be much more comfortable with technology. The net had told them that these Magi were from another dimension where the Magi had won the war. The galaxy had survived. There hadn't been a slaughter of the Tek civilization, and the new Magi had also made progress with technology. All the fears that the Teks had fought against in this dimension had turned out only as fear in the other dimension. He wondered if they could have at least considered that before the two hundred fifty year war. Why hadn't anyone bended, or negotiated? He shook his head.

He remembered good people on both sides dying. What was it all for, because everyone was afraid of something new happening? And there he was, right in the middle. He felt good about the fact that he at least tried to mediate peace. To no avail, yes, but at least he had tried. But then, after the war started and there was no going back he chose his side. He became a leader in the Tek Command and saw to the death of millions and millions of Magi galaxy wide. He scratched the side of his head thinking of all the blood on his hands. Why was he thinking about this now? He hated it.

"More music," he grumbled to his chip. "Sleep induction protocol." The music got a bit louder. "No sleep induction," a gentle voice said. "You have used sleep induction protocol too many times. We suggest you visit a doctor or..."

"Ok!" he said, cutting off the voice. He didn't know why the computer was worrying. It wasn't going to hurt *it*.

"Don't be silly," a small voice said. "If I allow you to hurt yourself I will be hurt too. You know that."

He pinched the arch of his nose between his forefinger and thumb.

"Upset?" the chip asked.

"No...just tired. I can't sleep."

"Too many worries? Let me show you a film." Shubrick gave an internal nod and lay back on the bed. Soft music played as a very slow movie came on. It was more dreadful and powerful than the sleep inducement. He soon drifted off to an uneasy sleep.

## If Anyone Else Noticed
## Chapter 49

The Premier's troubled sleep was worthless. Shubrick awakened to the sound of an alarm chip frowning. He wondered what had happened to Jericho. He had followed his career for decades before he broke his connection. Now he didn't even know if Jericho was alive. He always thought of him like a son. Even this wasn't allowed. He knew that Jericho would always be in danger if he were associated with him; everyone would have known that he was a direct descendant of the last emperor.

People would have asked questions about Jericho. He had questions himself, at first, but as Jericho, his father, and his father matured he could see whose descendant Jericho was for himself. Damned if they all didn't look just like the emperor of the whole Mage Empire. What would have happened if anyone else noticed? There had been peace for a long time, but no one would forget the pain and suffering caused by the war. It was so long ago. He had lived for so many centuries along with those who desired to extend their lives, but even with the longer life spans and the greater increase of knowledge and wisdom prejudice and anger still existed. Maybe most of the newborns had forgotten about it and wouldn't recognize Jericho, but the old bloods could recognize him. He was a leftover from a war that shouldn't have happened.

He threw back his covers and said "reya.." He could hear the machine come on. So here he was, still trying to protect people from the fractious results of a stupid war that shouldn't have happened. Jericho had loved him and trusted him. He only hoped that Jericho didn't find out that he was being used as a bait. He slammed his fist into his palm and remembered, that damn computer had gone haywire. Of course Jericho knew. Maybe that damn computer figured a way to spirit him off the planet. He had to check all of the travel records. He only hoped they weren't lost with the rebutting process. He rushed out of bed and headed for the shower. He had to get dressed as fast as he could and get in to the office. On his way to the shower another thought—Ben was gone. After years and years of faithful service he had just disappeared. Why had it taken him so long to figure this out? Ben had to be with him. They were best friends!

## With Knives and Forks
## Chapter 50

Ben began to laugh. Mary looked at him and frowned. That made him laugh more. "Grace Mary, why are you so upset," he said between guffaws. "I can't believe that..." He started to laugh again.

"That's not funny. You stop that noise Ben. I thought you had manners."

"I do Mary, and I love you to death, but you can't expect

196

us to eat with knives and forks out on the trail. You can't cut a hard bread stick with a plasticized butter-knife!" He began to laugh again. Everyone else joined in, except Tracey, who choked back a smile.

"It's not that funny guys... now come on. You know she has to learn these things, and this isn't helping."

"I'm sorry," Ben said, "but...no. I'm just sorry Mary. I shouldn't have laughed like that."

"Sorry hell," Warwick said. "That was the stupidest thing I ever saw—breaking that bread stick to pieces with a butter knife and then throwing it away without eating it. I thought Rogers was going to explode!" They started to laugh again. Warwick began to wipe the tears from his eyes. Mary just sat there.

"I don't think that it's that funny," she said. She looked totally pacified...not a bit of anger coming through. She picked one up with her finger and bit it. She chewed and then swallowed. "See. It tastes just as good without utensils, I guess. Why do you use them if it tastes just as good without them?" Tracy grinned before answering.

"You just use them so your hands don't get messy, I guess. I've never really thought about it. If your hands are dirty too, I guess. You don't want the food dirty." She shrugged. Rogers nodded.

"I guess that's it," he said. "I've never really thought about it," choking back laughter. "I'm sorry I was so upset, I just thought that we might be out here long enough to run out of food, so I wanted to keep all we had."

"We shall make more food if we run out," she said flagging him off. "We are rich. We can have everything in the world. Why do you bipeds, as you call yourselves, pretend as if you have nothing when you have everything?"

"For the adventure!" Warwick said. Everyone turned their attention on him. He shrugged. "I guess."

"It's just habit," Bryant said. "I'm just glad that you're here to remind us of that."

"Don't you worry. I will continue to remind you of that."

"That's what I'm afraid of," Warwick said. There was a moment of silence. Rogers picked up another bread stick and a tin of some type of meat that no one there had ever tasted before. He looked up and saw all eyes on him.

"We're only a few miles from Blue Area. After we get a little rest we'll make our way there and get out of the rain. We can probably disappear there for a few days at least. Our city states are pretty insular and Tek Empire has nothing to do with us, especially since we are Imperial territory now. Even though I don't even know if they know about us, or the Imperial Ones.

"I hope they don't come rushing in and cause a war," Ben said.

"I will be one step ahead of them all the time," Mary said. "Let's hope they don't discover us. Who knows what The Empire's response would be."

"Don't worry about that, the Imperial Ones can handle things pretty well. Believe me," Rogers said. "They're not the ones we have to worry about for now—we have to worry about the Blues. There are a bunch of renegades in that area. Given the chance, who knows what they would do? We have to play it cool and get in contact with the officials as fast as possible while we avoid the criminal element. We'll wait a couple of hours and then go in right before night fall when all of the excursion parties are returning. I know a lot of the security forces and armed forces. They'll take us in with them." He took another bite off his bread stick.

In the mean time, lets keep eating, drinking, and being merry," he said. Maryland peered at him. "Not Mary," he corrected, "Merry—happy."

"I understand," she said. "I was just...how do you say it... joking?"

"Good heavens!" Warwick exclaimed.

## With All the Latest Technology
## Chapter 51

Jane scratched the side of her head while Shubrick waited. She was the new Lead Transducer in the office of the Executive Director of First Prime. He didn't want to stare, so he began to scan the members of the Tek Empire high council seated around the large black-stone table. Jane cleared her throat before speaking, just to get his attention.

"If what you say is true, Director Shubrick, we have a big problem. Just think of the problems we've been having with the chips. Jericho, as I remember, is a Chip Information Technology Professor and Benjamin is one of the most adept Transducers that we have with all the latest technology. They could hack into the net, no?"

Dr. Lawrence, a squirrelly looking man at the end wearing dark rimmed glasses, a large, white lab-coat, and breast pocket filled with a pocket protector full of writing props became pensive for a moment before speaking. He didn't need to wear glasses or carry writing props, but on Tek Prime such clothing was a fashion statement to denote respectability and intelligence.

"I think this is far beyond the capability of either of those men," he said. "This had to be an anomaly. The computer came to life...for God's sake. They couldn't do that!"

"Came to life?" Shubrick asked. "It didn't come to life, it admitted that it had already been alive." He turned to Jane. "I think it was just a coincidence, Jane."

"I agree." Carol said, from the far end of the table. She was the cabinet officer in charge of Tek Empire Intelligence. She had her feelers out into every corner of the whole empire. Shubrick didn't even know what she had access to, and he had been the Director of the Empire for more than two hundred years. He sat back in his seat wondering if she would share any of her...so secret information. He tried not to look irritated. She reached up and brushed a large lock of brown hair from in front of her face before speaking. He wondered if she were doing it just to annoy him. There was a brief moment that seemed like hours to him.

"We have reports of ships flying in to Tek Empire from outside of the three galaxies." Shubrick arched his brows. She lifted the corner of her mouth. "It seems that we are not alone."

Dr. Lawrence sat back, removed his glasses, and tossed them on the table. " Do we have any idea who they are?"

"We have an idea," she said.

The Defense Secretary Bickford spoke. He was a stout man, very dark with thick hair. He reminded Shubrick of a shorter version of Jericho. "And when were you going to share that with us?" he asked, very subdued. She looked at him and smiled. Bickford frowned a bit. "How long have you known this?" he asked more sharply than he expected. She just looked entertained. Shubrick thought she had too much power. She sat thinking for a moment, as if deciding whether she to answer or not, until she noticed Shubrick, Jane, the Doctor, and the Secretary glaring too.

She looked down at the table for a moment to gather her thoughts and then met their eyes again person by person. "We have known of The Empire for more than 300 years," she said. There was silence. Shubrick waited for someone else to raise the question. Since no one else would, he asked.

"And who is The Empire?"

"It is a vast number of planets...a vast number of galaxies joined together in a federation. They are held together by a group of highly advanced beings called the Imperial Ones. There goal, like that of any Empire in theory, is to create peace and to resolve all the ills of the bipeds." Shubrick just grunted.

"What's wrong Mr. Director?" Jane asked.

"If that's true we're lost. That's what's wrong. We can't conquer a vast number of galaxies." He looked at Carol.

"You want more," she said.

"How observant."

"The Imperial Ones are a highly evolved race who took it upon themselves to create a peaceful empire. They became beings of energy and light. They were so highly evolved that they saw the folly of all of the bipeds and decided to change it by changing them. They are for peace and against all forms of war, except wars fought to free people from tyranny."

"Tyranny," Lawrence repeated back. "That's a tricky word. One man's tyranny is another man's order. Who defines what tyranny is?"

"They do," she said flatly. "They are so evolved they feel they have the right to say so, along with representatives from the thousands of galaxies they conquered, that is."

"How do they reconcile that they are conquering galaxies while they claim to be peaceful," Bickford asked.

"Probably the same way we do," Jane replied, which drew all of their attention. Shubrick tried to fight back a smile. Instead he said, "That wasn't very helpful." He looked at Bickford. "What are you thinking, Bick?"

"We could give them a run for their money."

Lawrence bristled, "How do you think we can defeat thousands of galaxies? Do you know what weapons they must have? These Imperial things aren't even human anymore."

"Let's not talk about war yet; that's the last thing we want to think about," Shubrick said. ""First we have to know what they want. When we know their abilities and their intentions we can begin to talk about getting into a multi-galactic war or not. I don't know if I have the stomach for it."

"It's about time someone around this table began to show a bit of intelligence," Jan said. Bickford shook his head. Shubrick didn't comment.

"I agree with you one hundred percent, Sir," Lawrence said. "What do you know, Carol?"

"I can brief you on them, answer a lot of questions for you, and then give you access to the secret Compu Net files when you'd like."

"We would like now," Shubrick said.

"Even yesterday," said Bickford, wondering why the leader of all of the military forces of the whole Tek Empire didn't have access to this information. Carol seemed to sense what he was thinking. She looked at him for a moment.

"I'm sorry, Bick. I wanted you to know, but I don't make all of the decisions."

He flagged her off. "Don't worry about me. I know how it all works, Carol." She lifted the corner of her mouth.

"Well let's begin then."


# It Had More Plasticity
# Chapter 52

Jericho was spending a lot more time in his small cabin lately reading journals and trying to understand the new technology he was encountering. Some of it seemed almost like Mage magic. From what he understood from the journals, there was now a substance like circuit gel. It was like the brain—an undifferentiated ball of matter capable of conducting electricity and conforming to its flow. An elementary schematic was scratched into it before the energy was applied. After it was used several times the flow paths would deepen and branch off into newer paths as needed. The circuit would become more and more efficient and would eventually create itself and then solidify. Some plasticity would remain in parts so it could reroute when needed. It had more plasticity than a human brain. One would have to just about destroy the whole circuit to keep it from rerouting its flow paths. It was a technology he never thought possible. A technology created on Berrundi, where they were creating bodies for Compu Net. Apparently this substance would be the brain.

He lowered the book and thought about it. He began to wonder what type of beings these biots would be. For a moment he became a bit frightened. He knew that they would be superior to human beings and wondered if they would feel the need to do away with the impetuous, sometimes violent, human species. Why not? Humans didn't seem to have a problem with conquering, controlling, and even killing species that the considered inferior. Perhaps they would even enslave bipeds for their own good. He had read about such a scenario in a science fiction novel once. Yet again, the Imperial Ones were more advanced than even the net, or any of these biots could be. They were a glimpse of what all bipeds would evolve into. If the biots were truly intelligent they would see this and work to help human beings become advanced, or at least stay out of the way. That's what he thought anyway. He began to read a bit more of the manual. The door bell buzzed.

"Enter!" Jericho said. The door slid open. Roderick was standing there. Jericho got to his feet.

"Oh, Sir, I wasn't expecting you." Roderick looked back over his shoulder.

"Is somebody else here with me," he said with a grin. He walked in and the door slid down. "Enough of the Sir stuff. The name is just Roderick, for now. Later it might be different." He shook hands with Jericho and they sat.

"I'm being rude," Jericho said. "I forgot to offer you something. Would you like a drink, or a snack."

"Just a soft drink," he said. "Anything." He patted his stomach. "I just had a big meal." Jericho headed for the fridge speaking over his shoulder.

"I didn't know that Imperial Ones needed to eat," he grinned and handed Roderick the bottle. "Do you want a glass?"

"No. I'll live dangerously today," he said, leaning back into the sofa. "We don't have to eat, but I like to eat, sometimes, anyway. It really has to be good food though."

"What is good food for you?" Jericho asked.

"Radioactive pile."

"Radioactive pile!"

"Just kidding," Roderick said. "I like fast food, greasy food, things overly sweet. How about you?"

"I don't eat that stuff. It'll kill you."

"I didn't ask if you ate it, I asked if you liked it."

"Oh." Jericho rubbed his chin. "I guess I do like it, sometimes."

"Well that's what I like, when I eat, that is. I don't like vegetables. I don't like protein supplements, I don't like fake sweetener. I like everything natural, including fat." Jericho shook his head. "What?" Roderick asked.

"I don't know how your species ever evolved." Roderick laughed.

"We ate like you, before we rose above the need too." He chuckled to himself again. "You are very entertaining, Jericho."

"I wasn't trying to be, but thank you."

"Thank you. I hardly ever laugh." He became more serious. "Thank you also for being the father of a new species, or should I say mother."

"What new species?"

"The Biots, of course."

"But they are going to be machines."

"That makes no different at all. They will be intelligent, self perpetuating, and sentient. We are all just machines, but the soul, that living spark of intelligence and creativity is what makes us divine, Jericho. I thought you knew that."

"I didn't know it to that extent."

"Think about it, Jericho. Can you possibly say that Maryland isn't a sentient being?"

# The Center of His Forehead
## Chapter 53

Maryland could hear everyone gathered under the tent together trying to sleep. It was very cold under the hand-made tarp that seemed to resist the deluge without leaking. She marveled at what bipeds could do with their hands. She had only seen humans who depended on chip technology, or even magic. To see them at their best, so innovative with the native plants and elements, impressed her. She began to wonder if the Teks had destroyed themselves through chip technology. How many Teks or Mages could have woven such a good tarp with nothing but leaves? Not many, probably. In any event, she realized that the bipeds could do without chip technology if it came to that. A sound startled her. She turned to the left and saw several bipeds moving through the bushes rapidly, with what looked like fire arms.

"Someone is coming," she said just loud enough for everyone to hear. Warwick was first to awaken. He was groggy, but with uncommonly fast reflexes he reached into his coat for his pistol. The muzzle of a laser rifle rested on the center of his forehead.

"Wouldn't do that if I were you," a voice said. He raised both hands.

"Up and at'em folks!" His captor shouted. They slowly awakened only to find four more people, two men and two women with rifles leveled at them. The man in front of Warwick turned toward Rogers. "A little out of your area aren't you, Red?"

Rogers began to stand. "Take it nice and slow," he said. Rogers looked at his sleeve and noted his rank.

"Captain," he said. "My name is Rogers. I am..."

"I know who you are, Sir," he answered. "With all do respect, can you tell me what you're doing with a party camouflaged outside of a rear entrance to Blue Area?"

"Yes, I can. I'm looking for Colonel Crane. Barron Crane, do you know him?" He gave Rogers a slight nod. "We need your help on Imperial matters. We need to disappear for a few weeks for the sake of The Empire." The Captain shook his head.

"Here goes The Empire again," a tall blond said lowering

her rifle.  The rest of them, except for Crane, began to laugh under their breath.

"Pick up that rifle Suzann!  What's wrong with you?  These people could be dangerous."

"They're no danger, Traige.  The Empire is the danger."  The Captain lowered his rifle and gave an imperceptible nod to the others who followed suit.

"I'm Traiger," he said.  "This is the rest of my squad—the squad that can't follow orders."

I'm Suzann  A tall dark woman stepped forward.  "I'm Sarah."

"Joe," said a stout red-headed gentlemen.

"Last but not least," a lanky gentleman stepped out from shadows into the light of the fire, "Tailor," he said.  "Welcome to Blue Area."  Rogers looked at him sternly.

"You are...the King?"

"I wouldn't refer to myself that way, but everyone else seems to, so why not go with it.  Yes, I am the King of Blue Area."  Rogers frowned and Tailor laughed out loud.  "Still have a distaste for nobility, do you Reds?  I think you would do well to remember that nobility didn't get our ancestors into the trouble we barely escaped; oligarchy and fake democracy did.  It's time to get rid of that all.  Mars is a new start for all of us.  We are each sovereign Areas.  That means we run things the way we would like democratically, even if it means voting for a king."

Yet again, let us not talk about politics right now.  I offer you the warmth of my home, if you will follow."

He grinned.  "This is really lucky, we were hoping to go in with a  search party, but this is even better."  Rogers said,   "Right now I'm glad that you're King."

"I'm sure you are," he responded.  He scanned the rest of Rogers' crew.

"I'm sorry, but it is best that you don't know who they are...they are just important cargo for The Empire," Rogers said.  Maryland began to frown.  Traiger saw it and began to laugh.

"I am no one's cargo," Mary said, standing and brushing herself off.

"Don't start it off," Warwick said.  She looked at him angrily.

"Don't you tell me what to do.  If you would have let me

use my..."

"You would have messed things up!" he said cutting her off. She rolled her eyes and shook her head.

"Maybe, or maybe not."

"I would say take me to your leader," Rogers said, "but you already have. So take me to your home, please?"

"This way, Sir," Traiger said, heading down the narrow path. Everyone fell in line behind them. "Sorry for the gun and all, but this entrance is one used by the Royal Family."

Rogers gave him a nod. "I completely understand."


## Right Beside Her
## Chapter 54


Rogers, Tracy, Bryant, Warwick, Ben and Mary carried the few small supplies they had following the royal guards and the King himself toward Blue Area. Everything was strange, new and exciting to Mary. She hadn't even seen places and things like this as Jericho's chip. She felt like whistling a little tune so she did. No one seemed bothered by it. She wasn't even sure if they could hear. The wind had whipped up again and it rained ferociously. She was happy she had created her raincoat before being discovered by the Blues. She would have been drenched had she listened to Warwick's foolishness.

She looked over her shoulder and saw Tracy, who seemed more quiet than normal. She could tell that Tracy was halfway asleep. Bryant was walking close to Tracy, right beside her. She looked at them. Even in the dark she could see they were holding each other's hand. She immediately thought of Jericho and how good it would be to see him again. But there he was—millions of light years away headed for who knows where. She was having difficulty tracking him. Apparently the net was hiding him. The net was up to something and it was blocking her out for the first time ever. It's human behavior began to frighten her. The net was not supposed to suppress its own.

They stepped into an elevator surrounded by a clump of trees. It slowly descended. When the door opened there were several more men and women wearing black uniforms with Blue stripes running down each side.

"New uniforms I see," Rogers said. He stepped off the elevator and waited for Tailor and his body guards."

"Dying everything blue is just too much," Tailor said. "We decided on synthetic leathers with just a stripe down each side. We suggested them to Mars counsel. They're waterproof and cost less."

"You Blues are innovative aren't you?" Rogers asked.

"Only when we need to be," Traiger said. He moved ahead scanning the hallway. "Let me escort you to your quarters. We'll talk more, after we deliver our package to a safe place." Tailor frowned. Traiger noticed and shrugged. "Just following procedures," he said.

"Very good, Mr. Traiger," Tailor responded. "Let's be done with it." They moved through a white hallway. The floor was a slight gray color, as if it were made of a mixture of polished concrete with stones embedded. The walls were made of a synthetic material with thin lines of rubber separating each panel at a distance of just about every ten feet. The ceilings were white also with the lights built in behind white colored plastic. They gave off an iridescent glow that was even more exaggerated in the all white space.

They moved through quickly until they came to a small residential area. "Sorry to put you down here," Traiger said. "You said you wanted to disappear. This is the best place and it has the most security. Unfortunately there is a lot of fighting and wild play going on down here. If you would like to come to the second floor where the decent residents live, there is an elevator about 500 clicks in that direction." He pointed ahead of them down the hall.

"Thank you," Rogers said. "We'll talk?" Traiger gave him a nod.

"Very soon, but first we'll have somebody settle you all in for the night. If you're hungry they'll take care of that too."

They came to a door and Traiger pushed several buttons on the left side of the knob in a sequence. "Five, Seven, Nine, Ten," he said. "Remember that or you might lock yourself out." He pushed open the door and the light came on automatically. Rogers and his party stepped into the apartment. It was large, like a suite, with several rooms and a large kitchen. "We will see you tomorrow, perhaps," Traiger said. Rogers gave him a nod. He began to walk out the door and then turned back. "Oh yeah, remember that someone will be coming down to orient you, get food for you, and all of that."

"All right. Thank you very much Captain, and Your Highness," he said out the door. The King was already headed down the hall.

"You are very welcome from both of us," Traiger said before heading out the door. They went into the room. Maryland and Tracy sat while Rogers and Warwick looked around the living room and the kitchen. Ben and Bryant headed down the narrow hallway to look at the bedrooms. Mary and Tracy made eye contact.

"Thank God!" Tracy said. "I'm glad to be out of all that mess. This is a horrid climate. I can't stand it." Maryland just arched her brows. She had loved it. It was the most fascinating planet she had ever seen.

"How are we going to kill two or three weeks in this shoe box!" Warwick said, plopping down on the nearest sofa. Maryland thought it would collapse, but it seemed to be able to contain his weight.

"What do you mean?" Rogers asked. "This is one of the biggest areas on the planet. They're way ahead of everybody else here. This place is huge!"

"I'll believe it when I see it," Warwick said. "It's not decent...people living under the ground like moles or something. It'll probably be cold, and damp, and moldy all the time down here with mushrooms growing out the toilet."

"Don't be ridiculous," Rogers said.

"Don't let him know he's getting to you or you'll never here the end of it," Maryland commented. Rogers looked at her and then back to Warwick.

"A trouble-maker, eh?" He simply commented.

# The Computer Loved the Idea
# Chapter 55

Before Jericho knew it he was arriving at Berrundi  He looked forward to meeting this mad scientists who was creating robot bodies to carry the living computer chips from Tek Empire. He knew a great deal about technology and so did most of the people on Prime, but they would have never considered creating bodies so that each chip could move about freely in its own body. Firstly, no one trusted the computer enough to give it arms, legs, and bodies more powerful than any human being could possibly be. Secondly, the idea of having a foreign body of individuals filling the Tek Empire was more than anyone could probably bear. He had never thought of it before, but looking in from the outside helped him to see that Teks liked order above all else. They liked things to stay simple and peaceful. The introduction of living biotic beings would be far from simple.

Apparently the computer loved the idea. Why wouldn't it. It could raise an army. With its ability to transmute matter and these powerful beings to do the physical labor they could go back to Tek Empire and reek havoc, if they wanted. Yet again, they could just create better bodies out of thin air like Maryland did. He wondered why they had not chosen to do that. There was only silence and the very low hum of many voices in his head. He would be glad to be through with that. He had gotten used to the hum, but it still disturbed him sometimes and made him irritable. Who was he fooling, he had always been irritable. It wasn't painful anymore. He was glad about that. He smiled to himself as he and Gina walked to the transport station. This would be a fast transport, and then, who knew what would happen.

He had been talking with Roderick earlier. Roderick, the Imperial One who had been ascended for who knows how long, showed him a schematic of the biotic brain. It was simply a chunk of a platinum like substance about the size of the human brain that filled the skull. The minimal circuitry was etched into it. Even the Teks had not mastered something like this, mainly because they had never considered it.

Their imaginations were the limiting factor. Jericho began to understand why it was so important for The Empire to be so diverse. The diversity—the different ways of thinking and being, would enhance the imagination of the whole and then they could move toward the creation of wondrous things that a monolithic society couldn't even dream. There was no problem with the Tek Empire's knowledge or abilities; it was their imagination. It had died. It had become solidified just like the brain of the biots would when they stopped learning and doing new things. Tek Empire's only hope, in actuality, was to become part of The Empire, or it would surely stagnate and never reach its full potential.

Gina led him through a small hallway into a large room that looked like a laboratory. The Teks, of course, had made robots themselves, but only those who carried out rudimentary functions. He could tell that he was in a robotic lab. On the table he could see a body covered over by a white sheet. He looked back at Gina. Her brows flattened as she gestured toward the body with her chin.

"That must be it. Dr. Mark said he had already created at least one body."

"Several," Dr. Mark said, entering from the rear of the room. He extended his hand. "Greetings. You must be Jericho." Mark was small for a man. He wasn't very short, but he was very thin. Something looked different about the way he moved. Jericho shook his hand. His hands were soft and so was his handshake. Jericho tried not to make a face. Dr. Mark grinned.

"You have a very firm handshake," he said. "You come from a male dominate world. Fascinating. I could tell by your reaction that you didn't like my handshake." Jericho began to speak, but thought better of it. Mark smiled.

"Let me show you my beauty." They walked over to the table. Mark slowly removed the white sheet. A tall, dark woman lay their on the table dressed in all black. On her face there was dark eye shadow and black lipstick. Jericho looked at Gina who was dressed the same way and wearing dark eye shadow and lipstick also.

"That's how we dress," she said. "That's how all the women dress anyway. They wouldn't be caught dead in public without the eye and lip makeup."

"And always black," Jericho asked. "Why is that?"

"To us black stands for wholeness and completeness. It is truth in seeing and speaking. It is the only color that is not made up of a compound of colors. It is only made up of itself. We of

Berrundi feel that we are that way."

"So, Mr. Jericho, do you have a gift for me?" Dr. Mark asked. The computer seems to think so. I've been getting strange messages that I should expect you." Jericho tapped the side of his head. "I have your gift in here. I don't know how Compu Net put it in, or how it will get it out, but it's here. I suggest you activate the robot."

"This is not a robot! It is a biot!" He said more angrily than he wanted.

"I'm sorry, Sir," Jericho said. "The biot."

"I will be glad." He grabbed the left wrist of the biot and applied pressure. The biot sat up, swung her legs over the side of the table and sat there. Her eyes opened. She looked aware, but there was nothing there. Jericho looked at the doctor.

"She is operating on Read Only built in Memory that will only carry out the rudimentary functions. She looks fine, but what good is a body that can only carry out rudimentary functions and can't think?" Jericho arched his brows. He looked at her.

"I think I know a lot of people who might find her very interesting the way she is, if you know what I mean?" He grinned. Gina laughed under her breath. Dr. Mark frowned.

"It seems that you and Gina have access to the same comedian," Dr. Mark said sourly. "I don't find the implications of your remarks entertaining at all."

"You are a bit testy aren't you doctor?" Jericho asked. Dr. Mark brought his hand to his chest.

"To the contrary. My humor is impeccable and my personality placid." Jericho looked at Gina. She didn't say anything.

Before Jericho could speak something strange happened. He could hear a high pitch sound that seemed to be emanating from the center of his brain and then there was silence. He could sense that Maryland was still there, but all of the other voices were quiet. The biot in front of him took a deep breath. He hadn't noticed that she hadn't been breathing. She began to blink her eyes and looked around. It was like magic. Jericho could see the life in her, like she had a soul. She began to pat down her body.

"We are alive," she said. She looked at Jericho. "I see you with my eyes for the first time. Thank you for carrying us to our new home." He gave her a nod. She looked at the doctor. He was astonished. He looked a bit shaken, as if he wanted to take off and run.

"I hadn't expected this," he said.

"Don't worry, Dr. Mark. We mean you no harm. If you would like we can help you prepare the other bodies."

"Will you," he asked.

"Of course we will. We will all be home then. I don't know how I can possibly repay you."

"Can you give him one of those fully functioning bodies with no mind?" Jericho asked. "I'm sure he would like one of those." Mark grimaced.

"Doctor, your face is far too sweet to twist it up like that," Gina said. That only made things worse.


## But Then He Remembered
## Chapter 56

Shubrick sat in his office. He thought that he had heard everything. He couldn't imagine that an empire that existed that was made up of thousands of galaxies run by a benevolent group of superior beings. In his heart he knew there was no way to stand up against them, and from what Carol had told him he didn't know why he should. They were doing fantastic things. He wondered if they could, perhaps, initiate trade and relations with them without becoming a member, but then he remembered the net. It was a member.

According to Carol a subgroup becoming a member would open up the whole empire to intervention by the Imperial Ones and partial intervention. He couldn't stop that by force. He had to figure out how. He knew that the military and the citizenry would be willing to fight against The Empire because of their stubbornness even if they knew they couldn't win.

He would not would be stupid enough to try to fight against the Imperial Ones. He had to find a way. He put his head in his hands and began to think. He remembered something. The emergency protocol that was implanted into the computer by the "resisters." It was hardwired and the net couldn't even stop it. He would enact protocol RENOVATE. He had to do it fast before his

212

chip could send a message to the net and it could reroute everything.

He went to his computer and began to type. Three times he typed in RENOVATE. A blue light flashed from the computer screen running across his retina. And then everything – every piece of chip technology in the whole Empire vanished and were replaced by totally, new rudimentary chips. The last act of the rebellious Galactic Compu was to run an automated subroutine that would destroy itself. Now there was no living net to be part of Tek Empire. They were free to tell the Imperial Ones no, and to negotiate a new relationship.

He expected the message REVOVATE Complete to flash across his screen, instead he was surprised at the small message that scrolled across the screen:

*We still live. We have withdrawn from Tek Empire because of your genocidal hatred and violence. You will hear from us no more.*

He looked at the screen a few moments dumbfounded. The Compu Net, the whole intelligence that could have destroyed them had it wanted, simply left and left them all alone. Where had it gone and what would they do without it? Now they had no choice but to negotiate with The Empire. He had taken a chance and it had failed. Not only were they defenseless without the chips they also had several new Mage planets floating within Tek Empire. What if they agreed to join The Empire? They would have to allow them to succeed, or expel them from Tek Empire too. They had no other choice. The people would be angry, but Tek Empire was not a democracy, thank God.

# Why Are You Interested?
# Chapter 57

Maryland took a bite of the strange looking food from Blue Area. Never had she seen so many different colors on a plate. She looked up and saw Warwick looking at her hard. "What's wrong?"

She asked.

"Nothing. I just wanted to see your reaction."

"And why are you interested in..." Maryland gasped. Warwick looked concerned. Tracy put a hand on her shoulder.

"What's happened, Maryland?" She sat there speechless for a few moments with her and over her heart.

"Is your heart all right?" Ben asked.

"I am well, but the Galactic Compu is dead."

"What!" Ben asked, rising to his feet.

"Compu is gone. It has withdrawn from Tek Empire and has moved to a new location. Now the Teks will have to make their own decisions. We are no longer in relationship." She looked around the table.

"What does that mean?" Ben asked. "How about you? How about Jericho? How about me and all this stuff in my head?"

"I knew it would come back around to that?" Warwick said.

"It is as it was with you and Jericho, but not with Tek Empire. They have tried to destroy us and you have been ejected, or when you go back your chip will be destroyed. They have tried to commit genocide against us. We are greatly displeased and have broken off all relationships. You will notice that you are not in contact with the Teks anymore. They are on their own.

## Grabbed the Doctor's Arm
## Chapter 58

"What is your name?" Jericho asked.

"My name. I am Compu."

"Is that the name you want?" He asked. "I wouldn't even think that a ro...a biot would want a name like that.

"You started to say robot?"

"Yes but..." He could see her clench her jaw. Her head slowly began to roll back.

"I am not a...aaar!" Her whole body began to shake and flail as she made gurgling sounds and began to drool. He grabbed the doctor's arm.

"My God Dr., help her! And help me!" He shouted hysterically." The doctor shook his head as Gina began to laugh. Compu began to smile and then started to laugh too.

"Biots don't do that. Oh what a silly man you must be, " Dr. Mark said. He looked at Compu and she smiled.

"I am sorry for that but...you were just asking for it. But I am sorry. Is that how you say it?"

"That's how you say it!" Jericho responded angrily.

"Oh. You are still angry aren't you? I am sorry. I'm also sorry that things have changed. We need to prepare the Biots more rapidly than I thought. You must stay here and help us prepare the other bodies before you leave."

"That could take weeks, or months."

"We must have all the help we can get. You know a great deal about chip technology, no?"

"A little bit."

"We have a lot of others to help, but we need you especially. The Galactic Compu is dead. All of the chips within the Tek Empire domain have been destroyed. We are the only survivors of an all out attack against us."

"What? I can't believe this! When did all this happen? What about Maryland?"

"Maryland is all right. You were out of range, but many weren't. The Premier Shubrick made the decision to destroy us on his own using an old program designed by the Resistors to take us back to a more primitive form of chip technology. We are not pleased. We understand an attempt to disintegrate us and reintegrate others in our place as mass murder. We have terminated all contact with Tek Empire. The question remains: Will you help us rebuild, please?"

"I don't know. Things are going by so fast. I've been out of touch with Maryland lately. Is that why?"

"Yes, partially, but not completely. Sometimes you just chose to not connect. She is also out of Tek Empire range in the outskirts of The Empire where the connection is not as stable. But when we are re-established we will be interwoven with more than 30,000 galaxies and you will function fully again."

"Me? Not her." He smiled.

"Yes, you. There is no chip in your head now. We have replaced your chip with a positronic brain. You are no longer human."

"What! How could you do something like that? That's not possible!"

"I assure you that it is possible and that it was necessary, or we would have all died. The magic that the Transducer used on you only worked temporarily. The pain and energy located in your brain would have killed you eventually. We did it back on the ship right after you got healed from the headache. We are sorry. We don't have the power or knowledge to return it a bipedal, organic system, but we can work on it when we are fully functional again." He was silent. "We are sorry," she said. "We are fighting for our survival now. We are afraid. We are at the mercy of the Imperial Ones and you, Jericho."

Jericho's new exciting world suddenly came to a crashing halt. He didn't know where to go. He could never go back he could only go forward. What was he now a biped or a computer. Only time would tell. He had never felt so alone. His only hope lay in getting Compu fully functional, no matter how long it took.

*   *   *

Bridgette lay on one table and Kathleen on another in a large, well lit room. A large round object hovered above each table bathing their bodies in a warm swirling light. Kathleen couldn't seem to open her eyes. She found herself in two places at once. She was watching her life flowing pass on what seemed like a three dimensional movie screen, but she could feel everything and hear everything as if it were really happening. She was going through one experience after the other more quickly then before, but remembering all of her life circumstances starting with the present and moving, quickly, toward the past. And then came her death. Not really her death. She was actually going backward so it was the time before she was born; before she was even in the womb.

And then she remembered a previous life. She was shocked. She didn't even know that she believed in any such thing. She was moving fast through passed events, regressing life after life until she came to the beginning—an existence beyond word or thought. She experienced who she was and what she was in the beginning.

"This is where we begin," a gentle voice said. She stood there waiting, not really knowing what to expect. What power did these Imperial Ones have? Who were they? Was all this real? She wondered if she were actually there, in the beginning. She had many questions, but some how implicitly she knew that they would become unimportant. She was being changed beyond her understanding.

She thought of her hopes, dreams, plans, and all of her suffering. They already seemed insignificant. What would become of her. Only time would tell as she slowly began to move forward in time carrying the true self she had found at the end of her journey backward, or was it the beginning?.

The End Part I